Alice MacDonald Greer Mystery Series

This is a work of fiction. All incidents, dialogue and characters, with the exception of some well-known public figures, are products of the author's imagination and not to be construed as real. Where real-life historical or public figures appear, the situations, incidents and dialogues concerning those persons are used fictitiously and are not intended to depict actual events or to change the entirely fictional nature of the work. Any legal issues and analyses are fictional and not intended or to be taken as legal analysis or advice. Coffee County and Coffee Creek exist solely in the author's imagination, where they are located somewhere in the Texas Hill Country between Dripping Springs and Fredericksburg.

Published by Stuart's Creek Press, LLC
Dripping Springs, Texas

SCP Stuart's Creek Press

Book Design: Bill Carson Design
Library of Congress Control Number: 2022923847
ISBN 978-1-7327229-2-7

For Stuart Dickson Currie

KUDOS FOR THE ALICE MACDONALD GREER MYSTERY SERIES

Ghost Daughter, Book 7 in the series, was named Finalist in the 2022 Eric Hoffer Book Award Grand Prize Short List, the 2022 Next Generation Indie Book Awards, and the 16th Annual National Indie Excellence Awards.

Ghost Cat, Book 6 in the series: "The atmospheric descriptions are succinct and vivid, highlighting the rugged and bountiful landscape of Texas Hill Country. Foster's skillful plotting, easy pace, and captivating characters will hit the mark for audiences craving a new mystery series to binge-read." BookLife

"With her extraordinary and narrative driven storytelling style, author and novelist Helen Currie Foster once again exhibits her mastery of the mystery genre with the publication of *Ghost Cat*, the newest addition to her consistently entertaining 'Alice MacDonald Greer' series of deftly crafted suspense/thriller novels." Midwest Book Review

OTHER BOOKS BY
HELEN CURRIE FOSTER

Ghost Cave

Ghost Dog

Ghost Letter

Ghost Dagger

Ghost Next Door

Ghost Cat

Ghost Daughter

Chapter One

White-Knuckled

Alice gripped the armrests as the Edinburgh-bound plane bounced upward through storm clouds above Heathrow. When the plane topped the clouds, she loosened her white-knuckled grip and took a breath. She'd raced from her British Air flight from Austin, forty minutes late, struggled through immigration and then security, barely making her flight.

Two days earlier, she'd fired off another email to the Aberdeen office of Her Majesty's Coastguard—the same email she'd sent every month for five years: "Any trace of the helicopter *Grampian* registered G-TBDR, en route from NorthOil oilfield platform Lucky Strike to Aberdeen?" Every month she got the same response: "Madam, no news. Very truly yours, etc." But this time the response said, "Madam, wreckage of *Grampian* found 54 nautical miles northeast of Aberdeen at depth of 100 meters. Wreckage retrieval is underway. Divers report two bodies."

One might be Jordie, her husband and father of her children. She'd forwarded the email to her kids. Ann, a college senior, was flying from Boston to Edinburgh. John, a grad student at the University of Edinburgh, had flown back from an interim course in Hong Kong. He would meet them at the Edinburgh airport on this wet November Monday and drive them to Aberdeen.

Would she and her children see the wreckage? The bodies? Would she be able to identify Jordie? The big Scot, her friends had called him. They'd had a whirlwind romance her last year of law school, then two children, busy careers. Then, at four in the morning, she woke in dread to a static-filled transatlantic phone call. "We regret to inform you...no trace...of course we are searching..."

No SOS from the chopper. No life vests floating in the frigid gray waters of the North Sea. No battered life raft spotted on a rocky coast. Nothing at all.

After the small chopper's disappearance, desperate for information, she'd engaged an Edinburgh law firm to keep her posted on the investigation. After a few months the head lawyer told her, "The Coastguard searched diligently but found nothing. Until they find the wreckage, we don't feel we can be of further help." Remembering, she felt a rush of anger—but at what? Fate? Weather? Five years of helpless waiting?

What if neither body was Jordie's? Could she bear another year of uncertainty? She'd tried to rebuild her life in the five years since he disappeared. But if Jordie was alive—unimaginable, but possible—an amnesiac in a Norwegian village? Living a double life in Inverness?—of course he'd come home. Wouldn't he?

*****

John and Ann met her outside security, their eyes wide with concern. She dropped her carry-on and pulled them both close into the family's traditional scrum, feeling their warmth, their strong arms, knowing they needed her strength too.

"No bags?" Ann asked.

"No."

They reached the red rental sedan. "You sit in front, Mom," Ann said. "You can watch John shift gears with his left hand."

"And you?"

"I'll be huddled in the back seat, navigating. We take the M90 north to Perth, then the A90 northeast to Dundee and Aberdeen. It's a little over two hours to Aberdeen."

"But that depends," John said, deftly moving into the airport exit, "on where we're going, Mom."

Alice blew out a breath. "Well, according to Her Majesty's Coast-guard, we go to the mortuary at the Scotland Police headquarters on Queen Street in downtown Aberdeen." She found the folded printout in her purse and passed it to Ann.

"Have you ever been to a mortuary, Mom?" John glanced sideways at her, then stared back at the M90.

"Not a real morgue. Only funeral homes, for my parents and grandparents."

"I don't want to go in," Ann declared. "I want to remember Dad just...just the way I remember him. Big and watchful, with the best hugs in the world. I miss his laugh, I miss his voice. I don't want to lose any of that." Her voice wobbled.

"I feel the same way," John said. "It's selfish, I know."

"It's not," Alice said. "I don't want anything to destroy your memories. But we need to know if we've found your dad. So we can celebrate him. So we can stop being angry that he hasn't come back, stop wondering if he's in a hospital in a permanent coma, stop wondering if there's something else we should be doing to find him."

"Stop wondering if he's thrown us over for a different family in France," Ann said with a little snort. "It's like being ghosted by your own dad," she continued. "Here today; tomorrow...not so much."

Silence in the car. Then John said, "Hey, Ann, remember the time you snuck out with your friends when you had a sleepover at our house?"

"Never!"

"And the police car brought you home? And Mom was having a conniption?"

"Are you sure that wasn't you, sneaking out?" Ann interjected.

"Remember what Dad said to you and your little buddies?"

"Oh, I remember."

So did Alice. She smiled, remembering broad-shouldered Jordie in his Japanese yukata lecturing the miscreant girls, mesmerized, lined up on the sofa in their den.

"Betrayal of trust, right?" John said. "Breach of hospitality?"

"And a lot more." Ann sighed. "My girlfriends loved him though."

Rainsqualls moved in from the coast and began pelting the car. John squinted through the windshield, turning the wipers on full blast. Ann spoke from the back seat. "There's the first sign for the A90."

They made their way through steadily more hectic traffic into Aberdeen. "First sign for Queen Street," Ann said. "Look, there's Police Scotland." John pulled left into a parking lot.

As they reached the street curb, Alice instinctively looked left and started across. John grabbed her arm. "Watch out, Mom! Remember, you've got to look to your right!"

"I always forget," Alice muttered, standing back from the passing car. She found herself reaching for her children's hands. She knew she had to stay strong, had to help them get through this—but she was grateful for the warm hands in hers.

Across the street loomed police headquarters. Alice marched into the first door and asked the desk officer how to get to the mortuary.

He sketched a small map, walked her back to the door, and pointed through the rain down an unpromising sidewalk toward an unwelcoming entrance.

The anteroom inside was even more unwelcoming: stained plaster walls, ancient wooden chairs, antique linoleum. Ann's face crumpled at the faint penetrating odor of formaldehyde. John's jaw tightened. In a corner sat a uniformed man, scrutinizing them. Alice went to a closed glass window and rang the bell on the sill. When the window opened, Alice said to a blank-faced clerk, "Alice Greer. Here to identify Jordan Greer." The clerk asked for identification. Alice handed over her passport and driver's license.

"Look up at the camera, please." Alice finally spotted the camera in the corner of the clerk's window. The red light blinked. The clerk disappeared, then returned in a few minutes. "Here you are." She passed Alice's documents back, closed the window, and vanished.

The uniformed man in the corner stood, a broad-shouldered, sturdy man with unblinking eyes. "Alice Greer? I'm Ian Blane from Her Majesty's Coastguard. You're Jordan Greer's...wife?"

"Yes. These are our children, John and Ann."

Blane nodded at them. "I know this is a difficult time. I've been assigned as your liaison. Perhaps we can speak after your visit with the mortuary folks."

Alice felt a wave of relief. At last, someone to help explain what had happened.

The door to the mortuary proper opened. A gray-haired woman in white jacket and trousers said, "Mrs. Greer? I'm the pathologist, Dr. Rose White. Please come with me." She paused, looking at John and Ann, then back at Alice. "Would they wish to come?"

After a glance at Ann, John said, "We'll wait here."

Dr. White walked quickly down a hall and held the door for Alice to enter the mortuary itself. The building—yellowing plaster, chipped paint, worn hallways—felt ages old. How many bodies had lain here, waiting for someone to claim them? Alice's heart thumped, her stomach tight. She clutched her shoulder bag against her belly for protection.

Dr. White turned, blue eyes intent on Alice's face. "I did receive what appear to be Mr. Greer's dental records from a dentist in Austin, Texas, forwarded by someone called Silla. Your assistant?"

Alice nodded dumbly.

White went on. "Can you recall whether Mr. Greer had broken any bones?"

Alice nodded. "He broke his left wrist, playing rugby. When he was about twenty."

"Any other medical issues? Allergies?"

Ah, Alice thought. "He wore a medic alert bracelet because of his reaction to penicillin."

Dr. White seemed to relax. "We found such a bracelet. This body also had an old wrist break. The dental records appear to match as well. Are you ready to see the body?"

Alice nodded. "What—how much is left? Was he found inside the helicopter?"

"Yes, he and the man we believe was the pilot. I understand the wreckage is a four-man helicopter. I must warn you that, after this many years in seawater, the remains are basically skeletal."

She held the door open for Alice. And there was the lumpy white sheet.

Dr. White gently pulled back the top of the sheet, revealing a skull. A few stands of hair remained on the cranium. Alice stared at the crack along the side of the skull, unable to move her eyes. But she needed to know.

"May I see his hands?" Her voice sounded quavery and far away. She pressed her lips together, fearing she might faint, might find herself collapsed on the grim concrete floor. She mustn't fall apart.

Dr. White paused, holding the sheet. "As you can see from the cracked skull, the crash damaged the bodies. The damage to the wreckage suggests the helicopter fell sharply into the water." Alice kept her eyes riveted on the sheet.

Dr. White pulled it down further. Yes, some neck vertebrae looked disconnected. Alice could see scraps of a shirt across the chest. One button remained. She could still read the embroidery—"Greer"— on the empty pocket. She'd loved Jordie's hands. The bones of the right hand, some broken, were loosely reassembled inside the sheet. The left hand looked intact. "Was there a ring?" asked Alice, trying to control her voice.

"Yes," said Dr. White. "In the wreckage. It wasn't actually on a body. Can you by chance remember any inscription?"

"'Jordie,' then a dash, then 'Alice.'"

Dr. White allowed Alice a small smile. "Excellent." She seemed to reach a decision. "We also have some of the items found near him or in what was left of his clothing—his wallet, keys, a small waterproof bag with a phone, notebook, pen." She pressed a buzzer and a young man peered in through another door. "Can you bring Mr. Greer's effects, Duncan?" He reappeared with a large labeled plastic bag. Dr. White handed it to Alice, who opened it and looked inside. At the bottom lay a folded yellow waterproof jacket labeled "Greer." Atop that lay a small clear plastic bag containing Jordie's ring, medic alert bracelet, travel wallet, and keys, as well as a small orange notebook, pen, and phone, and a small orange REI waterproof bag, pocket-sized—the sort Jordie favored and often hooked to a belt loop. Maybe he'd put the notebook, pen, and phone in the bag? Things he wouldn't want to get wet. But after five years? She tried without hope to turn on the phone. Dead as a doornail, of course.

"Based on the dental records and your further information, I'm satisfied at least that this body matches the information we have so far on Jordan Greer. I'm willing to recommend that we release the body unless you have further questions."

Did she have further questions? Yes! The blood flooded her face. She took a breath. "I want to know what happened to Jordie!" She faced Dr. White across Jordie's remains. "Why did this particular helicopter crash? Did someone shoot it down? What does the damage to the helicopter show? Did these two men drown? Were they dead right after they hit the water? What happened then?"

Dr. White nodded. "I see. No one's told you anything about the chopper yet. But I deal only with bodies. I see no evidence of any trauma to either body that could have been caused by anything other than being inside a small helicopter that fell from a distance and hit the water." She paused. "I'm afraid that's rather like hitting concrete."

She looked into Alice's eyes and said, "Do you understand what

I'm saying?"

"You've identified the two bodies still inside the helicopter. Perhaps they died when the helicopter hit the water. Or perhaps not. Is that it? After five years, what do I tell my children? Not just how their father died...but why?"

The pathologist sighed. "I'm afraid that's it. I can feel your anger, your frustration. I wish I had the answers you need as to why this helicopter crashed. I'm hoping the Coastguard can provide some help."

Alice turned back to the shrouded body. She lifted the sheet and touched the bones of the left hand, then the cracked skull. She heard Dr. White tell her to stop, but she couldn't. She traced the crack, smoothed the brow, and burst at long last into tears, mopping her face with her neck scarf. After a moment she said, "Thank you," and started toward the door, then stopped dead and turned around. "Oh! What are you—when do you release the body to the family?"

"Not today, I'm afraid," said Dr. White. "When there's an ongoing investigation into the crash, I can recommend release of the body, which I'll do today, but I can't permit actual release until I get official approval."

Like the medical examiner back in Austin holding onto a body until it was clear no homicide was involved...

"Will you be taking Mr. Greer's body back to the States?" White asked.

"He's from Broadview," Alice said. "His mother still lives there." She thought of Gran, at her farm outside the little town on Scotland's southwest coast, overlooking the Irish Sea. She remembered Gran showing her the spot in the churchyard on the hill above Broadview where Gran wanted to be buried. During the years when Jordie was missing, Gran—being the exemplary mother-in-law she was—had never suggested to Alice that she wanted Jordie buried there too. But maybe that was the right decision. Alice decided she'd discuss this with John and Ann. Once she was sure she knew what they wanted, she'd talk to Gran and Jordie's peppery sister, Robbie.

And if anyone asked what Alice wanted? Jordie had lived as long in Texas as he had in Scotland. He loved their Coffee Creek ranch. He'd planted trees, found the burros, built the treehouse. But she knew his heart beat for Scotland.

She walked out the door and back down the hallway, mulling over what to tell her children, and opened the door to the anteroom. Three pairs of eyes stared at her, waiting.

Chapter Two

Incompetence? Negligence? Indifference?

John and Ann seemed to know from Alice's face that yes, the body was her husband's. Their dad's. They sat like statues, staring at her.

John stood, then Ann. Alice gathered them in her arms, hugging them both. No one spoke.

Blane rose from his chair. After a moment he cleared his throat. "Sorry to interrupt. I do have some information to share, and some questions. Do you feel like talking?"

Alice held tight to her children for another long moment, then released them. This guy's clearly not a parent, she thought, straightening her shoulders. "Okay. We've come all this way. But surely not in here?"

"Right." He pushed open the door Alice had just entered. The hall was empty. He peered around the first doorway, then stopped, waving them in; Alice saw a grim conference room. The wooden chairs, the oak table, the window sills all had the patina of a grubby old age, of a century of sad hands gripping armrests. Blane noticed their sidelong glances. "Sorry for the surroundings. The city approved a new mortuary, but the budget keeps changing."

The children sank into wooden chairs on either side of Alice. First, ignoring Blane, Alice looked from one to the other, then patted the plastic bag in her lap. "Here's your dad's jacket and some personal stuff. We'll look at it later." Then she stared at Blane. "Dr. White said the Coastguard has more information. Tell us."

She noticed Blane's blue eyes didn't blink often. He opened a small notebook, then looked up at Alice. "We believe the helicopter was pretty far off the expected flight path to Aberdeen. There were severe thunderstorms and strong winds in the area when the platform lost radio contact. Potential causes could include weather, or a mechanical issue, or damage. Now that we have the wreckage, we'll do forensics and also check the maintenance records again."

"Is this another case of shoddy maintenance on a damaged rotor, like that crew transfer helicopter crash over nine years ago?" asked John. "That killed at least sixteen people, right?"

Alice noticed Ann nodding as well; her face held no surprise. Her kids must have been doing the same despairing research she had.

"We don't know yet," Blane said.

"But this wasn't the usual crew transfer helicopter, was it?" John asked.

"Right, the crew change helicopters hold at least sixteen people. This was just a four- passenger chopper. The next crew transfer was a week away, via the offshore crew boat, and Mr. Greer had finished and wanted to leave."

"Only two bodies were found?" John asked.

Blane nodded. "Yes, inside the cabin. The flight records showed another passenger was originally scheduled, but he'd left two days earlier on the offshore crew change boat."

"Who was that?" asked Alice.

Blane looked down at his notebook. "A geologist with a company called GGI."

"Why didn't he fly?"

"He'd apparently finished his work and had a flight to make."

Alice leaned forward. "Did you confirm that?"

Blane frowned. "We haven't been able to reach him."

"Why not?"

Blane shook his head.

Alice sat back for a moment. "Can't you tell us anything more?"

"Not at this point. We may know more after we look at the wreckage."

"You don't know why they were off course, what happened to the helicopter, why one passenger luckily—or conveniently—left earlier? And why the wreckage wasn't found for five years?" A pulse throbbed in her temples. Incompetence? Negligence? Indifference?

Silence. Finally Blane said, "We'd like to know that too."

Alice's litigation instincts revved up. "I want copies of the documents. I want copies of any flight plan, any transcripts of radio chatter. I want copies of everything you've got."

Another silence. "I'll do what I can," Blane said. "The Coastguard investigates...but we're dealing with multiple parties. A private company owns the chopper. The oil company manages the drilling platform."

"I want it all," Alice said. "We're entitled to every scrap." She didn't know that for certain. Scottish law? English law? She had no idea. "We're entitled not just legally but because we're talking about a beloved husband and father who was killed on someone's watch."

A very small smile from Blane, which didn't reach his eyes. "We want to be of whatever help we can."

So far, that's not much, she thought.

"Hey, Mom, remember we've got a drive ahead," Ann interjected.

"Flying out so soon?" Blane asked.

Alice just nodded, seeing no reason to tell him they were on their way to Luce Bay on the southwest coast of Scotland to see Jordie's mother. She rose, gathering her shoulder bag and the plastic bag of Jordie's belongings.

Blane's eyes were on the bag. "Would your husband normally have carried more?"

Alice paused, remembering. "His backpack and maybe a small carry-on. But I assumed they weren't in the wreckage, right? Otherwise, wouldn't Dr. White have provided them?"

For a moment his face was blank. Then, "I didn't see them on the wreck inventory. Could've disappeared in the currents. I'll look into it." His eyes fell to the plastic bag in Alice's hands, the orange notebook visible. "They gave you only a few items?"

For some reason this question bothered Alice. It felt...prying. He wasn't entitled to see these pitiful remnants, the ring and bracelet that had touched Jordie's skin. Refusing to satisfy his curiosity, she clutched the plastic bag—all she could retrieve of her husband, except for the bones beneath the sheet. She moved toward the door, then turned to say a stiff farewell.

John and Ann rose. "Thank you," muttered John, then Ann.

Blane said, "I'm sorry for your loss."

Alice detested that phrase. So pat. But at least he'd offered sympathy.

"As your liaison, I'll be in touch," he added.

Alice and her children marched out to the dark hall, back through the cheerless anteroom, and out to the sidewalk.

Let it be that it happened fast, Alice prayed. That he hit his head on the way down and didn't know anything more. Let him have peace. Even though the rest of us will have none. Until I find what really happened on that rig, on that flight...

Chapter Three

So It Was Quick

Rain pelted their car almost all the way. They escaped Aberdeen via the A90 to Dundee and Perth, then took the M90 to Edinburgh and followed the loop south to the A702. By the time they passed through New Galloway and Newton Stewart, John and Ann had agreed they wanted Jordie's bones to stay where he grew up, in Broadview. At Whithorn the rain ended. Traveling west on the coast road, they caught their first sight of the heights of Ben Cathair, gold in the last of the fall sunlight.

"I can't wait to get to the top again," Ann said. "Who's coming with me?"

"I'm in," John said. Alice remembered her own first hike up Ben Cathair, with Jordie. Her half-Scottish children had climbed these headlands from childhood.

They drove through Broadview on Harbour Road and turned into Hardie Farm. Somehow Gran heard the car. She stood on the front steps of the farmhouse, waving madly as the car slowed and parked. Sue, her border collie, stood next to her, tail wagging.

Gran pulled them inside, hugging, kissing, patting their cheeks. "You're here. You're here!" She tugged them into the kitchen, where a fire blazed in the old stone fireplace and the kettle sang softly on the Aga. "Hot tea, that's what you need, after such a day."

She didn't even ask, Alice thought. She knows somehow.

"Oh, Gran!" Ann exclaimed. "Scones! And clotted cream!" Alice poured their tea and watched, smiling, as her children fell upon the scones. Her own cheeks felt stretched. Probably the first time she'd smiled all day...

Gran bustled back to her old blue Aga. With a flourish she pulled out a pan of toasty brown, puffy, delectably buttery-smelling pastries.

"Butteries too, Gran? Oh, man." Watching John dive into the tea pastries, Alice realized how much older he looked; he was paler than Jordie, taller and thinner than Jordie, but was finally growing into those shoulders.

Ann's usual merry twinkle hadn't quite returned, after the devastating morning in Aberdeen.

John finished his buttery and brushed crumbs from his fingers onto the plate. "They're always even better than I remembered," he said.

Watching Gran, Alice saw that she too looked older: more silver in her short hair, more crinkles around those clear eyes. Alice loved Gran, loved her honesty, her courage, her discipline.

Gran sat down at the table. She gave Alice the "okay, tell me" look.

Alice said, "They found Jordie's body in the wreck of the helicopter. The broken wrist, the penicillin ID bracelet. His wedding ring. The pathologist suggested he could have died on impact, when the chopper hit the water." She paused, watching Gran's all too knowing eyes, the eyes of a woman who had seen and dealt with death.

"So it was quick, then," Gran said. "He didn't drown, alone in the sea." She turned quickly to the stove, pulled a dishcloth from the rail, and rubbed aimlessly at the counter.

Alice buttered a scone but put it back on her plate. "Gran. Would there be room for Jordie's body in the churchyard, near your plot?"

Gran burst into tears. But she was smiling, turning to John and Ann. "Are you sure?"

"Oh, yes," they chorused. "We plan to drop by often."

"Right!" said Gran.

Ann and John rose from the kitchen table, thanking Gran. They disappeared down the hall, then burst back into the kitchen, pulling on jackets. "We're taking Sue for a sunset walk," John announced. "Then the pub." The border collie glanced up at John and trotted to the door leading outside, then turned, head cocked. "I mean Sue's taking us," John corrected himself, opening the door. The trio hurried out, leaving Alice and Gran with a breath of cool fall air and a glimpse of pink and orange clouds.

"They always go for their sunset walk, don't they?" Alice said. "They love it here."

"I hope they still will," Gran said, face serious. "With their dad lying up at the churchyard."

"They'll love it even more." Alice's throat closed. Tears stung. She blinked them back.

Gran paused, then said, "I'll tell Walter to tell the funeral director. He'll get it handled." Walter McAfee was the pastor at Gran's church. Alice had heard him preach on Cain and Abel after the murder of a young man at the local whisky distillery.

A door slammed in the front of the house. Rapid footsteps followed. "That'll be Robbie," Gran said. "We've—we've talked. She wanted to do something special."

Jordie's younger sister strode into the kitchen. An artist, tall, with a halo of light curly hair, she still rowed with a women's crew on the Firth of Forth. Wordless, she hugged Alice, then Gran, with those strong arms. Her hands were paint-stained. "I've brought it," she said. "You'll have to tell me if it's right."

She hurried out of the kitchen, then hurried back in, hoisting a roll of white canvas at least as tall as she was.

"I didn't think Jordie could be wearing a suit, after five years in the ocean," she said brusquely. But nervous eyes darted back and forth between Gran and Alice. "But I couldn't bear to think of him alone in a coffin."

"Let's see," Alice whispered.

Robbie unfurled the canvas. As background, she'd painted the Saltire, the Scottish flag, its four blue arms reaching diagonally toward each corner of the white canvas. She'd overlaid across most of the flag one of her distinctive landscapes: heather-clad waves of the Galloway Hills like a green ocean, topped by the rocky face of Ben Cathair. Below she'd added hints of Broadview—a spire here, houses there, Gran's small farm to the left, the harbor disappearing below.

Robbie and Gran watched Alice's face.

"It's perfect," she breathed. "Like...like a shroud? Only beautiful." After Dr. White lifted the sheet from Jordie's bones, grisly worries invaded Alice's mind: would the funeral director, even for a mere interment, insist on dressing the skeleton, insist that she bring in shoes and a suit and tie—whether or not she or her kids or anyone else wanted Jordie's remains costumed like that? She couldn't bear the thought, yet the vision of a naked skeleton, alone in its coffin, haunted her.

Now, in her own way, Robbie had leaped the gap. Alice closed her eyes, glad Jordie would be surrounded by so much of what he loved. She managed to say, "Jordie would be smiling," before all three women converged in the family scrum.

Alice's phone pinged in her pocket. After a moment she extricated it and stared at an email from Dr. White. "Our office will release your husband's remains effective tomorrow at eight a.m. Please contact the mortuary to make arrangements."

Then a second ping: email from Ian Blane: "By tomorrow morning I expect to have part of the information you requested."

"What does he mean, 'part of the information'?" she muttered.

Chapter Four

Are You Gran?

Ian Blane's email attachment pinged precisely at eight the next morning.

Alice was standing by the Aga in Gran's kitchen. She grabbed her phone, popped open the email, and waited for the attachment to load, tapping her foot impatiently. Page one: short transcript with communication from the helicopter pilot back to the oil rig, the morning the helicopter went down. Pilot: "*Grampian* to Lucky Strike. En route with one passenger, Jordan Greer. Aberdeen weather was iffy when we left. Severe thunderstorms predicted. If it starts closing in I may try for Peterhead. Over and out."

That was it.

Page two, on NorthOil letterhead: "Interview on Lucky Strike platform re GGI geologist who arrived at the platform Thursday of last week at 16:00 hours via small boat with Belgian flag. GGI employee stated boat was only transport available from his location."

Nothing further.

Page three, on NorthOil letterhead, a memo titled "Global Geology International Contract": "Company engaged GGI as geology consultants to review seabed scans, evaluate existing sampling protocol, and take additional samples. GGI provided geologist who arrived Thursday (a week prior to helicopter incident on following Friday). Geologist completed assignment early and left on following Wednesday with crew change group on offshore crew boat to make international flight to Singapore leaving that day. Awaiting final written report which is expected to be satisfactory."

Nothing more.

Alice felt cold fury. She punched Blane's number into her phone and stalked out of the kitchen into the yard.

After three rings, an answer. "Ian Blane."

She tried to control her voice. "I've received three pages. You've sent nothing explaining what happened to the helicopter, nothing about who found the wreckage, nothing about the weather. You've sent nothing about any search and rescue, including any effort by your own Coastguard. Were there no further transmissions between the helicopter and the rig, or Aberdeen, or Peterhead? Didn't anyone care that the helicopter went missing? Then this geologist: you've sent nothing about who the heck he is. Resume? Bio? And where's the GGI contract? Where are the lab reports for any seabed samples? Where are the seabed videos he was supposed to see?" She took a ragged breath. "And where's your so-called forensic examination of the helicopter and—and the bodies?"

Ian Blane's officer-like tone: "Mrs. Greer, we just found the wreckage. We don't have the forensics yet. That could take weeks. Months."

"What about the other information I've asked for? This happened five years ago! On a North Sea project worth millions! After five years, *someone* must know who the geologist is. *Someone* must know what happened to that helicopter and why it was so far off course." She paused. "I'm here with my husband's mother, sister, and children. We want the truth. Are you going to get us any answers? Or do we have to do this ourselves?"

I'll go to the papers, she thought. Or Gran will. Sue the oil company and the helicopter company. *I will find out.* Silla can dig out every detail on safety records, maintenance records, not to mention GGI personnel. Her indispensable, indefatigable smart-as-a-whip legal assistant Silla, the red-headed Oklahoma barrel racer, could make a computer sing as it spewed forth information.

Blane again. "I apologize there's not more to report. The pilot was flying under visual flight rules, no air traffic control contact required. We'll provide all the forensics from the wreckage, including the maintenance records. Those may provide answers." He paused. "Your husband's possessions, which the mortuary returned? Did you find anything that might help us? Any suggestion in his notebook of concerns or matters that should be reported?"

An odd question. "No." It hadn't occurred to her that the Coastguard wouldn't have checked. Was this apparent omission evidence of some weird Scottish sense of privacy?

After a pause, Blane said, "As to the GGI guy, the rig personnel say the phone numbers they had five years ago are no longer working. They can't track him down."

But I bet Silla can, Alice thought. She'd text her as soon as she hung up.

"If there's documentation you haven't sent, please don't edit it.

I want the original materials."

"You return to the States when?" Blane asked.

"The interment is Wednesday. I'll leave Thursday." She hung up, then emailed Silla: "See if you can locate a company called GGI, geologists, and a list of past and present personnel."

She felt again the weight of five years of loss, grief, and frustration. After running her fingers over Jordie's cracked skull—she discovered she was at this moment actually rubbing her thumb gently over those same fingertips—she felt divided, split. On one hand she was desperately trying to right her family ship, rolling in heavy Scottish seas. On the other hand, for five years, after the chopper vanished, she'd tried to rebuild her life while living in limbo, waiting for some final word about Jordie. She'd sold their Austin house, moved her law practice from Austin to Coffee Creek, and now lived full time in the place she and Jordie had built in the Hill Country. She'd become part of the Hill Country landscape, where involuntary solitude was at least bearable. New friends, new work.

She loved the ranch. John and Ann now considered it home.

But always lurking in Alice's mind was the sense she'd failed—failed to help their children find their lost father.

The phone pinged again—a text from Ben Kinsear, four thousand miles away in Texas: "Thinking of you. When you have a chance, let me know how things are and whether there's anything I can do. Regards to Gran. Here when you need me."

She took a deep steadying breath. Kinsear, still there, but not pushing her. She remembered what Gran had said after meeting him the summer before. "Good man, that."

She looked down Gran's green fields toward the sea and then uphill toward the heights of Ben Cathair. A lark high above sang its song. Breathe, Alice told herself. Breathe. You'll get through this. You'll track down the GGI geologist. Even if his early departure was perfectly innocent...perhaps he could tell her something.

"Mom?" John closed the kitchen door behind him. "Gorgeous, isn't it?" He tilted his head toward the view.

She hugged him, realizing he was taller now than Jordie. Grown, almost. She ached to have him back safe on the North American continent.

"Mom. About this Hong Kong thing."

She took a step back, searching his face. The Scottish university had awarded him a six-week fellowship in Hong Kong to study Chinese economic policy.

She managed a smile. "I'm really proud of you. What's the timing?"

"I'll fly back to Hong Kong next week. After Dad's—after the service."

A wave of fear washed over her. Hong Kong. Her only son disappearing into Asia. But she said, "Do you have everything you need? Sheets and towels?"

He laughed. "They do sell those in Hong Kong, Mom." His face sobered. "Listen, can we take a look at Dad's things? I'd like to see what he had with him."

They walked inside. John followed Alice upstairs. She retrieved the plastic bag Dr. White had provided and said, "Let's find Ann." They should do this together, she thought.

The three sat together on the window seat at the stair landing.

"Not much in here," Alice said. "Here's what I want to see." She pulled out the small orange notebook, the engineering field book Jordie always carried, with waterproof cover and paper. He had a shelf of such notebooks from past projects, all full of his compressed square printing.

"Engineer style," Ann commented.

"Yup." Three heads leaned together, peering down at what Jordie had written.

The entries, brief, succinct, described Jordie's project work, sprinkled with his idiosyncratic abbreviations ("dk" for don't know, "wkg" for working, "diff" for different, and so on). They turned to the last entries. "Arrived onsite w/replacement crew. Met w/ spvr and EHS mgr."

"Environmental health and safety?" asked Ann.

"Yeah," John said. "Looks like he had questions on operations."

They turned the page. At the top: "JJ here Fly out Fri Ck Cigars?"

Jordie was John Jordan Greer. "Why would Dad put his own initials in here?" Ann demanded.

"If they're not his, whose are they?" John wondered. He studied the small notebook, leafing through the pages. "Hey. The last page is gone." Sure enough, someone had apparently torn it out.

Alice rose and trotted downstairs to find Gran rooting through her cookbooks in the kitchen. "Gran? Can you come see Jordie's field notebook?"

Gran was up the stairs like a shot, Alice behind her.

Wordlessly the kids made space between them on the window seat for Gran and held out the small notebook, open to the last entry. "'JJ here,'" Gran read aloud. "He didn't mean himself. He meant JJ's here. Jameson Jeffrey Greer. His faux-bro, Jordie called him. The brother he didn't have. His cousin, five years younger. I called him Jamesie; Jordie called him Jimmie. They were very close."

Alice felt memories stir: Jimmie, Jordie's best man at their wedding. He hadn't come to Jordie's memorial service at St. Giles in Edinburgh, the service without a casket, the family following behind the piper, the high dome of St. Giles echoing to "Scotland the Brave." Gran had said Jimmie was out on a ship doing research on the Great Barrier Reef or some such thing.

"Where is he?" Alice asked.

"Good question," Gran said crisply. "I wrote him in Australia to tell him about Jordie's service at St. Giles. After that he wrote me back, sent birthday cards and Christmas cards for a couple more years, all postmarked somewhere in Asia. Then—nothing more."

"Do you have a phone number?"

Gran shook her head no. "Last mail from that lad was a postcard from Indonesia, maybe almost two years ago, with no return address. That was it. He lived with us as a child when his folks were out of the country. He always stayed in touch. Not to send me a word, that's not like Jimmie." She glanced at Alice. "I try not to imagine what would keep him from calling or writing. I'm very worried."

*****

Late Wednesday afternoon, word was out. Parishioners gathered in the Broadview parish church, atop the ridge above the town. Promptly at four the pastor, Walter McAfee, walked to the front of the chancel and lifted his hand. The quiet murmuring ceased.

"A few years ago, when no sign of his helicopter could be found, we celebrated Jordie's life at St. Giles in Edinburgh," he began. "Today, finally, we can place his bones at rest in the place he loved, here on the side of Ben Cathair above the Irish Sea. Today we too seek peace, because our brother, our father, our son, our husband, our friend Jordie is also at peace. His family can now come here to sit at his side in the churchyard, stare out at the great ocean, feel the breeze from Ben Cathair, and celebrate his life and his love for them." He looked briefly at Gran, then said gruffly, "I read from Psalm 103. 'As for mortals, their days are like grass; they flourish like a flower of the field; for the wind passes over it, and it is gone, and its place knows it no more. But the steadfast love of the Lord is from everlasting to everlasting...and his righteousness to children's children.'" He looked up again. "We flourish in this beloved place, yet our days are like grass. What remains is steadfast love. Jordie had that, and gave it. As the psalmist concluded, 'Bless the Lord, O my soul.' Now we can truly say to Jordie, 'Rest in peace.'"

McAfee nodded at John, Robbie, Ann, and Neil Gage, owner of the Broadview pub. The four rose and grasped the handles of the plain polished casket, so light with its burden—only bones. From the church entrance came the piper's call: "Scotland the Brave." The congregation stood as the pallbearers passed down the aisle, followed by Gran and Alice, and out the open doors. As she passed the last pew, Alice noted a stranger, a woman maybe mid-forties, tanned and fit, with straight blonde hair in a short bob.

The procession reached the open grave at the corner of the churchyard, where the view across the Irish Sea disappeared into the "back of beyond." The funeral director and his men gently lowered the casket into the pit as Ann's clear soprano joined the piper: "Hark when the night is falling, Hear! Hear, the pipes are calling, Loudly and proudly calling..." John and Neil Gage joined in: "Down through the glen," and the congregation added their voices: "There where the hills are sleeping, Now feel the blood a-leaping, High as the spirits Of the old Highland men."

Alice and Gran took ribboned armfuls of the late wildflowers and dropped them into the grave. Walter McAfee pronounced a benediction. Townsfolk surrounded the family, hugging, reminiscing, shaking hands; then suddenly everyone began moving downhill toward town. Most split for Neil Gage's pub, including Robbie, her blonde head visible amid a protective gaggle of friends.

Gran shooed the rest of her family back to Hardie Farm. Alice opened a bottle of wine; Gran put the kettle on for tea. At the front door Sue began barking. Gran turned from the stove. "Someone's at the door." Alice followed her.

On the doorstep stood the blonde woman Alice had seen in the last pew at church. Tentatively, blue eyes fixed on Gran, the woman said, "I'm Emma Linden, from Antwerp. Are you—are you Gran?"

Chapter Five

Too Many Unanswered Questions

The woman unbuttoned her jacket, pulled a battered postcard from an inside pocket, and handed it to Gran. Gran examined both sides, then looked up and said, "I am indeed Gran. Come in. We were just having tea."

Alice followed the two women down the hall toward the kitchen. She signaled John and Ann, perched on the staircase, to join them.

Antwerp?

Seated at Gran's kitchen table, Emma Linden pushed aside the straight bangs on her forehead. "I saw in the news that the helicopter was found. I had no news of my Jimmie. I came to—to pay my respects, is that right?—to his beloved Jordie. I was told to find Gran." She spoke excellent English, with a slight accent.

"I'm Jordie's wife," Alice said. "How do you know Jimmie? And who told you to find Gran?"

Emma's blue eyes moved from Gran to Alice.

"I got this postcard." She pointed at the one Gran still held. Gran handed it to Alice.

On one side the battered postcard showed a wide-angle shot of Hong Kong's Victoria Harbour. She flipped it over. The postmark and stamp were from Jakarta, Indonesia. The message, in colored pencil, consisted of a hand-drawn yellow flowering potted plant with green leaves. Below, hastily scrawled in blue pencil, were these words: "See the gran broad view? And mum for you! Ck cigars." No signature.

"You see?" Emma asked. "It's Jimmie's drawing. He was great for botanical sketches."

"When did you get this?" Alice asked.

"Last week," Emma said. "It took six weeks to reach me. But you see why I came?"

Gran scrutinized the message. "You think Jimmie wanted you to come to Broadview. The 'broad view.'"

"And to find Gran," Alice added.

"There's more," Ann said, leaning over Alice's shoulder. "The potted plant looks like a chrysanthemum. A mum. Could he be warning you, Emma, to keep mum?"

Emma looked puzzled.

Alice explained. "'Keep mum' means 'keep quiet.'"

"Oh. Maybe so," Emma said.

"But this last bit—does he mean 'check cigars'? Did Jimmie smoke?"

"No," Emma said.

"The card was mailed in Jakarta," John interjected, "but the picture shows Hong Kong."

The tea kettle whistled. Gran jumped up and poured boiling water over the tea leaves in the brown teapot. Alice gathered cheese, bread, butter, pickles, and jam, and passed out plates and glasses. John opened a bottle of wine. Gran served tea as well.

When they were seated, Alice turned to Emma. "Tell us everything."

"I met Jimmie in Australia, six years ago," Emma began. "We fell in love. We traveled everywhere. Then he joined a geology firm with a big mining contract in Myanmar. I went back to Belgium to teach. Maybe a year later, he showed up in Antwerp. He'd joined a new company—GGI—that wanted him to do some North Sea work, then fly back to Asia. I actually took him out to the oil rig platform on my boat. He was excited about meeting his cousin there—he wanted to talk to him. He hoped to spend a few more days in Scotland, and then with me, before he had to fly back. But he called me after he left the rig on the offshore crew boat, barely made his flight to Heathrow, and was about to board for Singapore. He said GGI ordered him back; the ship was ready to leave." She paused. "That week I read in the news that a small helicopter disappeared later with your Jordie on it. I am so sorry."

"Did Jimmie know about Jordie?" asked Alice.

"Not until he got to Singapore."

"But you stayed in touch?"

"For a while. We called, we wrote. He was so upset about Jordie. But he was tied to GGI's survey schedule in the Pacific. I did fly out to see him a few more times, but I had trouble feeling I had any future with a man like Jimmie. He was in love with the Pacific, in love with what he was doing, surveying seabeds. We'd talk, we'd email, but... I began seeing a fellow teacher in Antwerp. Not as interesting as Jimmie, but Jimmie didn't call often. Then his calls stopped. I don't know why." She glanced at Gran. "He'd said something strange on his last call—said he'd begun to think his old Myanmar mining clients were criminals. He hoped never to see them again."

Alice pressed on. "And you didn't hear from Jimmie again until you got this postcard?"

Gran poured more tea. Emma went on.

"For close to two years, I heard nothing. His phone number stopped working. Then two things happened. This postcard arrived, and the papers announced your Coastguard finally found a wreck with two bodies, the pilot and Jordan Greer. So I came to Broadview, to pay my respects. And see if Jimmie's here. I was sure he'd come for this service today, because he—he treasured Jordie."

Her eyes traveled from Gran, to Alice, to John, to Ann, and back to Gran. "Have you seen my Jimmie?" Her face fell as she watched them shake their heads.

"We've heard nothing," Gran said. "I'm sorry."

Alice heard the front door open; Robbie appeared in the kitchen, cheeks flushed. Gran introduced Emma and handed Robbie the postcard. "We think Jimmie sent it." Then she showed Robbie the puzzling page of Jordie's notebook. Robbie narrowed her eyes as she read it, then peered back at the postcard.

"Does that last bit mean 'check cigars'?" Robbie queried. "Could he mean my old cigar box upstairs in the studio? Where we used to leave each other messages?" She raced back down the hall and upstairs. In a moment they heard slow footsteps on the stairs. Robbie placed on the table an ancient pasteboard cigar box with a gloriously lurid sunset on top. She opened the lid. The box held old paintbrushes, and a two-piece metal cigar case. With all eyes watching, Robbie slid open the cigar case and pulled out a tiny slip of paper with tiny square printing. She read aloud, "Emma Linden. 24 Vrieland, Antwerp," then a phone number starting with the 32 country code.

They all turned to Emma. "That's my address," she said. "And my phone number."

"And Jordie's writing," Robbie confirmed. "But when—?"

"You weren't here, Robbie, when Jordie visited me before he flew out to that platform," Gran said. "He must have left it then."

"Looks like the last page of Dad's notebook," Ann said. John nodded.

Jordie was in on this, Alice realized. How much had he known about Jimmie's work? Why was Jimmie so eager to talk to Jordie?

"The Coastguard says Jimmie was scheduled to leave on the same helicopter Jordie took. But Jimmie left two days earlier with the crew change on the offshore crew boat. Jordie was still finishing his project, still writing his report," Alice said, eyes focused on Emma. "If Jimmie said he was eager to talk to Jordie, we need to know as much as we can about what Jimmie had been working on."

Alice took notes while Emma told everything she remembered about Jimmie's work. The Myanmar mine was on the China border. Jimmie was relieved to quit that job. He was excited about GGI, the new company he'd joined, because he'd be assigned offshore, out in the Pacific Ocean.

"His bosses were interested in rare earths. Metals for batteries, I think. He was protective about the information, wouldn't talk specifics, said the information was really valuable and his bosses were big on secrecy. He even thought he'd been followed after he quit the Myanmar project. In one of his last emails, he sent me a picture of some guy lurking outside his hotel in Jakarta. Lurking, is that the right word?"

"Did you see Jimmie again? After he sent that picture?" Alice asked.

"No." Emma looked at the kitchen clock and stood. "I must return to Edinburgh. I'm flying to Antwerp."

Alice wrote down Emma's phone number and the school where she taught. Ann spoke up, face serious. "Don't forget what the postcard says, Emma. Please be careful."

John added, "Because if someone was really shadowing Jimmie, maybe he knew something dangerous."

Emma nodded, her face somber. "I have had that feeling. I'll leave Gran the postcard. Thank you."

Alice walked Emma to her rental car and waved goodbye as the taillights disappeared in the dusk. She was sorry for Emma, arriving full of hope, leaving with hope dashed. But she also felt there were too many unanswered questions about Jimmie. If he was so glad to see Jordie, why did he leave the platform early? Okay, GGI reportedly needed him back, so he wanted to make his Singapore flight; but she couldn't help wondering if Jimmie knew it wasn't safe to take the later chopper flight. Could that explain why he hadn't bothered to come home either for Jordie's memorial service years ago or the burial of his bones? He'd sent no excuse. Where was he now? Alice frowned, dismayed at the thought that Jimmie might have known something that saved him—but killed Jordie.

Ann met her on the front porch. "Mom, we've got to pack. John says if we don't leave by five tomorrow morning, we'll miss our Heathrow connections."

Alice groaned and followed Ann upstairs. As she packed her carry-on, she reviewed the week: the text from the Coastguard, Dr. White lifting the sheet from Jordie's skull at the mortuary, Ian Blane's infuriatingly skimpy report, the burial this afternoon under the blue November sky. Then Emma, staring at her from the back pew, and the postcard.

Too much unfinished business here. What about the answers Ian Blane failed to give? Why did the helicopter crash? What would forensics show? What did Jimmie know? And what, if anything, had he told Jordie?

And if that wasn't enough, ahead lay the fraught prospect of saying goodbye to her children: John, flying back to Hong Kong; Ann, returning to her New England college. She could only hope they'd both be safe.

And she'd be back in Coffee Creek. Her phone pinged. Text from Kinsear: "I'll pick you up at the Austin airport."

She'd had a fairly serious fling with Ben Kinsear when they met in law school. Then, ambushed by a dizzying romance with the North Sea oil expert she worked with during a Houston summer clerkship—Jordie—she surprised herself by marrying him. She heard Kinsear accepted an offer in New York for hedge fund work, then later cashed out and bought a ranch in Fredericksburg. After years of no contact, after Kinsear's wife died jumping her horse, after Jordie's chopper disappeared and Alice moved her practice to Coffee Creek, she and Kinsear had encountered each other in a Fredericksburg beer garden. Last spring he'd asked her to marry him. "I think...yes," she'd said. But she was still in limbo.

Now she was flying back to Kinsear. After this week, how would that feel?

*****

Kinsear returned her "I'm here" text immediately when she made it down to the baggage claim on Thursday at the Austin airport. She felt her heart speed up when his veteran Land Cruiser made the curve in front and slid to a stop. He was out and opening the door before she reached the car. A quick side hug, but no kiss—that's what she got.

"How was the flight?" Polite routine question. Friendly but not intrusive. Hmm.

"Pretty great, flying direct from Heathrow."

"How's Gran?"

"Amazing. She sends her regards."

"The kids are okay?"

"Fine, given they had to accompany me to the Aberdeen Mortuary."

He squinted, made a face. "Alice. That sounds awful."

"Not something I looked forward to." She waited for another question. None came. She realized he was trying not to invade her space, trying not to presume things were still as they had been, with a wedding in the works. In case she'd changed her mind. Or perhaps, more optimistically, in case she merely needed more time.

She adjusted the visor so the western sun wouldn't glare in her face.

Had she changed her mind?

Had he changed his?

This week had been all Jordie. Jordie, the big Scot. Jordie, Gran's son. Her children's father. The man she'd fallen so hard for, two decades ago.

But sometimes, as Kinsear joked, you take the bull by the tail and face the situation squarely.

"Flying out of Heathrow, I could see the tip of Cornwall," Alice said. "That's a hike I'd love to do, across that little peninsula they call the Lizard."

She silently counted one chimpanzee, two chimpanzees, three

chimpanzees...then Kinsear replied, "If that's an invitation, I accept. Lemme know when."

Alice settled back in her seat, took a deep breath.

But no, he didn't spend the night. He dropped her at the ranch and explained he had an evening meeting in Fredericksburg and another the next morning.

Sometimes he was almost too tactful.

*****

Silla was not tactful. She threw open the office door the next morning and greeted Alice. "At least you won't have to file papers to have your disappeared husband declared dead before you get married again!"

Alice rolled her eyes.

Silla was right.

Silla continued. "Do not make lunch plans. Your young friend Mischa from your old firm?"

"Yes?" She'd mentored Mischa, who handled securities cases.

"She and Nanette Ferris want you to come to lunch today. Noon at the Beer Barn. They want to pick your brain about a new job for Nanette."

Alice had met Mischa and Nanette when the two young women were law students and Alice had volunteered to judge a Moot Court competition. Mischa was the bubbly one, outgoing and gregarious. Nanette seemed shyer and more reserved. Both were strong Moot Court contenders. They were good on their feet, sharp as tacks, and seemed to love what they were learning. Given Nanette's quiet demeanor, Alice had been gobsmacked at her efficient, forceful arguments at Moot Court.

The two students so impressed Alice that she'd stayed in touch with them. After they finished law school, she'd recommended Mischa for a securities law slot at her old Austin firm. Nanette, her heart set on the world of private equity, had joined a solid Austin firm with a big practice. "I've got to make some serious money, Alice," Nanette had told Alice. "I've got to pay off my student loans so I can help my parents. Ranching in New Mexico's a tough gig these days. And I'm an only child. Meaning, if I want that ranch someday, and I do, I need to help keep it going."

Every year, they'd met for birthday lunches—Alice's, Mischa's, Nanette's. When Alice moved her practice to Coffee Creek, Nanette and Mischa had surprised her with a champagne party on Live Oak Street, ceremoniously bashing her new sign—Alice MacDonald Greer, Attorney at Law—with a bottle of bubbly.

Now, thinking back, Alice realized it was over a year since she'd seen Mischa and Nanette. How had that happened?

Silla went on. "Guess what? That new building off the Old Hays Road, the one we all wonder about? Gated driveway, lots of security lights? I hate those lights at night. Too big, too bright, no shields. Don't people want to see the stars anymore?"

"With that huge chunk of limestone by the gate engraved with a giant S?"

"You got it." Silla added smugly, "Tax records show it's owned by a hedge fund—Simpson Strategic Assets. The billing contact's Patrick Simpson. I looked him up. He's a lawyer—general counsel for the company."

"I haven't seen him at any law gatherings around here. Where's he from?"

"New Jersey area, apparently. So's his brother Ron. Ron manages the hedge fund."

Alice grinned, shaking her head. Silla could find out anything. Those flying fingers...

"And that's where Nanette works now." Silla handed Alice the bio Mischa had forwarded for Nanette: after doing private equity work at Betts & Smith, she'd made a lateral move just over two months ago to Simpson Strategic Assets.

Huh, Alice thought. She was stunned Nanette hadn't called to let her know she was actually in Coffee Creek. Why in the world had she left Betts for Simpson? And why does she want to move again, so soon?

Alice refilled her coffee mug. She hoped to stay awake till noon without falling asleep on her desk. What did Kinsear say after returning from Europe? "My body may be here, but my soul's still over the Atlantic."

At her desk she dug through the mail, organized into neat stacks with sticky notes by Silla: "Done." "Sign here." "Read this stack first." She picked up her pen, started signing, then didn't wake up until she heard Silla at her door.

"Alice! You'll be late for lunch!"

Chapter Six

All One Happy Family?

Just before noon she walked through the swinging doors of the Beer Barn, the beloved Coffee Creek roadhouse that not only offered the best music in town but also served bar food from 11 a.m. to 11 p.m. In prior incarnations the building, well over a century old, had been a livery stable, then a feed store. In the 1980's some Coffee Creek residents decided the town needed a dance hall and added a stage and a dance floor. The three current owners—Jorgé Benavides, Bill Benke, and Bill Birnbach—were Alice's treasured clients. Jorgé ran the music; Benke ran the beer; Birnbach ran the numbers. They claimed a beer hall run by a Latino, a Czech, and a German was likely immortal. "How can we lose?" they said.

Today the outdoor sign by the parking lot read, "I prefer my kale with a silent K."

Alice commandeered her favorite table, in a darkish corner off the far end of the polished wooden bar. So far, the other tables near the bar were empty. "Iced tea, unsweetened," she told the lone barkeep as she took her seat.

Across the room the front doors swung open. In came Mischa, medium height and slim, her straight brown hair in a ponytail, and Nanette, a bit taller. Alice hugged them both, delighted to see them again. Mischa was appealing, with her dimples and grin. Nanette was quietly beautiful, with porcelain skin, black brows over wide gray eyes, and a short black bob.

Both women wore a combination of tailored pants and a floaty top over a shell. How did they put these combos together? Alice wondered, glancing down at her own chino pants and linen shirt. She didn't have a single floaty top... But since it was Friday, at least she was sporting her Goodson Kell boots. Confidence inspiring.

She found herself grinning. "Two professional women dressed to the hilt for the Beer Barn! Bringing chic to Coffee Creek."

Nanette carefully hung a stylish but apparently heavy orange Longchamp tote on her chair. A silvery MacBook stuck out of the tote's corner.

"You lugged your laptop in?" Mischa asked.

"Can't afford to lose it," Nanette answered.

Hmm. Pretty security conscious.

"Nanette, you're in big trouble," Alice teased. "Why didn't you tell me you were working in Coffee Creek? Think of the lunches we've missed!"

Nanette blushed. "I know. I meant to call every minute, but once I got here it was like being on a luge run—just barely staying alive."

The barkeep hustled over. Like Alice, the two young lawyers ordered iced tea.

"Must be a serious lunch?" Alice ventured. Friday—but no beers.

Mischa gave Nanette a quick look. "Nanette wants your thoughts. She's thinking of leaving Simpson. Even though she's moved to Coffee Creek. Right, Nanette?"

"Yes. My hours run so late I couldn't manage the commute from Austin any longer. A couple of months ago, I found a decent apartment at Limestone Lodge."

Alice smiled. Coffee Creekers called the converted warehouse the "Convict Arms." In the 1880's convict labor had quarried the limestone slabs for a building on the edge of the small settlement. Now an enterprising contractor had managed to create two floors of loft-style apartments—a new concept in Coffee Creek.

She wanted more background. "I didn't know you'd left the Betts firm. What brought that on?"

"Filthy lucre," Nanette said, somewhat ruefully. "Simpson offered me fifty percent more. I'll finally be able to pay off those student loans. Plus, I've got to help my parents. To hang onto our ranch, they had to sign another mortgage. I want it paid off."

Alice had lifted her eyebrows at "fifty percent"—way more than would be typical for most law firms. "That's a huge bump."

Nanette nodded. "I've been wanting to call you, Alice, but getting a free minute's not easy at Simpson. It's a zoo, especially at the end of the quarter."

Alice knew private equity lawyers went nuts at the end of each calendar quarter, when deals had to close.

"So I insisted on a reunion," Mischa broke in.

"I like it. Remind me—when did you two first meet at law school?" Alice asked.

"First year, first day of class," Mischa said. "Faraday and Ferris, side by side. Civil procedure prof put us all in alphabetical order. We bonded."

Nanette nodded. "Little girl from New Mexico—I knew no one. Mischa knew everyone. I'd never have survived if she hadn't adopted me."

A friend like that...invaluable in the fraught world of first-year law. The barkeep returned with their drinks and took orders: taco salads for Mischa and Nanette, tortilla soup and a side of guacamole for Alice.

When he left, Alice said, "So why leave Simpson, especially with that raise? Sounds like a pretty lucrative practice. Simpson must have some well-heeled clients."

Mischa snorted. "You should see the cars in the parking lot. This morning when I went to meet Nanette, I saw an Aston Martin, a Bentley, a red Maserati convertible, three of the biggest Teslas. Plenty of money in that parking lot."

"That makes it a big day for Anton, the security guy," said Nanette. "He manages to meet clients in the parking lot, brown-nose them, polish their cars in case there's a little Coffee County dust on the hood. Sometimes they let him drive their cars around the parking lot." She smiled. "Anton's not so bad."

Mischa added, "Yeah, I saw him making eyes at you. But I was so intimidated I stashed my little Subaru in the back row, by your car, Nanette."

"It's not just the clients who like to show off. My boss, Pat Simpson, just got a new Tesla. And his brother, Ron, got the new Mercedes SUV. So my boss upped the ante with a Hummer, for rough work. Not sure what Ron will come up with next."

"So the hours are punishing, but the money's good?" asked Alice.

Nanette nodded.

"Is there time for anything but work? Sports?"

"No. I'd love to go diving again. Sounds crazy, for a child of the New Mexico desert, but the ocean's magical." She sighed. "Maybe after I get the loans paid off—and the mortgage."

"So probably no time for volunteering?"

Nanette's face softened. "I tutor a little boy at Coffee Creek Elementary. Benjy Patch. I've fallen in love with Benjy." She hauled her laptop out of the orange tote. Alice saw a grubby Mario Brothers sticker on its lid. "He gave me his precious Mario Brothers sticker. And look." She opened the laptop. The screensaver was a childish crayon drawing of a woman's face. The dark hair and gray eyes looked like Nanette. The drawing was signed, "I love you. Benjy."

"Benjy and I meet every Wednesday at nine," Nanette said, returning the laptop to her bag.

"Any social life?" Alice asked.

Nanette blushed. "A little."

That sounded interesting, but Nanette offered nothing more.

"What about that Michael Greene you've been talking about?" Mischa teased. "Your voice goes all mushy when you say his name! Admit it, the snow queen has finally fallen in love!"

Nanette's face was bright pink. She shot a look at Mischa, then stared down at her plate. Alice recognized the mix of feelings on her face, remembering when she first met Jordie—the shock of such promise, such potential joy, along with the almost paralyzing fear of losing that chance for joy, followed by her blind leap of faith, toward Jordie.

"I'd like to meet Michael Greene," Alice said. "So, with this new man, a young friend like Benjy, and a significant salary, why would you leave?"

Nanette turned and surveyed the nearby tables—still empty of customers. "Kind of a long story."

"Go ahead," urged Mischa.

"You know about the private equity market these days? Really busy, stock market's up, investors awash in money."

Alice wasn't awash; she was paying tuition for two kids. And she wasn't a private equity lawyer.

Nanette continued. "At Betts I did a bunch of private investment deals, including for investors based in Asia. The Simpsons said that's one reason they pursued me—the Asia connection. Anyway, you know how, some deals, you've got a whole raft of entities involved? Parent companies, subsidiaries, affiliates, and so on? Figuring out who's got the real money is like peeling an onion. Layer after layer, trying to find who holds the ultimate purse strings."

Mischa added, "Which is why we have private equity mantras!

AML! KYC!"

Oh, yeah. Her long-ago securities class floated back into Alice's brain. "AML!" meant "Anti-Money Laundering!" and "KYC!" meant "Know Your Client!"

The barkeep returned with their lunches.

Mischa dug in; so did Alice. Nanette ignored hers, fiddling with her silver. Her gray eyes stared into space. "Back at Betts I worked for several partners who were outside counsel for various hedge fund clients. But now I've joined the Legal and Compliance Department at this hedge fund. So the hedge fund's my employer. Pat Simpson's my boss—he's general counsel. His brother Ron manages the hedge fund."

"All one happy family?" Alice was horrified at the potential conflicts of interest...if indeed any party identified, much less cared, about conflicts of interest. Nanette had lost the protection of outside counsel status. Now she was just another employee.

The Beer Barn's front doors swung open again, and Alice saw a young man in a blazer enter. His eyes swept the room, stopping briefly on the back of Nanette's head. When he noticed Alice watching, he walked toward a small table at the far end of the bar. Once he sat, Alice couldn't see him.

Nanette didn't answer Alice's "happy family" question. She kept her voice low.

"Ron Simpson went after new business from an investor entity that had already done some very lucrative deals in Florida," she said.

"So my first assignment was to take charge of onboarding the new investor entity, called Springs Ltd. This new entity would make a big contribution to the Simpson Strategic Assets hedge fund, a contribution that was key to success in some real estate deals the Simpsons had in mind. The private placement memorandum generally described the types of future investments the hedge fund could make, including Texas real estate. You know, 'commercial and vacation properties...no guarantee...solid track record...excellent air and road access'...that sort of thing."

Nanette picked up her fork, laid it back down. "Onboarding Springs meant getting a properly completed subscription agreement where I could check all the boxes—make sure Springs was a qualified purchaser and accredited investor, establish wiring instructions, and so on. I asked my boss who was handling AML. He just said 'You don't need to worry about it. Not your issue. Just get the subscription agreement signed and our money wired.' So I assumed someone else was handling the standard AML—vendor, firm administrator, someone like that.

Then my boss said, and I quote, 'Get this done. And no digging around in the investor's business. This outfit's very, very private.'"

"Meaning you were not to do any digging on the investors? He told you that?"

Nanette nodded. "Yes. Very clearly."

Alice had some recollection from law school of the Securities and Exchange Commission's due diligence requirements. "The hedge fund's registered with the SEC, right?"

Nanette nodded.

"So doesn't Simpson Strategic Assets have an anti-money-laundering policy in place?"

"Yes, we have the AML policy. And of course we need a paper trail for the SEC that shows appropriate KYC due diligence, in case Simpson Strategic Assets gets investigated."

"So what did you do?"

"I forged ahead. I tracked down the Springs representatives, got their signatures, gave them wiring instructions. They signed the required agreements. But I didn't feel quite comfortable. I might not have worried so much if Springs had been a U.S. entity, but no. It was a British Virgin Islands limited company." She glanced at Mischa. "As you well know, BVI is a high-risk jurisdiction for due diligence. Do you remember the Pandora Papers? A lot of shady people were using BVI entities to evade taxes and reinvest money to legitimize ill-gotten gains."

Alice wondered what she would do in Nanette's situation. "Nanette, am I right that you did some due diligence on your new investors? Despite instructions?"

"Yeah, I did," she sighed. "But by myself, and on my personal time. At Betts, the lawyers didn't do due diligence. We used vendors. But I wasn't sure Simpson was running the traps, and somehow I felt we needed to confirm that, despite BVI being a high risk jurisdiction, the investor passed muster."

Alice knew law firms preferred to shift due diligence work outside. That way, if a due diligence vendor made further requests—passports, addresses, certifications of company documents—and further delayed closure of a deal, blame didn't fall on the lawyers.

"Without a vendor, I was on my own," Nanette continued. "I managed to get the Springs formation documents from the BVI registry. Then I Googled the designated directors, followed up on their names. That made me nervous enough that I went to the Treasury's Office of Financial Assets Control sanctions list. I checked other sanctions lists as well, the UN's, EU's, and so on.

"One director on the certification of formation was General Shwe Sone. He's a retired Myanmar military officer who headed troops at a rare earths mine in Myanmar, on the China border. I found an article on organized crime in Myanmar that mentioned smuggling of rare earths."

"Was there evidence this Sone guy is involved?" Alice asked.

"Just rumor. But two other directors, both Miami based, got my attention. There's a young director, John Vitale. Per the Internet, his first cousin is Tino Vitale, reportedly Miami mafia. A second director is Ivan Johnson. Turns out his maternal grandfather is Dmitri Novikov, reputed head of a Russian crime family. Russian mafia's pretty busy in south Florida. Organized crime's gone international, with sophisticated protective cover, often using what look like legitimate entities. But if you get suspicious and start digging, and one name with a spotless reputation turns out to be related to another name that's not so spotless, you might worry that the ultimate owner's someone you don't want near your investor roster."

"Yikes," Alice muttered.

Nanette continued. "I wondered—if I found it, how was it missed by whoever's doing our AML? Then I noticed the Springs financials included income from interests in metals contracts. Some were for rare earths—lithium and something I'd never heard of, something not in the periodic table back in the day."

"Like neodymium, right?" Mischa put in.

Alice hadn't heard that in high school chemistry, or ever. She pricked up her ears.

Nanette nodded. "Neodymium oxide. Apparently it's used in batteries for electric cars. That same contract mentioned delivery of polymetallic or manganese nodules."

"Which are?" Alice asked.

"Had to look them up. They're nodules, some bigger in diameter than a softball, on certain seabeds," Nanette said. "One big area's the CCZ—the Clipperton-Clarion Zone—out in the deep Pacific between Hawaii and Mexico, on what's called the abyssal plain. They're in other seabed areas as well. The nodules are mainly manganese but can include silver, gold, copper, cobalt, zinc, and some rare earths." She took a sip of iced tea. "Marine biologists worry that harvesting those nodules by plowing the seabed may kill ocean species that no one's even identified yet."

Alice frowned. "Don't you need a permit for undersea mining?"

Nanette nodded. "The UN's International Seabed Authority requires permits for seabed mining outside any country's economic zone. Those permits allow only exploration, not mining, until ISA gets enough information on potential environmental damage. I found no evidence of any mining permit. Environmental risks can create big-time controversy. So I asked my boss whether Springs would care about potential bad publicity." She glanced at Alice. "He said Springs wouldn't care. The environment? 'It's not a client.'"

The three women sat silent.

Nanette went on. "He gave me my second assignment—again a rush. I had to close a big Texas real estate deal, asap. My—my hesitation began with the first email." She sighed. "My boss told me Ron wasn't paying us to reinvent the wheel. He said, 'Just copy the Florida documents.'"

Alice leaned forward. "But obviously you have to be sure the documents work for a Texas deal."

"Obviously," Nanette said, her face set.

"And your boss's position on the new investor's instructions?" Alice felt her stomach knot, thinking of Nanette's predicament.

"My boss said, and I quote, 'Get this done. Use the existing damn documents.' That's when I realized—the new Springs money was going right into this land deal. But by then I had other worries."

"Tell her about the asset prices for this deal," Mischa added.

"Well, besides the concerns that Springs is based in a high-risk jurisdiction and I'm instructed that due diligence is not my job, a surprisingly large amount of money's involved. The first deal involves Texas ranch property, west of here, and a spring-fed river, for a huge purchase price."

Alice raised an eyebrow. A spring-fed river? Sounded like a Texas treasure. She wondered who could ever sell such a treasure. But for a huge purchase price? Still, a piece of your soul...

"As I'm trying to draft proposed closing documents for the land sale, the land price seemed high, based on comparables. Yet I was seeing no price negotiation going on. Again I went to my boss—he said, 'Just close it.' So," Nanette said, "now I'm worried about money-laundering. The cash Springs is investing in our hedge fund? Maybe it's from illegal mining or smuggling. And I'm scared my employer's helping launder it via this land deal." Her face looked pained. "I'm worried we're not following established AML policy for a high-risk jurisdiction. I'm afraid shady people are involved. The Office of Foreign Asset Control could come in and freeze all the hedge fund's assets. I could be out of a job, under subpoena, with my reputation ruined. And I'm part of the Legal and Compliance Department! Simpson could leave me holding the bag." Her eyes filled with tears. "I can't be part of this. My parents would just die if I was charged with a crime."

"Nanette," Alice began, full of trepidation, "does anyone at Simpson know you've been doing due diligence? Despite those instructions?"

"I don't think so," Nanette said, wiping her eyes. "I've tried to be careful." She looked at Mischa, then at Alice, clearly weighing her words. "One more thing. I've got the sense that the hedge fund's needing a big win. It may need more liquidity, may need the cash infusion from this deal. I mean, a hedge fund always worries that existing investors may decide to withdraw or redeem their money."

Whoa, Alice thought. Nanette had been careful, had revealed no confidential information about her employer. But Alice could only imagine the acid indigestion the Simpson brothers would suffer if news of possible financial weakness got out. To have investors bailing out of your hedge fund and demanding back their investment would ruin your day. And your nights.

Mischa shook her head slowly. "This is a terrible spot for an associate lawyer. The senior partner gives orders, but—like you always told us, Alice—a lawyer's got to protect her own reputation, her own character."

"It's more than that," Nanette said. "Going to an in-house law department is so different from what I envisioned. Now I'm just an employee. I feel like...like I've lost my autonomy. Lost my independence as a lawyer." She looked at Mischa, then at Alice, face desperate. "I'm afraid I made a terrible mistake, moving to Simpson."

Mischa leaned forward. "Alice, you've got contacts. Can you help Nanette get a new job?"

Alice had friends at other law firms handling private equity deals. They always fussed about being slammed at the end of each quarter, when the deals closed and financial statements were issued. Surely they'd be eager to snag an experienced senior associate? "You haven't put the word out yet, Nanette?"

"No."

"Okay. I can think of three people to call," said Alice. "I'll start this afternoon."

Nanette leaned forward, face anxious. "Don't let them call me at Simpson! Ask them to call me on cell. Preferably at night."

"Hey, Nanette, you're not obligated to stay if your integrity's at risk. Your boss knows that. He's got to know you're a hot commodity."

"Maybe, but..." She looked up at Alice. "I feel pretty isolated out in that building. It sounds paranoid, but it feels like people in my office keep their eyes on me."

Alice suddenly realized a man had materialized at Nanette's shoulder. Silver hair, slim, tan, bespoke jacket, expensive LA jeans. "Nanette! Introduce me to these ladies!"

Nanette jumped. Her face turned even paler. "Alice, Mischa, meet Pat Simpson, my boss. Pat, meet Mischa Faraday and Alice Greer."

Alice didn't extend her hand. "Hello." Mischa managed a small smile.

Pale eyes surveyed Alice, then Mischa. A sudden grin showing very white teeth. "Ladies who lunch. Not so many choices in Coffee Creek, are there? So what's today's topic?"

None of your business, Alice thought. "Just catching up," she said easily. "We're old friends. What brings you to the Beer Barn?" She looked past his shoulder. "You came alone?"

He hesitated then said smoothly, "My secretary likes the enchiladas. I had an errand and said I'd get her some to go. It's the end of the quarter, too busy for her to leave the office." He looked down at the top of Nanette's head. "Though some of us here seem to be all caught up, hey, Nanette?"

"Everything's under control at the moment," she answered.

"Well, nice to meet you," Alice said, in her "we're through, have you noticed?" tone. "Ask Luis in the kitchen to give your secretary both the green sauce and the special salsa."

Pat Simpson looked momentarily blank. "Oh, the enchiladas. Indeed. Thanks for the tip."

He turned toward the bar.

Nanette stared down at her salad. Mischa made a face, then said in a carrying voice, "So, Nanette, did you catch any of ACL this year?" She meant Austin City Limits, a two-weekend fall music fest.

Nanette looked up gratefully and answered the same way. "Yes, I had out-of-town friends stay with me. We saw My Morning Jacket and some other folks."

"Me too," Mischa continued. "You, Alice?"

Alice didn't want to explain that she'd been at the Aberdeen Mortuary instead of ACL. "No, but why don't we have our next lunch at Shade Tree Barbecue? Before it gets too chilly outside?" She watched Pat Simpson at the bar, pulling out his credit card. She wondered how long his enchilada order would take.

"Agreed," said Mischa.

"Nanette, you may not have much time for pro bono work, but let me tell you about the Library Board." Alice took her time describing the issues she worked on.

The kitchen door opened at the end of the bar and Luis hurried out with a go-box.

"Thanks," Simpson said. He picked up the box carefully and sauntered out the swinging doors to the parking lot.

"He's gone," Alice said quietly. She found Nanette's anxiety disturbing.

The barkeep brought the check, which Mischa insisted on paying. "I knew you would help, Alice."

The three women gathered their bags and began walking out. But Nanette stopped dead when she reached the small table at the end of the bar. "Brett! What are you doing here?"

"Oh—um, hi, Nanette. I just wanted to try this place..." said the young man, face paling. "I'd heard about the food..."

Nothing on his table but a Coke.

"Spying on me again?" Nanette said, face set, eyes narrowed.

"Of course not!" he said. "I mean, not too many choices here in Coffee Creek, y'know."

Alice caught the eye of the barkeep—a grad student everyone called History, still finishing his dissertation. He lifted an eyebrow at her.

Nanette marched away, back rigid. Mischa steered her into the restroom. Alice followed. Nanette was trembling with rage, trying to take some deep breaths. "At least he can't follow me in here!" she said. "Brett Bradley followed me to Simpson from the Betts firm, Alice. Second-year associate from Duke Law. He drove me nuts at Betts. I was supposed to be his mentor. He was in my office twenty times a day. Standing between me and the door. Standing too close. Asking me out for drinks. Staring at me at meetings. He's another reason I left."

"But why didn't you warn Simpson?"

"Pat Simpson hired him last month without telling me. Said he assumed I'd be pleased." She rearranged the heavy orange tote on her shoulder. "I carry my laptop everywhere after finding Brett in my office, snooping."

Mischa interrupted. "He's a stalker, Alice."

As the three women walked outside to the parking lot, Nanette stiffened again, gazing at the parked cars. Alice looked where she was looking. In a black Tesla sat a silver-haired man, holding a phone to his ear. Vanity plate: "Simpson."

Mischa snorted. "So much for getting those enchiladas to his precious secretary."

Nanette managed a smile. She thanked Alice, then said, "Mischa, we'd better beat my boss back to the office." With Mischa close behind, she hurried to a small red Mini Cooper. They exited the parking lot while her boss was still on his phone.

Alice blew out her breath, thinking she'd call her contacts as soon as she got to the office. Money laundering plus having to put up with a twit like Brett Bradley? Nanette deserved better.

Then she wondered about Brett Bradley. He'd appeared, followed by Pat Simpson. Coincidence? Or had he told Simpson where Nanette was?

As she watched the Mini-Cooper leave, Alice heard footsteps and turned. "Jorgé!"

"Saw you having lunch, Alice. Can you talk for a sec? Got something I want you to look at."

She followed him back inside to the office he occupied together with Bill Birnbach and Bill Benke, the triumvirate that ran the iconic roadhouse.

Jorgé handed her a one-page document. "We got this bare-bones proposal for a band festival weekend in Coffee Creek that apparently would take place here at the Barn. It seems to involve some sort of collaboration with the Events Committee at the Chamber, but it's very sketchy as to what, if anything, the Chamber would provide. We need you to check the terms, specifically the liability provisions. I'm not sure what we'd get out of this. Looks like maybe we just wind up holding all the bags."

"I'll take a look," Alice said.

Jorgé's cell phone rang. He looked at the screen and made a face. "Gotta get this."

Alice smiled and left his office. On her way back out she checked the bar area. Brett Bradley had disappeared.

When she reached the parking lot again, the Tesla was still there, Simpson now leaning on the hood, still holding his phone. Weren't those enchiladas getting cold?

A typical Coffee Creek pickup, dusty, slightly battered, cruised slowly from the back of the lot toward the exit. It braked sharply as a large white Mercedes SUV wheeled in, spraying gravel and narrowly missing the pickup's fenders. The pickup driver leaned on the horn, then leaned out the window. "Where you from, buddy? That's not how we drive here!" he roared, glaring down at the Mercedes.

The Mercedes ignored him and pulled into an empty space near the Tesla. A tall man emerged and strolled over toward Simpson.

They could have been twins. Except for his dark hair, the new guy was a dead ringer for Pat Simpson—similarly tanned and slim, with sunglasses perched on his head.

Alice's car was parked past Pat Simpson's. Would he hail her? He did.

"Alice Greer, right? Come meet my brother, Ron Simpson. He manages the hedge fund."

"Hello," she said, noting the arrogant eyebrows and assessing the silk shirt, the stylish jeans. She preferred Kinsear's typical style—boots, chambray shirt, and real jeans, a bandana always handy in his pocket. Pat glanced at his brother, then back at Alice. "Alice has a local law practice. Formerly in Austin. Right?"

"What happened? Didn't make partner?" Ron drawled.

Obnoxious. "Wrong," she said. "I was a partner; I enjoyed my Austin practice for many years." Not that it was his business. "I hear you're from New Jersey. Why'd you set up a hedge fund in Coffee Creek?" Texas already had over a hundred hedge funds, with more than twenty in Austin. Alice refrained from asking, "Couldn't compete in the big city?"

"These days everything's connected. Capital can move anywhere. Might as well be where the real estate's cheap and there's no state income tax," said Pat. "Our Florida backers had their eyes on some Texas opportunities. We've already invested in a privately-held local construction company."

"Besides, we focus on high-end clients." Ron added, adjusting the tilt of his sunglasses. "As part of our service we try to shield them from publicity. Not much of that around here."

Right, Alice thought. If Nanette's suspicions were correct, their clients couldn't afford publicity, couldn't afford to attract attention from the authorities.

Pat spoke. "Alice was having lunch with Nanette and someone named—what? Something like 'Mochi'?"

Alice didn't correct him. Mischa didn't need to be involved. "I've known both those talented young women for years." She almost said "talented lawyers" but didn't want these guys to suspect she intended to abet Nanette's escape.

She gave a short wave and climbed into her green Discovery, thinking about Nanette, deciding which of her contacts she'd call first. New job for Nanette: she was on it.

When she reached her office, she Googled the Simpson brothers. They weren't currently on LinkedIn. She looked harder. Their online presence? Missing. The Simpson brothers were Internet ghosts. The website for Simpson Strategic Assets was polished and uninformative: "high net worth...risk-adjusted superior returns...holistic portfolios..." No phone number and no owner pictures, which she found interesting.

Alice began calling. Anyone need a really hard-working private equity lawyer? Two of her three contacts perked up at the thought and responded, saying they'd ask Nanette to visit with them. Alice left Nanette a message on her cell phone, ending, "Sounds promising."

Chapter Seven

A Constant Worry

Alice spent a solitary Saturday morning at the office, playing catch-up. She reviewed her notes for a long-scheduled probate hearing on Monday, then settled down to review the proposal Jorgé had asked her to look at, suggesting a December event involving the Beer Barn and the Chamber of Commerce. The proposal was merely a wish list. Proposed activities were vague. Indoor? Outdoor? Music? Selling food? Which party would handle which activities? The Chamber didn't seem to be undertaking any responsibilities. Alice frowned at the sketchy indemnity provision. No way would the Beer Barn indemnify the Chamber. She began drafting.

Finally, neck stiff, she took a break. The office felt too quiet without Silla. Alice's muscles ached from too much airplane. Which made her think of Scotland, the mortuary, and Ian Blane—all depressing. She checked her email. Nope, not a word from Blane. She emailed him: "What's the status of the forensics investigation? I've requested that you forward all maintenance records for the helicopter." Then she added, "Also please forward all information concerning the flight schedule and weather conditions. When can I expect those?" What else?

Her phone pinged—a text. Not from Blane; from Nanette, also apparently spending Saturday at the office. "Thanks for your message, Alice. Just had another 'discussion' with my boss, who announced money's already been wired. I shared my discoveries, but no luck. Am convinced I must leave. I have sent you my resignation letter. I'll leave it on my boss's desk tonight. Thanks for all your support. Nanette."

Alice saw no attachment. She checked her office email account and found an email from Nanette with no subject line but with these words pasted in: "Dear Mr. Simpson: I have recently raised certain concerns about ongoing work projects in which I'm involved at Simpson Strategic Assets. At this point I feel obliged to turn in my resignation. With best regards..."

Short and sweet, Alice thought. Maybe that's all Nanette should or could say. Must have been quite a discussion. She hoped she'd hear back quickly from the friends she'd called about a new job for Nanette. She looked at her watch. Just past four p.m. Central Time: not too late to call John, six hours ahead in Edinburgh on Saturday night. She wanted to catch him before he flew back to Hong Kong. John sounded breathless. She heard voices and music in the background. "Sorry, Mom. I'm out with some people."

"No worries," she said. "You're all packed up?"

"Yes. Everything's set. I'm on an early flight tomorrow from Edinburgh to Heathrow, then a direct flight to Hong Kong."

"You've got everything you need?" The eternal mom question.

"I'm fine, Mom." The eternal answer.

Alice looked out her window at the autumnal afternoon; in Edinburgh it would soon be midnight, and then her precious boy would be alone in Hong Kong. She shook her head.

"I'll miss you tons. Safe flight, darling."

"Love you, Mom."

Parenthood. Motherhood. A driving force for her, and a constant worry at the back of her mind. John and Ann seemed so able, so ready to tackle the world. Yet the world held surprises, some unpleasant, some she could not bear to contemplate.

Okay, now for Ann. Only five p.m. Eastern Time, but again, noise and music in the background.

"Mom!" Ann always sounded so joyful, so ready for fun.

"What are you up to?"

"Going to the opera, for my roomie's birthday. *Carmen!* What I get for rooming with a music major! Can you believe it? We are so dressed up!"

"Tell me!"

"Slinky dresses from the vintage shop! I'll send you a picture."

"Do you have dates?"

"Mm-hmm. Gotta go. Love you, Mom!"

Alice's phone pinged. She tapped the photo to see a selfie of Ann, with her glossy brown hair, her face alight with mischief, rocking a gold satin thirties-era dress, and her college bestie, similarly decked out. They were seniors now, full of ambition, plagued occasionally by uncertainty, about to be "lost, lost in the wide, wide world." That depressing lyric came from an antique ditty in Alice's college songbook, an earworm a century old, but still occasionally applicable.

She locked the office and headed home. Late sun slanted across her pasture. Big Boy, standing in the gravel drive, self-designated as her official greeter, brayed his traditional welcome.

Alice tugged on running clothes, determined to get in a short run in the cool air before the light faded. The burros clustered around the wrought-iron gate that kept them out of her yard, ready for their cocktail carrots. She broke the carrots into halves, fed the burros, patted Big Boy (the smallest), then Queenie, then Princess, the youngest. As always, she felt her heartbeat slow, felt her breathing grow deeper, when she stroked the burros. Odd, given how jumpy burros could be.

She trotted down the drive and made the turn onto the shoulder of Old Hays Road, hitting a slow stride and thinking about Kinsear. He'd invited himself for dinner tomorrow. "Potluck, Alice. I'll bring steaks to grill."

Running toward the orange sunset, she let herself consider what tomorrow evening might hold. She loved her children, who teetered on the edge of the nest, flapping their wings, preparing to leap into the air. She had compelling legal work, for which she was grateful, and which absorbed her attention enough to take her mind occasionally off her children. And now she'd touched the naked bone of Jordie's broken skull. Again she found herself rubbing her right thumb with her fingers, remembering that moment.

But tomorrow...moonlight? Dinner? Kinsear? Life, in fact?

She kept running, thinking of Kinsear, until the orange dimmed, and turned for home. Surely tomorrow would bring peace.

Chapter Eight

Stay Here, Ma'am

Sunday morning's sky brought the gray threat of the first fall norther, the sudden visitor from the plains that occasionally blasted the Hill Country. She heard the wind pick up. Outside in jeans, sweater, and barn coat, Alice shivered as the first gusts hit. The burros stood huddled in their shed, watching her tug open the barn door and drag first one, then a second haybale into their pen. She cut open the bales, her nose tickling at the grassy odor, and broke the straw into a bed for a cold night. The burros immediately began eating their bed.

Alice hurried back inside. Just after nine: maybe she'd make butternut squash soup. Kinsear liked it, and standing over a hot stove sounded comforting.

Her phone vibrated in her pocket. She dug it out, hoping for Kinsear. The number was vaguely familiar, but it wasn't his. "Hello?"

"This is Alan Joske, Coffee Creek Sheriff's Department. Who—who's speaking?"

She frowned. It couldn't be about Ann or John...what was wrong? She'd met Alan Joske before; he worked with Detective George Files. Sturdy, red-haired, very smart. Why didn't he know whom he'd called?

"This is Alice Greer."

"Oh," he said. "Ms. Greer, I'm investigating an incident at Limestone Lodge."

"Oh no," Alice breathed.

"It's a young woman. We found a phone nearby. If it's hers, she sent a message to your number yesterday afternoon."

The only text she remembered was Nanette's. "I had a text from Nanette Ferris. Is that who you're calling about? What happened?"

"We're not sure yet. The victim was possibly hit by a car."

Alice grabbed her fob. "I'll be right there."

"But"—

Alice hung up quickly. She bet he was about to tell her not to come, not to invade a possible crime scene. If indeed it was Nanette, Alice felt she owed her—what? Care. Attention. Because she'd agreed to help a lonely young woman. But she prayed: let it not be Nanette.

*****

Minutes later, speeding south down the creek road toward Coffee Creek, she turned left onto Navarro Street, then braked for the right turn onto Kestrel Lane. The Limestone Lodge property was still enclosed by its original limestone walls, the stone turning a soft gold with age. On the west it was bordered by Kestrel Lane, and on the east by Harrier Lane; both roads dead-ended at the fenced-off pipeline right-of-way on the south boundary of Limestone Lodge. As she drove slowly toward the end of Kestrel, Alice saw yellow crime scene tape fluttering across the west entrance to Limestone Lodge. She parked behind two Coffee County Sheriff's Department SUVs, and walked toward the west entrance, directly across the parking lot from the east entrance on Harrier.

Limestone Lodge itself sat on a small rise, to Alice's left. Downhill, on the right, she saw the tenant parking spaces, next to a grassy area with a picnic table, lawn chairs, a shrubbery border, and several live oaks. Tenants had easy access to Navarro via either the west entrance on Kestrel, or the east entrance on Harrier Lane.

Alice stopped, scanning the scene: an ambulance; EMTs standing nearby; two Coffee Creek deputies keeping watch; several crime scene techs in their white coveralls, walking slowly across the parking lot, examining the asphalt. No one was hurrying. She took that as a bad sign. She caught movement in the upstairs windows of the Lodge: residents, staring down at the grim activities below. Downhill from the tenant parking spaces to her right, just past a familiar red Mini Cooper, she spotted Alan Joske. He was bent over, searching the ground beneath a live oak near the edge of the shrubbery, his distinctive red hair hard to miss.

Again she prayed: let it be a mistake, let it not be Nanette. She started to duck under the crime scene tape. One of the deputies hurried toward her. "Ma'am, you can't enter."

Joske's head lifted. He spoke up. "Is that Alice Greer? I want to talk to her."

"Stay here, ma'am," the deputy said.

Alice complied, shivering in the gusty north wind.

Joske walked across the parking lot toward her, face impassive. He ducked under the tape and stood at her side, staring back toward the residents' cars.

"Is it Nanette Ferris?" she asked, hoping against hope he'd say no.

"Describe her."

Alice blew out a breath. "Tall and slim. Black hair in a bob. Gray eyes."

He nodded. "Sounds right."

She looked at the ambulance, sitting quietly in the parking lot. She heard the slam of a door. At that moment the ambulance began rolling slowly toward the east entrance onto Harrier Lane. A deputy moved aside the crime tape. The ambulance rolled away. "Is she dead?"

"I'm afraid so."

A blast of chilly air blew leaves across the parking lot. "Let's go sit somewhere warm." He looked across the street. "That your car?" She nodded. He walked her across the street but stopped in front of her Discovery, scrutinizing the grille. He looked back at the deputy waiting at the parking lot entrance and made a face, shrugging. Then he climbed into her passenger seat.

Alice got behind the wheel, glad she hadn't hit any live animals on the highway lately. Of course he had to check her car, but her heart thumped nevertheless.

Joske pulled out his notebook and turned toward her, eyes neutral. "Okay," he said, pencil poised. "First of all, tell me where you were last night."

"Home. Alone."

"How do you know this Nanette Ferris?"

"I've known her since she competed in a Moot Court competition I judged. I was out of the country last week. When I got back into town Friday, Silla, my assistant, told me I had a lunch date with Nanette, set up by another young lawyer friend from Austin, Mischa Faraday. I met Mischa at that same Moot Court competition." Joske made her spell Mischa's and Nanette's names.

She went on. "Mischa told Silla she hoped I'd help Nanette find a different job. We met at the Beer Barn Friday at noon." Only the day before yesterday, she thought.

Joske requested details—Mischa's current home and job contact info, a copy of the bio Mischa had sent. "So why was this Nanette needing a new job?"

"Nanette—Nanette worked on hedge fund deals, for Simpson Strategic Assets. It's in that new building on the Old Hays Road." She wondered if Joske knew anything about the Simpson brothers.

He frowned. "What kind of law is that? Is that what you do?"

"No." Alice gave a short description of Nanette's work. How much should she say? Could she share everything Nanette said? What if the Simpsons were completely above board? What if Nanette's suspicions were groundless?

"First, what happened to Nanette?" she asked. "I need to know."

"Why?"

"She seemed pretty anxious about her boss finding out she was job hunting."

Joske gave her a sharp look. "It appears she was hit by a vehicle."

"Here? In her own parking lot?"

"Hit at a high rate of speed."

Puzzled, Alice stared across the street into the parking lot. Could a car get up enough speed in that small parking lot to kill someone? Maybe some kid, out joyriding late at night, came racing into the lot from one street, planning to loop out the other side, just as Nanette climbed out of her car. Alice imagined her, exhausted from the long day at her office, gathering her belongings, locking her car, and starting uphill across the parking lot toward the safety of her apartment. On the other hand, if this was no accident, how could someone know so precisely where Nanette was at that moment? Sit parked, waiting, and then ...? She watched the crime scene team duck under the yellow tape and cross Kestrel in front of the entrance. Now they were peering down at the scraggly grass along the asphalt paving.

"Was it deliberate?" she asked Joske. "Not just some kid joyriding, too scared to stop?"

Instead of answering her question, he asked, "Why'd you drive over here after I called?"

She took a deep breath. "I started worrying about Nanette, after that lunch. And I kept worrying."

"Why?"

"Because she was worried." Alice's eyes widened. Mischa! Mischa could be walking across her own parking lot, on this quiet Sunday morning, unaware of danger. "Listen, shouldn't you call her friend Mischa?"

"Should I?"

"Yes! She may be at risk too! Okay, here's what Nanette said she was worried about." Alice tried to explain about contracts for rare earths, investments Nanette feared might be attracting unsavory investors. Face impassive, Joske took notes. But when she mentioned possible money laundering, Joske's eyes narrowed. She had his full attention.

"On Nanette's phone..." Alice began.

He raised his eyebrows.

"You have her phone, right? You saw my message to her. So did you see the text she sent me? About leaving Simpson Strategic Assets? And her resignation letter?"

"No, just your phone number, when you called and left a message on her cell."

Alice reached for her own phone, found Nanette's text, and showed it to Joske. "She asked me not to call her at the office, just on her cell. She felt people were keeping an eye on her." Alice remembered Nanette at the Beer Barn, arranging the heavy Longchamp tote by her chair. "Did you find her shoulder bag? Orange canvas? I'll bet it had a laptop in it."

"We found an orange bag under the bushes, but no laptop."

"But you did find her phone." Obviously he'd found it, since he'd called the last number. Must have gotten a techie to open it.

Joske nodded. "Under the green crew cab pickup in the far corner of the lot."

Alice wondered how it got there, then had a sickening thought. "Maybe she was holding it when she was hit?" The slim body, hurtling into the air, landing with a thud, the phone flying out of her hand... She looked at Joske.

His eyes met hers. "It's possible."

"When did this happen?"

Joske frowned, appeared to be assessing how much he could say. "Some time after midnight. That's preliminary only."

"And she wasn't found until morning? Lying in the parking lot?

Surely somebody would have seen her?"

"One of the residents went out to walk his dog about six a.m. and found her. The body was dragged under those shrubs behind the picnic table."

Alice closed her eyes, shook her head, trying to erase the image in her mind. "So you've been out here since, what, six-fifteen?" He nodded.

Then Alice remembered. "What about Mischa?" She grabbed her own phone.

Joske raised his hand. "Just give me the number. You stay here." These guys kept telling her that. She felt rebellion rise.

Alice recited Mischa's number while he punched it into his phone. He climbed out of the car, phone to his ear, and ducked back under the yellow tape into the parking lot. He turned, facing Alice's car. She watched him talking, staring across the street at her. Then he ducked under the tape and walked back to her car.

Alice rolled down her window and stared up at Joske. What now?

"Mischa Faraday's not answering her phone," Joske reported. "We've asked Austin police to check on her."

Alice stared out the driver's side window, looking at him, thinking, worrying. "We'll take care of it," he added, frowning at her.

"Okay, I'm out of here," Alice said. She started the engine and did a reasonably slow u-turn, avoiding Joske, who was striding back to the parking lot, phone again to his ear. She hoped he was calling George Files, head detective in the Coffee County Sheriff's Department. She wondered why Files hadn't answered the call in the first place. Maybe he was senior enough that he no longer had to crawl out of bed on Sunday mornings to look at a dead body.

Chapter Nine

Wash Away Such Sins

As Alice passed the H-E-B grocery, on impulse she turned abruptly into the carwash. Irrational, she knew, but she wanted to wash the taint of Limestone Lodge off her dusty Discovery. Only one car ahead of her in the carwash—a big white Land Rover SUV—but she could see from the lighted board listing the carwash options that the driver had bought the full monty: undercarriage, wheels, extra polish, spot-free rinse. She settled down to wait. Fancy Land Rover, she thought. Brand new; still had the paper license flapping from the rear. Now the multicolored soap foam covered the car; up came the spray bar to wash it off. Alice liked that multicolored foam. Times were changing in Coffee Creek. The longtime residents swore by their dusty pickups, but lately, with the market way up, she saw pricey new SUVs everywhere. Alice's vehicles were doomed to perpetual dust from her caliche driveway; she'd bet the Land Rover rolled home on a smooth, dustless asphalt drive.

Her turn. She pulled in, her car jiggling from the hard spray on the undercarriage.

Something made her glance at the rearview window. To her shock she saw a big white Land Rover SUV waiting behind her. Were there two in town now? Then she was blanketed in multicolored foam.

Polished and air-dried, she exited. Curiosity made her double back around the car wash, on her way to the gas pumps. She glanced back at the Land Rover. She couldn't tell if the driver was male or female. Yep, new paper car tag, flapping in the spray. She couldn't see the numbers. Two times through? Who would want to sit still that long in a carwash?

But suppose you'd crashed into a human being?

She remembered Joske scrutinizing the grille of her Discovery this morning. "Hit by a vehicle," he'd said.

Could a modern carwash with colored foam and high-speed spray wash away such sins?

If you'd hit a human with your car, would your first instinct be to run through your local carwash—twice?

No. Hightail it out of town fast, maybe use a chemical spray to get rid of anything a lab could find... Besides, wasn't the carwash open all night? Surely, if you'd just hit a human sometime after midnight, you wouldn't wait until mid-morning to wash your car? She shook her head, trying to erase the images. Cut it out, Alice.

In her momentarily spotless car, she headed for the creek road, and paused. Sunday morning. Almost eleven. Again on impulse, she turned toward downtown Coffee Creek instead of heading home.

After Jordie's death, Alice had abandoned church for a time, furious that someone as alive as Jordie could suddenly be swept away. Furious with God, furious with human frailty, furious with mortality. She'd returned in the last year, drawn by the honest words, the humanity, of the current pastor, oddly comforting. She pulled into the parking lot at the Presbyterian church and slipped through the entrance just as the choir members took their seats in the chancel at the front, music folders in hand. A white-haired usher smiled and handed her a bulletin. He didn't blink at her jeans and muddy boots.

Alice found a seat in the back pew. The choir rose, watching the choir director, who raised her hands. Softly the singers began, in unison, a single melodic line, rising and falling. Then the voices—soprano, tenor, alto, bass—began weaving their separate lines into a tapestry, alternately calming and disturbing, passionate and resigned. Was it Latin? Alice looked at the bulletin, then the translation. "Media vita in morte sumus..." "In the midst of life we are in death...of whom may we seek for succor?" Composer: John Sheppard, 1515-1558, who sang in the Chapel Royal at the funeral of Queen Mary I and the coronation of Queen Elizabeth. Plague years, Alice recalled, war years, plenty of death around. The composer had died at forty-three, carried off by a new infection sweeping Europe. Only a couple of years younger than Alice... She stared again at the bulletin. "In the midst of life..." Hours ago, Nanette was still alive.

Alice sat for the appointed hour, standing with the congregation, sitting again, listening. Images intruded: the dreadful sheet over bones in the Scottish mortuary. The ambulance carrying what once was Nanette, rolling away toward the waiting medical examiner. The faces of her precious children, so alive, so vigorous...so vulnerable.

She slipped out with the benediction still echoing in the rafters—"go in peace."

Maybe the burros would like extra carrots. She could lean on them, stroke their delicate long ears, feel her breath slow as they munched. Burro peace.

*****

On the creek road, driving home, Alice tried Mischa's number. Mischa answered immediately, sounding anxious.

"You're okay?" Alice blurted.

"I spent the night with my boyfriend. I heard about Nanette just now, when the police called." Her voice choked.

"Mischa. Did the police tell you to be careful?"

"Yes. They said her death might not have been an accident. Can that be true?" Her voice rose into a wail. "How could anyone hurt Nanette?"

"I don't know. But honestly, Mischa, I have a bad feeling about this." What a cliché. "Listen—what if you stay with your boyfriend a couple more days?"

"Why?"

"First, the police told you to be careful. Second, someone knew where Nanette lived. You parked in Nanette's office parking lot on Friday. Someone could likely figure out where you live too."

A long silence. Mischa sniffed, then cleared her throat. "I guess I could stay away from my place a couple of days, if you'll keep me posted. The police didn't say diddly about the facts." She began crying. "I feel responsible! I brought her to lunch! Her boss saw her! It was my fault! If I'd just minded my own business…" Her voice trailed off miserably.

"Look, Mischa, we don't know who did this. I doubt it has anything to do with you. But I want you to be careful."

A slow "okay" from Mischa. Then: "Will you please let me know what's going on? Call me?"

Alice agreed.

*****

Her phone buzzed as she reached her ranch gate. Kinsear's voice, very alive, very welcome. "What if I come over a little early? So the steaks can be at room temperature when I grill them?"

She grinned to herself at the feeble excuse. "Yes!"

When he arrived, Kinsear dusted the steaks with his homemade dry rub—the recipe still veiled in mystery— and left them on the counter to reach the correct temperature. "What's next?" he asked. He helped Alice toss more hay into the burros' pen, then offered to help put insulation over the outside faucets. Alice knew there'd be more lovely Indian summer days after this norther disappeared, but she needed to prepare for the occasional sharp freezes that hit the Hill Country.

He opened a bottle of cabernet while she told him about Nanette—the lunch Friday, the message Saturday afternoon, the dreadful news Sunday morning.

"I am so sorry," Kinsear said. "But I'm glad you didn't find the body, this time."

His face grew thoughtful. "The hedge fund world," he mused. He'd retired early after serving as general counsel to a hedge fund and still occasionally provided some advice. "And rare earths." He shook his head, handed her a glass of wine, poured one for himself. Then he looked up, holding her eyes, face grim. "Listen, you need to stay far, far away from this mess. Money laundering? This will be the feds. You don't want to come to their attention."

She nodded. He was right. This had nothing to do with her, except that she'd agreed to help Nanette find another job. And now she could do nothing more for Nanette.

He sipped his wine. She sipped hers.

"I believe the steaks need a little more time before I light the grill." He put down his wineglass, then took hers and placed it, with all deliberation, on the kitchen counter. He waited, eyes on her face. She moved into his arms, remembering the first time he'd kissed her, back in law school, before Jordie. She still remembered that kiss. The steaks might be reaching room temperature, but she felt her own temperature rising.

Which is how they wound up in Alice's bedroom.

Much later, as she watched him carry the sizzling steaks from the grill back to the kitchen, she thought how very at home this felt: Kinsear in her house, in her kitchen, in her bed. Despite the horror of the remains in the mortuary, the body on the medical examiner's table, for a moment at least, in the midst of death we are in life.

Chapter Ten

Plain Brown Envelope

Arriving at the office Monday morning, Alice found Silla had not only beat her in but had already picked up the mail at the post office.

Silla brandished her paper knife. "I'll bring your copies in a sec," she announced. She virtually never handed any original document to Alice, trusting her only with copies. "But this looks personal. I opened it, and it's only printouts, as far as I can tell."

She thrust a plain brown envelope into Alice's hands.

Alice stared down. No return address. Her address was handwritten in capital letters. She didn't recognize the printing. She walked into her office, tugging out a thin stack of paper, clipped with a bulldog clip. No transmittal letter; no handwriting on the top sheet; no sticky note of explanation. She peered back into the envelope: no, she hadn't missed anything.

At her desk she began turning pages. The Internet printouts varied. Some were websites of companies she'd never heard of; some were press releases reporting transactions—sales, acquisitions, mergers—again, for companies she'd never heard of. Some were newspaper reports of a crime, a trial, in Myanmar or elsewhere: Los Angeles, Las Vegas, Tampa, Miami. An article from a Miami newspaper on the expansion of the Russian mafia into south Florida mentioned Dmitri Novikov as a crime boss. A fuzzy telephoto shot in a Miami paper was labeled "Tino Vitale and Dmitri Novikov celebrating at Hialeah Racetrack."

On the last page, under a newspaper photo, one name was circled with a yellow highlighter.

Alice had learned the first summer of her first law internship never, never to mark on any document that might in future become an exhibit. If no clean copy was available, a copy with marks had to be explained. The only permissible mark involved a yellow highlighter which—at least back then—did not appear on a copy of the marked document.

Nanette? She'd follow the same rule. Did Nanette send these?

Highlighted on the last page: "General Sone visits Hong Kong's Victoria Harbour." Blurry photo of an Asian man wearing a blazer, standing on what looked like the white prow of a yacht. She flipped back through the other pages. No other mention of Sone.

Knowing Files might not like her next move, she took the stack and envelope to Silla. "Please make a copy, including the envelope front and back. The way you always do."

Silla stared up at her. "For what file?"

She hadn't yet told Silla about Nanette. "I'll explain in a minute," Alice said. "Can you wear gloves while you're handling these? I'm afraid I've already got my prints all over them."

Silla raised her eyebrows, then headed for the copier, red ponytail swinging.

Alice's mind raced. She should call Joske. But instead, she'd call George Files. He was Coffee County's senior detective. Joske might complain, but she had more history with Files. Perhaps they both viewed her with suspicion, but Files made it less obvious.

She found Silla at the copier. "About Nanette." Silla looked up, wary. Alice told her about Joske's Sunday morning call, her race to Limestone Lodge, the ambulance disappearing with the body.

"Someone hit her with a car? In the parking lot? And left her there?" Silla's face crumpled in horror.

"But maybe took her laptop."

Silla's face changed. She looked at the stack of copies, then the brown envelope.

"You think she you sent these? On Saturday afternoon? Why?"

Alice remembered Nanette's worried face at the Beer Barn, the slender fingers toying with the fork, food untouched. "She wanted our help."

"So these are going to George Files." Silla put the originals back in their envelope, then put the envelope into a manila mailer and handed it to Alice, adding, "Don't forget—you've got Rotary at noon."

Which made Alice remember: she should call Jorgé, ask about this festival proposed by the Coffee Creek Chamber of Commerce. She was bound to hear more about it at Rotary. Suddenly a vision rose before her: a Coffee Creek version of the long-running Austin Armadillo Christmas Bazaar. The Beer Barn would be perfect. She was reaching for her phone when it rang.

Jorgé. "Listen, Alice, I've got an idea."

"About this festival?"

"Yes. How did you know?"

"Tell me." She grinned, enjoying as always how their brains worked in sync.

"What if we call this the Beer Barn Holiday Bazaar? We could let the church folks sell their tamales, cookies, candied pecans, out in the parking lot."

"So they don't invade your kitchen and get the health department on our necks."

"Exactly. Inside, people could sell arts and crafts. We'd set up tables along the walls. But any big metal sculptures of longhorns would have to stay in the parking lot."

"What about music?" she asked. Irate neighbors would complain about too much outdoor amplified music.

"Maybe inside, with a different group every couple of hours? They'll play and sell some music. Also, that'll bring folks in to buy the arts and crafts. Here's another thought: how about a grand finale dance contest on a deck outside in the parking lot? The Mexican dance troupe at the high school is begging me."

"Sounds great."

"What I'm thinking is, if this works, we might have a new Beer Barn tradition. Benke and Birnbach are on board."

"What about a polka contest too?" Alice asked.

"Great."

Alice told Jorgé she wanted all dancers, sellers, musicians, and purveyors of any stripe to sign releases.

"Whatever you say. Put it all in our response to the Chamber."

"Who's your contact there on the Events Committee?"

"Guess. Large, loud, and obnoxious."

Alice had several candidates in mind. But the largest, loudest, and most obnoxious? "Louie Gumbert?"

"You got it."

Alice groaned. Gumbert was a lawyer who liked having his fingers in a lot of pots. He was both lazy and persistent, the type who never thought he'd made a final deal, always thought he could come back and re-trade. So tedious. He swaggered around, Alice thought, like he imagined himself the creative impresario of Coffee Creek. She looked up to see Silla at the door, holding up an invisible phone.

"Gotta go. I'll save you a table at Rotary." Jorgé hung up.

Silla announced, "Some guy named Blane's calling, from Scotland. Says he's returning your call."

Fear, anxiety, and anger assailed her. She picked up the phone. "Officer Blane. Your phone service has been restored?"

Chapter Eleven

Possibility of Sabotage

"There's been an issue with the forensics examination." His voice was dry, matter-of-fact, but she sensed a pressure behind it. "It appears there were issues with the chopper's performance, more than we would have predicted, even accounting for weather, tidal action, and the chopper's speed and elevation."

Over and over Alice had imagined the helicopter falling helplessly, out of control. Trying to dispel that image, she squeezed her eyes, then opened them.

Blane continued, voice still dry but somehow alarming. "The damage has puzzled the investigators. They had wondered about poor maintenance."

Nameless fear rose in her mind. She realized she'd hoped all along that the crash was caused by weather, weather impervious to human blandishments—not by human error or negligence. She didn't think she could bear living the rest of her life knowing Jordie was killed by carelessness or neglect.

"The company maintenance records look solid, but of course we'll take a second look."

Alice's worst fear was taking shape, the scenario she'd never let herself consider. "So...?"

"The investigators need to rule out the possibility of sabotage."

"Sabotage?" Someone might have killed her husband...deliberately? She couldn't take it in. She'd tried to prepare herself for the horror and unfairness of an accident, maybe metal fatigue, maybe sloppy human maintenance; she'd read up on the dangers of unexpected weather that might cause a pilot to experience vertigo, causing the helicopter to spin and fall out of control. She still couldn't get out of her mind the vision of Jordie and the pilot terrified and helpless, maybe killed immediately with the force of the helicopter hitting the water, maybe living just long enough to drown. But killed by persons unknown?

"Why would anyone sabotage that helicopter?"

"Now, Mrs. Greer. That's not our final conclusion. It's a possibility we must consider."

Her mind raced. "Why? Because the second passenger didn't fly as scheduled?"

"Right. We understand he'd finished his work and chose to leave earlier. So we'd like to talk with him."

"Did anyone on the oil rig see anything suspicious, see anyone messing with the helicopter?" she asked.

"No. But at shift change, mealtime..." His voice trailed off.

She took a long breath. Blane was silent. Finally she said, "What's next?"

"The investigation's ongoing." He paused. "Mrs. Greer. Is there anything else you can tell me? Did your husband say anything to you that might help? Maybe something he knew, or suspected?"

"About what?"

"Perhaps he'd heard something that might require reporting to authorities."

"I know of nothing like that." Well, she was telling the truth. But Alice was unsure what more she should—or could—say. What about those cryptic notes in Jordie's notebook? Had Blane seen them? She didn't think so. And for some reason—despite her questions—she didn't want to mention Jimmie. "I assume the Coastguard examined his personal effects?" She hated the thought of anyone touching the bracelet, the ring, the notebook.

"We followed procedure. So, yes." Alice heard background noise. Then Blane, in a hurry: "Sorry—may I call you back?"

"Yes."

He hung up.

She sat, digesting the conversation, thinking of Jordie aloft with the pilot, watching the coast of Scotland approach, then—what? Storm? Wind? Lightning? The notebook with its cryptic hints. Emma Linden: "Have you seen my Jimmie?"

She'd almost reached a state of peace, after reading about iffy Aberdeen weather. Maybe she could live with weather. But Blane's suggestion of sabotage—and his question about what Jordie knew? What Jimmie might have told him? Her stomach churned.

"Time for Rotary!" Silla called.

*****

One good thing about her Rotary meeting at the Chamber of Commerce: today was enchilada day. Alice inhaled deeply in happy anticipation. The lunch buffet held bubbling hot pans of cheese enchiladas, fresh tortillas, guacamole, salsa, pico de gallo and a vast bowl of corn chips. A second good thing: the three Beer Barons had saved seats at their table for Alice and her best friend, Red Griffin. Nicknamed "Red" for her favorite color (today she sported her red Armani suit), Red owned Red's Rescue Ranch for abused horses. Alice and Red sat down, ready to dive into their enchiladas.

A large shadow fell across the table. Red flinched as Louie Gumbert's elbow invaded her space. He lowered himself and his plate simultaneously. One highly decorated enchilada rolled off his plate, splattering Red's iced tea with sour cream and salsa. "Whoops!" he said, replacing the enchilada on his plate. "Gimme back that glass, Red!" He scraped the sour cream off the glass back onto the enchilada, then wiped Red's glass with his napkin and planted it by her plate. "Here you go."

Red recoiled, staring at her besmeared glass, momentarily speechless. She scooted her chair slightly away from Gumbert's bulk.

"Okay," he said. "Let's talk turkey here, now that I have you three boys trapped."

"Nothing we say here counts, Louie," said Jorgé. He glanced left, then right. Birnbach and Benke nodded.

Benke rose and grabbed a clean glass of iced tea for Red and handed it to her, then sat. "It's Alice you've got to satisfy." He carefully spooned salsa onto his enchilada, took a bite, nodded in satisfaction.

Gumbert looked at Alice, surprised. "Oh, yeah," he said. "You're lawyered up."

"Indeed," Birnbach said.

Gumbert leaned across Red toward Alice. "Listen, Alice. The Chamber came up with this plan for an event. We've got great ideas."

Red scooted her chair two inches further from the table.

"I'm sure you do," said Alice. "Of course the Beer Barn's got the venue, the reputation, the equipment, and the know-how. It's not our first rodeo. We'll send over a contract to the Chamber this week."

Gumbert returned to his enchiladas, then said, mouth full, "No need, little lady." He swallowed. "I sent over the basis for a contract."

"Hardly," Alice rejoined, putting down her fork. "The Beer Barn received merely a short wish list. We'll draft any contract. Pass the salt, please."

"And Alice is not your 'little lady,' Louie." Birnbach's voice was hard. "You don't want to piss her off." He leaned back. "We can go it alone if we have to."

Jorgé, on cue, played good cop. "But of course we're happy to partner with the Chamber, if it works out. I said 'if.' Who else is on your committee, from the Chamber?"

Oh, smart, Alice thought. Give us another contact.

"Um, what's her name, the bank girl. Mirabel? Something like that. And Leo, from Central Garage."

"You mean Miranda, who manages Madrone Bank?" Alice asked. She, Red, Miranda, and their friend Jane Ann were in the same book group.

"Yeah. But she's only on a need-to-know basis at present." Gumbert swigged his tea and crunched some corn chips. Crumbs flew.

Alice was about to ask whether Gumbert needed to keep anyone else at Chamber informed, when Benke put down his fork and switched topics.

"What's the program today? Isn't Mayor Wilson speaking? Let's move up so we can hear. We can pick up dessert on the way." The Beer Barons and Red and Alice rose and decamped to chairs near the podium.

"Hey! I'm not quite through," Gumbert called. He headed back to the buffet.

Jorgé said, in Alice's ear, "You know, I think it's rude to comment on folks' table manners. So I'll just say I don't want to sit across from Gumbert again. Lost my appetite. Even on enchilada day."

"I'll get a draft contract to you three asap," Alice said.

"Great. And if we can't work with Gumbert—" his white teeth gleamed—"we'll have our Bazaar anyway."

*****

After lunch, Alice marched back to her car, oblivious to a rising wind and spatters of rain. Mentally she drafted a division of labor. For the Beer Barons, book the bands; get the word out to churches who wanted to sell tamales or baked goods; run an ad in this week's *Coffee Creek Caller* about reserving space to sell crafts; get barbecue trucks lined up; and order banners. For the Chamber, rent picnic tables; provide space for additional parking and more food trucks; hire enough off-duty police to manage parking outdoors and behavior indoors; provide trash and garbage pickup; and totally indemnify the Beer Barn for anything other than gross negligence. What else?

When she reached the car, she called Miranda, who'd missed the Rotary lunch. "I hear you're on the Chamber Events Committee for a possible holiday event?"

"I was absent! I missed one Chamber meeting and learned I'd been appointed," Miranda groaned.

"Your colleague Louie Gumbert mentioned you—oh, wait, no, he mentioned someone named Mirabel."

"What I do for this bank," Miranda said. "'Mirabel'? Honestly."

"Can you and Leo outflank him? Even though he says you're only 'need-to-know?'"

"Do you doubt me? But Louie's way ahead of his skis. This so-called committee hasn't even met."

A helicopter buzzed overhead. Alice stopped, paralyzed.

"Alice?"

"I'm here." She'd never hear a helicopter again without thinking it was about to drop from the sky. "Well, could you let me know if your committee actually meets?"

"Sure. Don't hold your breath. Hey, mark your calendar for the Madrone Bank holiday cocktail event for our wealth management contacts. We've reserved that new French restaurant on Highway 290 for the Tuesday afternoon before Thanksgiving. They promised some nice hors d'oeuvres."

"Cool."

"Bring Silla too."

They hung up.

Alice unlocked her car and glanced at the brown envelope on the passenger seat. Now for Files.

She parked at Courthouse Square and walked to the Sheriff's Annex. She asked the desk officer, a middle-aged man with a crewcut and a serious face, for Detective George Files.

"He's not in. What can I do for you?"

"I need to get this to him." She handed over the envelope along with her business card.

"He'll know what it's about?"

"If he could give me a call, I'd appreciate it."

Back in the office she worked up a draft contract and emailed it to the Beer Barons for review.

****

When she got home at six, she called John in Hong Kong. Thirteen hours ahead—he'd be up.

She could hear traffic when he answered. "Hi, Mom! I'm walking downtown to catch the bus to my classes."

"You're safely there? What's the monastery like? Is it like your dad described it?" John had applied for a room in the same unusual Zen monastery Jordie had stayed in on his post-grad trip through Asia.

"Hang on." In a few seconds he said, "Yes, and believe it or not, the old monk still remembers Dad. He even gave me the same room. I've sent you some pictures. The room's just big enough for a twin bed and small desk. At least it's got a window, looking up toward the Peak. Same view Dad saw." He paused. "It's funny. I really like this place. It's so minimal, just like Dad said. No closet, just a couple of shelves. No elevator, just stairs. Tile floors. Sink in the room. I had breakfast downstairs—oranges, tea, and congee, you know that leftover rice? I put dried fish and scallions and soy sauce on mine. Pretty monastic!"

"Hey, I like the picture on your desk."

"Christmas six years ago, right? You and Ann and Dad and me. Remember? Little touch of home."

She couldn't stop smiling. "So, who else lives at the monastery?"

"It's like a hostel, but more long term. Pretty friendly. A couple of grad students have rooms near me. I met them at breakfast. We all put our cards in the nameplates on our door so we can learn names. There's one older guy I haven't met—no card on his nameplate yet. I saw him going upstairs, though. Hey, here comes the bus. At least I think it's my bus. I'll call later." And he was gone.

You wanted him to be independent, she told herself. But thirteen hours and a vast ocean away?

In the kitchen she turned on the news, washed an apple, and sliced some cheese. She found an open bottle of Petit Verdot and poured a glass. She sat, thinking about Blane's call. How much should she tell Blane? Why did she feel so reluctant? Was there anyone she could trust?

She called Kinsear. "Can you come over?"

Chapter Twelve

Fatal Attractions

Kinsear arrived bearing a cast-iron pot of chili and a couple of beers. "Hope I didn't get it too hot this time," he said. "You got any avocados? A little guac will cool the tongue. Or some sour cream...?"

He opened the refrigerator. "Aha. Fireman's Four for me. What about you?"

Alice felt the tension leave her neck and shoulders. Kinsear had priorities straight for dealing with stress. Chili, offset by a cold beer, and of course a vegetable—i.e., guacamole. But his eyes searched hers.

"Let's talk first," he said. "By a fire. It's getting cold."

He busied himself at the fireplace. Alice found a lime and some cumin and mashed two avocados into submission.

"Tell," he said, pointing to the chair by the fire. Flames wavered, then caught. Alice sat.

"Gran has a nephew," she began. "Jameson Jeffrey Greer. Jimmie. Jordie's cousin."

"You're using present tense, I see."

She nodded. "I met him at the wedding. He didn't make it to Jordie's memorial service in Edinburgh. The kids also met him at Gran's when they were eight and ten." She took a breath, not quite ready for the next bit. "The helicopter went down with only two passengers. Or at least they found only two bodies and identified both. One was Jordie."

Kinsear watched her face.

"When they gave me his 'personal effects,' there was a little notebook. Jordie had written, the day before he was scheduled to leave the platform, 'JJ here Fly out Friday. CK Cigars?'" She glanced at Kinsear's alert face. "The Coastguard says a seabed geologist from a company called GGI showed up at the platform via a motorboat based in Antwerp. He was scheduled to fly out on Friday, in the helicopter, but apparently finished his work early and left two days earlier with the offshore crew boat, to make an international flight. Gran says 'JJ here' means his cousin Jimmie Greer."

"So he left earlier. And then the chopper went down?"

Alice nodded.

Kinsear gazed at Alice, thinking through the last comment.

"Where's Jimmie now?

"Maybe still in Asia." She took a breath. "Gran was worried that she hadn't heard from Jimmie in a couple of years—said that wasn't like him. Okay, after the burial service in Broadview, we were sitting in Gran's kitchen when a Belgian woman named Emma Linden shows up asking 'Have you seen my Jimmie?' She claims she took him out to the oil rig platform five years ago on her boat. Emma says he hadn't liked rare earths mining in Myanmar and was glad to move to the Pacific. At some point he told her he thought he was being followed, thought his Myanmar clients might be criminals. He and Emma stayed in touch for a couple of years; then he quit calling. She didn't hear from him until she got this postcard a few weeks ago, mailed from Jakarta." She showed Kinsear the photos of both sides of the postcard.

Kinsear stared at the fire, then looked directly at Alice. "And the Scottish Coastguard guy didn't mention this, so maybe he didn't know, and you didn't tell him about this family connection. Is that where you are?"

She nodded, appreciating as always that quick mind.

He went on. "Because even though people on the platform knew this cousin wasn't flying, your husband's chopper still went down?" His face darkened. "Who the hell is this woman who showed up at Gran's? I don't want Gran dragged into this." He and Gran had bonded the previous year when he and Alice hiked in Scotland.

"Gran said Jordie came by before he flew out to the platform and promised to stop back by," Alice said, her stomach in a knot. "The day of Jordie's burial, when we searched, we found he'd left Emma Linden's address hidden in Robbie's treasure box."

"You've told this Blane guy none of this?"

"So far."

"You don't trust him?"

She thought about that vague feeling. "No, for some reason. Maybe because he doesn't trust me. I don't know, Ben. It takes them five years to find the chopper. This guy Blane said today they're still trying to rule out poor maintenance or—or sabotage. I find out Jordie left cryptic messages—didn't tell anyone he was meeting Jimmie. Why not, do you suppose?"

"I can think of several reasons. First, maybe his cousin Jimmie wanted to entrust some confidential information. But what was it? Second, your husband didn't want to endanger his family. But he dropped some breadcrumbs in case things went south. Third, this rare earths business, along with Jimmie's fear he was being followed, and his current radio silence—this scares me." Kinsear stared into the fire, then shook his head slowly. "Bad ju-ju, looking for rare earths. Lots of jostling, lots of sharp elbows in that trade," he added. "I mean it, Alice. Don't touch this stuff. You don't have any idea who might be involved. For instance, who the hell is this Emma Linden?"

"She says she's a teacher."

"But you don't really know. Seriously, you and Gran should stay far away from the world of rare earths. Rare earths could have fatal attractions."

He stood. "Time for chili. Can we just sit by the fire?"

He put on another log, sending up orange cinders and the smell of cedar. Alice spooned chili into large bowls. "Want cheese on top? Sour cream? Salsa? Guacamole?"

"The whole nine yards. And perhaps another beer. What about you?"

"I have a lovely chili wine in the fridge. Grenache and Mourvedre. Some attitude there."

They settled into chairs by the fireplace. Alice felt peace steal over her. She felt safe, here in the Hill Country, sitting by the fire with someone she trusted, far from the North Sea, far from rare earths.

Then she thought of Nanette.

Her phone buzzed. She checked the incoming message from George Files: "Need to see you about the packet you left at the desk, as soon as possible. I'm out of town but will be in by seven on Wednesday."

Chapter Thirteen

So Safe, Coffee Creek

At seven a.m. on Wednesday, Alice parked at the Sheriff's Annex at Courthouse Square and marched in, clutching her go-cup of coffee. She asked at the desk for Files. If he wasn't in yet, after that snippy demand on Monday night...

He was in. She heard his footsteps in the hall, measured, firm. He took her back to his small, cluttered office. He waved her to the familiar steel chair with its chipped paint and unforgiving seat.

The brown paper packet lay on his desk blotter.

"George, this chair's for perps, not for cooperative citizens," she said, trying unsuccessfully to find a comfortable position.

"Saves me time, usually," he said. "People want to leave as soon as they can."

She snorted. "Okay, I'll play. That packet I brought you arrived in Monday's mail."

"After Nanette Ferris was killed."

"Right. Postmarked Saturday. I know she worked late that day at Simpson, because she texted me saying she was going to leave a resignation letter on her boss's chair. At the same time she also emailed me the letter."

She scrolled to Nanette's email and handed Files her phone.

Reading, he raised one eyebrow. "So what's this packet about?"

"I've got a question first. Where have you been? This is Joske's case, right?"

Files said, "Then why'd you leave this for me, not Joske?"

She paused. "He's just a baby, though a bright baby. But I did wonder where you've been?"

"Training. Financial crimes unit, in Austin. Feds and locals."

"Good."

"Why?"

"This may involve financial issues."

Files said nothing, so Alice continued. "Did you look at the packet? You checked for prints, right? Silla's are on there, and mine. And, I'll bet, Nanette's."

He nodded. "I've got your prints on file. I'll take your word about Silla. Then some from the post office. Okay, any idea why Nanette sent you this?"

"She—she was worried her deals might involve money from illegally mined rare earths, maybe from the Pacific. She was scared the deal she was supposed to close might involve money laundering. She thought she'd found a link to organized crime."

"Shwe Sone."

Alice nodded. "You know anything about him?"

Files gave a lopsided smile—the kind that didn't reach his eyes. "Exquisite wife, impressive yacht. He just hangs out in Hong Kong—his business interests are reportedly Pacific-wide, mainly commodities and shipping. No dirt found yet, that's the general view."

She watched his face. "But not yours?"

Files grinned and shook his head. "No idea yet."

"What about a guy named Tino Vitale? She thought he might have some connection."

"Hmm." Files's eyebrows shot up.

"Apparently friends with someone named Dmitri Novikov. Russian mafia? South Florida?"

Now Files was focused on her face. "Possibly," he said.

Alice sat still, thinking. Small Texas town, far from power centers. "Surely we wouldn't have organized crime showing up in Coffee Creek?"

"Chamber of Commerce wouldn't approve," Files grunted.

Alice still thought of Coffee Creek as her refuge, with its small-town atmosphere, her stalwart friends, her beloved limestone hills. She imagined her Chamber colleagues, pooh-poohing the possibility: "So law-abiding, so safe, Coffee Creek." Yes, except for our murders, our human trafficking.

She sat silent, then said, "I can't believe this was a random hit-and-run on Nanette. The timing can't be a coincidence, assuming she left that letter on her boss's desk."

His face sobered. "Don't make assumptions. Could've just been a drunk kid with a fast truck on a Saturday night. But don't overlook anyone." His two mantras. He sat up straighter, twiddling with a pencil. "This still smells local, to me."

So shouldn't she tell him about the new white Land Rover SUV, the two-timer in the carwash?

She did. He looked bemused. No, she admitted, she hadn't gotten the temporary tag number. No, she couldn't see the driver, couldn't tell if the driver was male or female.

She watched. He'd made a note. A very short note.

Alice said, "Whether or not Nanette left that letter on Pat Simpson's desk, she still told us she was worried about this deal, and she wanted to leave. Her friend Mischa might be helpful. She practices securities law. She'll be good at explaining Nanette's work and the due diligence aspect."

Files lifted his head, staring at her, brown eyes thoughtful, then nodded. "I'll talk to her.

*****

Alice was back in her office by eight a.m. It was already Wednesday evening in Hong Kong: John didn't answer his phone. She'd already left one message and cut off her second call without leaving another. Don't bug your son: he's over twenty-one, she thought. Grad student, working on his master's degree. Entitled to some freedom from maternal fidgets, right?

She didn't believe that. John always called her back—even if for only a minute.

He was half the world away.

She called Ann.

"Hi, Mom." Subdued voice. "You know he's met this new girl? He said she took the same bus that he does, three days in a row—that's his bus to Hong Kong University. Turns out she's taking some of his same classes. Says she's getting her master's too."

"Really? What's her name?"

"Rose Chu." Ann paused. "He seems intrigued. But you know what I think?"

"No. What?"

"I think she's stalking him. I mean, showing up on the same bus stop at the same time three days in a row?"

"But Ann, why is that odd? Especially if they have the same class schedule?"

"Because John's hostel—that Zen monastery—is on Kennedy Road close to downtown Hong Kong. Not a very residential area, so where's she coming from? It just sounds staged to me… Also, he sent me a picture. He said he had to snatch a photo on the bus—she doesn't like to be photographed."

"Huh."

"I'll send you the picture. You can decide."

"Okay. When did you last talk to him?"

"Yesterday."

"I wish he'd call me back. It's not like him."

"I know. I sent a snarky text after we talked. He hasn't answered."

Alice felt the same grip on her vitals as when Ann had called from the road after a friend's accident, as when John's college roomie had called to say he'd taken John to the emergency room after a pick-up game. "Will you let me know if you hear from him?"

After she hung up, she still felt that unrelenting maternal anxiety.

Time to work. On her desk lay a will and a sticky note in Silla's firm handwriting: "Call Mr. and Mrs. Ferris, Nanette's parents, in New Mexico. Nanette had told them about you. They emailed Nanette's will. They need help dealing with it." Alice flinched at the thought. Her deepest terror was losing her own children. How to talk to someone who'd just experienced such loss? She shut her eyes, imagining Nanette's crushed body, stuffed beneath bushes, her phone found beneath a truck...

She read through the will, took a deep breath, and picked up the phone.

The call wasn't as bad as she'd feared. Nanette's parents had talked to Mischa and the police. Their voices sounded quiet, resigned, but still thick with tears. They were executors under the will. Alice explained the process. Then she said, "I need to tell you about my recent lunch with Nanette." She recounted Mischa's call, their lunch, and her agreement to help Nanette with job contacts. Then she told them about the packet Nanette had mailed the next afternoon, which Alice had given to Files. Nanette's parents asked her to hold while they talked. When they returned, they asked her to help them with probate. She waited a moment, trying to assess any conflicts, then agreed.

"I'll need an engagement letter," Alice said. "And a key to her apartment."

"Mischa's already sent you one. We asked her to," said Nanette's mom. "Send us the engagement letter. We'll send it right back." Her voice trembled. "Thank you for helping Nanette."

If I did, Alice thought. She hoped her lunch with Nanette wasn't the trigger event for her death. But what was?

In an hour the Ferrises had returned the signed engagement letter. Alice drafted an email to Pat Simpson: "As counsel for Nanette Ferris's parents, who are her executors, we will be visiting Nanette's office in your building to inventory and remove her personal belongings. We plan to come Friday afternoon."

Silla stuck her head around Alice's office door, waving a key. "Got this from Mischa in today's mail." She laid it on Alice's desk and swung back to the door, where she turned to say, "You have nothing on the calendar this morning."

"Okay, okay." Alice fingered the key. Nanette's packet didn't contain much, did it? Just speculative Internet grazing. She'd swing by Limestone Lodge, take a look...

On second thought, going alone to Nanette's would be a dumb move. Alice needed unimpeachable records for her clients—Nanette's parents. And what about Files? The skimpiness of that bare-bones packet of Internet printouts nagged at her. She had the feeling a lawyer as thorough as Nanette had found—and perhaps concealed—more. But what? And where?

"Silla? You'll come, right?"

"Well, of course." Silla finished locking the office. She and Alice, each toting an empty banker's box, headed for Alice's Discovery. "What're we looking for?"

"Good question. Maybe it'll be like what Justice Potter Stewart said about pornography. 'I know it when I see it.'"

Chapter Fourteen

He Hadn't Even Known

At Limestone Lodge, late morning sun glinted off the back window of Nanette's car, still sitting in her reserved space. The physical reality of her death hit Alice once more. Nanette would never again feel the joyful independence of sliding into the front seat, heading—wherever she wanted.

For a moment, Silla didn't speak. Finally, she said, "Well, I'll add that car to the inventory." Most of the parking spaces were empty. "Looks like everybody's already at work."

"Wonder what the rents are here?"

"Pretty hefty, for Coffee Creek," Silla answered. "High ceilings, historic building, I'm thinking this place appeals to techies working on the outskirts of Austin."

Alice unlocked the front door. The entry held the tenants' post office boxes. The building was quiet. A classic Hill Country restoration: polished stone floors, polished wood trim, creamy old limestone walls. Alice and Silla carried their banker's boxes upstairs to Unit 201, one of four units on the second floor.

Alice unlocked Nanette's door. They entered a lofty space that occupied a front quarter of the building. To Alice's immediate left, a kitchen area and small dining table sat below windows overlooking the parking lot. Opposite the entry a balcony faced west, with two pristine deck chairs arranged by another small table. Inside was a seating area, with a wood-burning fireplace flanked by bookshelves. Nanette's furniture was minimal: a large gray suede-cloth sectional, one teak rocker, and two brass lamps with geometric lines. The air was still, with the faint smell of fireplace ashes and the woody scent of a candle on the mantel.

Alice stood for a moment, envisioning Nanette walking out to her balcony, holding iced tea or a beer, to watch the sunset light up the oaks and cedars beyond the building, then coming inside to curl up by the fire with a book. But was that Nanette's life? Instead, Nanette typically worked way past sunset, probably so late that staying up to build a fire seemed impossible.

Alice believed a person's books could be revealing. She checked out the bookshelves by the fireplace. Jacques Cousteau; a world atlas; a paperback on Texas rivers and springs; and Anne Hillerman mysteries—a New Mexico touch. On one shelf, a small frame holding a photo of

Nanette, standing by the stairs to Austin's Moody Theater, grinning in joy at a tall pale boy next to her, his arms around her shoulders. Hmm. Nanette looked different with that joyful smile.

Then she and Silla explored the layout. A short hallway to the right led to a bath and two bedrooms, one large, one small. The small one, windowless, held bookshelves, a desk, and a futon. The big one had the same sunset view as the balcony, and a queen-sized bed with a handmade quilt in pink and green calico. By the bed, a pottery lamp on an antique oak bedside chest. A touch of ancestors here.

Time to get going.

Silla pushed open the mirrored sliding doors of Nanette's closet.

"Wow," said Alice, who struggled to keep her closet in some sort of order. But Nanette's immaculate clothes hung in labeled groups—pants, skirts, dresses, tops, jackets. Her boots and shoes stood neatly on a rack next to a tall rolling cart with pull-out drawers.

"Intimidating!" Silla said. "Tidiest closet I've ever seen. Full-tilt Marie Kondo." She pointed at the folded undies, shirts, and workout clothes, in labeled drawers. "Everything's folded perfectly, except..."—she pointed—"someone disturbed the undies." The neat stacks of lacy bits were disarranged.

"Probably the cops. That's where I hide stuff," Alice said. "My underwear drawers." Despite her best Marie Kondo efforts, Alice found those drawers persistently disarranged, a challenge, with panties sidling beneath yoga togs and ancient notes from her children stuffed under socks.

Alice filmed Silla rolling out each drawer.

She moved to the bedside chest, filming a book on the Great Barrier Reef and a small book of meditations.

Silla's turn to film. "Top drawer, jewelry," Alice recited. She began opening the row of small velvet cases. "Pearls. Maybe her grandmother's?"

"Why don't we still wear pearls?" Silla asked. "They feel so nice on your neck."

Alice tried to imagine Silla in full rodeo regalia, with pearls instead of a bandana.

"Pearl earrings," Alice went on, snapping boxes open and shut.

"Gold chain with small diamond. Next, pink velvet box with multiple bracelets. One is rose gold with initials that aren't hers. Another plain gold, two Navajo silver. All four look antique." Silla took a picture. "Earring box, multiple pairs." She held it open while Silla filmed. "Nothing else in the drawer." All spare, tasteful, and with a nod to family, or heritage.

She opened the doors below the drawer.

Nothing but neat stacks of scarves and gloves.

"Has she no secrets? No old love letters? No traffic tickets? No ragged t-shirt from a really wild concert?" Silla asked.

"Let's hit the bathroom."

In three minutes they were done. "How does she live this way?" Silla wondered. "Nothing out of order, nothing hidden, nothing stashed at the back of a drawer? And only one photo."

Then the kitchen. Pantry shelves: sparse. Everything visible. Only two cookbooks. Alice held them sideways and riffled the pages. Nothing fell out. Refrigerator and freezer: no surprises. Looked like Nanette's diet consisted mainly of yogurt and various brands of water. With some dark chocolate—yes, 79% cacao. Alice sighed.

Last stop: Nanette's office, silent and orderly. Briefcase, empty. Printer on a side table, mouse on the desk, but still no sign of Nanette's laptop. On the bookcase, folders labeled "Taxes," "CLE requirements," "Car," "Insurance," and "Personal mail."

"Mind-numbing and frustrating," said Silla as she finished filming the contents of the insurance folder. "Anything in the closet?"

"Look at this." Alice lifted a bag to the desk. Inside, a folder labeled "Benjy Patch." Drawings signed "Benjy," neatly dated on the back, apparently by Nanette. "I wonder if he brought her one every week." The last crayon drawing, recognizably Nanette, with her distinctive gray eyes and black hair, was signed "I love you. Benjy."

"That's the screensaver she showed us at the Beer Barn," Alice said. "Looks like she'd already bought Benjy's Christmas presents." She pointed at a plastic container with a clear plastic top, labelled "Young Artist." Stacked neatly inside stood boxes of calligraphy pens, colored inks, chalks, drawing paper, and a book titled *How to Draw Anything.* Next to the art box lay a new t-shirt, child size 8-10, bearing the name

"Austin FC"—the popular Austin soccer club.

In the top right desk drawer, open boxes held pens and pencils. Alice saw a blue Waterman fountain pen in a holder, along with small boxes of blue and black Waterman ink cartridges. "Who still uses a fountain pen?" Silla asked.

"She's—she was a funny mix of old and new, wasn't she," Alice said. She herself had a Waterman, beloved, but almost never used. She took another look at the small box of black ink cartridges. Its lid didn't quite close. She opened it, with Silla filming.

"Folded piece of paper," Alice breathed. It wasn't just folded; it was folded and rolled like a fat joint, just a bit longer than an ink cartridge, and taped shut.

"Huh." She looked at Silla. "Passwords? Love letter?"

"Something she didn't want found." Silla handed her a zip-lock bag. "Let's don't lose it."

Alice stuck the folded cylinder back into the ink cartridge box and into the bag. She found herself slipping the little packet into her bra. Shades of younger escapades. But at least she'd make sure this was... unavailable, if anyone else came to search the empty apartment.

"Let's load up and get out of here," Alice said. They boxed up the personal folders and the bag of gifts for Benjy Patch, then doubled back to the bedroom for the jewelry. At the door Alice took a final sniff of the faint cold ashes from the fireplace and the woody perfume of the candle. She walked back to the fireplace, took the poker, and gently stirred the ashes. Nope, no discarded love letters, no work papers, hastily burned. Only in British mysteries.

"You think the police took anything with them?" Silla asked.

"I don't know. We'll ask Files. He's on the case now."

Alice felt strong curiosity about the folded paper, so carefully hidden. She wished she could ask Nanette about it. Was it something of Nanette's that she wanted no one else to see? Or something not hers, something she didn't want others to know she had? As to the inventory of Nanette's property...did the inventory require identification of each document? Was her own office safe from cyber spying? Why was she having such thoughts? Finally, who had Nanette's laptop?

They carried their boxes out Nanette's front door and relocked it.

"Who are you and what are you doing in Nanette's apartment?" asked a sharp voice. They looked up at a grim-faced young man, tall and pale, brows furrowed, arms crossed.

"I'm Alice Greer. I'm a lawyer. This is my assistant, Silla. I represent Nanette's parents," Alice said. She set down the banker's box and tugged a business card from her pocket and held it out. "They'll be her executors. Who are you?"

Puzzlement as he stared at the card, then the horrified realization of the implication of "executors," washed across his face. "What's—where's Nanette?"

"Tell me your name."

"I'm Michael Greene. Nanette's—Nanette's friend." He tilted his head, indicating a unit across the hallway and further down. "I'm in 204."

Belatedly Alice recognized him from the photo on Nanette's bookshelf. "I'm sorry to tell you Nanette was hit by a car. She's—I'm so sorry. She's dead."

A deafening silence.

Alice saw the suitcase across the hall.

"Did you just get here?" Alice asked.

"Yes. I had an early flight to Boston on Sunday. Business. I just got back. I was going to ask Nanette—" Tears rose, and Michael turned away, wiping his elbow across his eyes. "I was planning—" He stopped, shook his head, and took a breath. "I kept texting, but she didn't answer." Finally he focused on Alice's face. "What happened? Where was she?"

He'd had an early flight... "What time did you leave for the airport Sunday morning?" Alice asked.

"Around quarter to four, for a six a.m. flight. I never really got to sleep."

She mentally crossed her fingers and asked, "Did you see anything, or hear anything?"

He lifted his head, remembering. "Yes. A car roared away up the street."

"Did you see the car?"

"Yes, a white SUV. I saw it from my bedroom window. Might have been around two a.m." His eyes sought Alice's. "Does that matter?

Do you mean...?"

"Nanette was hit in the parking lot early on Sunday. The police will want to hear about that SUV."

"But I was in that parking lot when I left for the airport! I didn't see—I didn't see anything!"

Alice didn't want to tell him that someone had dragged Nanette's body under the hedge, that she hadn't been found for hours. That she might have been dead when he carried his luggage to his car. She switched gears: "You and Nanette were planning something?"

"I got tickets for a concert I thought she'd like. We liked a lot of the same things. Diving. Archeology." He paused. "But we didn't have enough time to..." He turned away, elbow again raised, wiping his eyes.

Alice knew that feeling—the shock of abruptly losing one's beloved. Like falling down an elevator shaft. She waited, then touched his arm. "May I have your contact info?" She needed to let Files know.

He peered at her business card and texted her his phone number. Then he dug out a business card and handed it to her.

"Thanks," she said, glancing at his card. ArcheoStat? Archeological statistics? She would have asked more but the grief on his face forbade any cross-examination. "Michael, if you want more information, call me any time. And tell the police about the white SUV."

Michael Greene nodded, jaw clenched, face set.

*****

While Silla arranged the boxes in the back seat Alice called Files, left a message about the encounter with Michael Greene, and forwarded his contact info. At the office Silla locked the banker's boxes on one side of the conference room closet.

Alice unlocked the massive black antique safe, ornamented with gold, that took up most of the conference room closet. She'd bought it from Cowman's Bank when it closed, just as she was opening her Coffee Creek office. She'd had the safe bolted through the floor to the joists beneath.

She retrieved the small plastic bag from her bra, tugged the little taped cylinder from the box of ink cartridges, and turned it over in her fingers. Why did Nanette hide this paper so carefully? And what should Alice do with it? It could be totally personal. And irrelevant.

Or it could have everything to do with Nanette's murder.

Pat Simpson had threatened her against removing his firm's work product. Indeed, a lawyer had heavy ethical responsibility not to violate protections for another lawyer's work product—material prepared or mental impressions developed in anticipation of trial or litigation. She tried to think through her conflicting obligations—protection of Nanette's privacy; a proper inventory of Nanette's property, needed by her executors; her own ethical duties when confronted with a possible crime or fraud; her duties as a citizen to assist the police investigation.

For now, lock it up. She shut the heavy safe.

Back to her desk. She checked messages and email. Still nothing from her son, John. Nothing from Ann either. She felt her breath come faster and her lips clench, felt the unstoppable anxiety of motherhood. Surely he was fine, busy in an exciting foreign city. He'd been just as lax about calling home his freshman year—except when he needed something, like money or his hiking boots. But still...

Michael Greene's grief-stricken face rose before her. Nanette had died days earlier, and he hadn't even known. Far from home, without her family or even her apartment neighbor knowing, she'd died alone.

Far from family, like her son.

Stomach in a knot, Alice texted Ann. "Any word from John?"

Quick response: "He's fine. Am at library finishing term paper due today. Talk later."

At least he was talking to Ann. She sighed. Parenthood.

Chapter Fifteen

She Needs Your Help

Thursday began with Silla's sticking her head around Alice's office door, announcing a call from Louie Gumbert. Silla rolled her eyes and lifted her upper lip in an excellent sneer.

Alice rolled her eyes too, then put Gumbert on speakerphone. "I've made a decision," he barked. "I've decided the Beer Barn's the wrong place for the town's Christmas bazaar. I'm moving forward with tents at the City Park." Alice heard the sound of chewing, then swallowing. What was the man eating? Lord, now he was belching.

Alice squeezed her eyes shut, trying to shut out the images. "That's an interesting idea, tents when it's in the thirties. Doubtless you'll have chosen a date with good weather. Of course, the Chamber can always hold its own event. Nevertheless, my clients are already publicizing the Beer Barn Holiday Bazaar. They're lining up vendors and bands."

"Well, they can just stand down," Gumbert insisted. "I want more control over how this shakes out. I want my stamp on the event. It's well known that people have confidence when I'm in charge, y'know."

"Look," Alice said, fuming, "my clients plan to proceed with the Beer Barn Holiday Bazaar. Of course, nothing stops you from proceeding with a separate event." She paused. "I'm sure you can make appropriate arrangements for all the contingencies."

"Whaddaya mean, contingencies?"

"Oh, you know. Adequate plans for insurance. Safety. Bad weather. Traffic. Parking. Liability releases. Logistics. Power. Water. Plenty of toilets. Sanitation. Trash removal. All the usual."

Short pause, then Gumbert said, "I'm sure City Hall can handle all that for me. They've got people I can call. I mean, let the little people deal with the details—I'll handle the concepts."

Alice recalled her role in helping the mayor deal with logistics for the town's first barbecue competition. "Tell me about your concepts here, Louie."

"Oh, I don't want to overshare right now. But it'll be spectacular, like all my deals. I mean, that's my trademark, thinking big. Thinking outside the box."

"Want to give me a hint? Beyond the, uh, tents?"

"Well, tents send a message, don't they? Kinda western? Of course, I'm not necessarily tied to tents."

Alice giggled to herself, imagining Louie tied to a tent. Then she imagined the big guy pulling up stakes and starting across the City Park, the tent billowing behind. "I'll be interested to hear your concepts. Meanwhile, the Beer Barn's already decided on dates, including Thanksgiving weekend and the first three weekends in December, reserved bands and equipment, and, like I said, gone to work on the contingencies." Then she added, "Saturday and Sunday, indoors and outdoors at the Beer Barn, with music, dancers, vendors, food and fun, that's our concept."

He harrumphed. "You'll hear more from me on this. I'm in charge of this Christmas event. Mine's gonna be like those German Christmas festivals, what are they called. You know, snowflakes and hot chocolate."

"You're in charge, for the Chamber," she said. "The Beer Barn's like the dog in charge of itself. Going ahead with the Beer Barn concept."

He hung up.

Alice immediately called her friend Miranda at Madrone Bank and reported her call with Gumbert. "He's decided the Beer Barn's the wrong place for a holiday festival. Instead, and I quote, he's 'moving forward with tents at the City Park.' He envisions a German-style festival with snow and hot chocolate, and he wants to put his stamp on the event. He also demanded that I send over all the documents we're drafting for the Beer Barn event."

"Gumbert hasn't got a clue, Alice," Miranda groaned. "The so-called Chamber committee still hasn't had a single meeting, just one long garbled conference call where he interrupted anyone who tried to talk. I've heard nothing about tents in City Park. Good lord." She switched to her banker's voice. "Just so you know, the Chamber has committed no money to this project."

Alice called her three clients at the Beer Barn. Jorgé Benavides, Bill Benke, and Bill Birnbach all joined the call. "Oh, for God's sake, Alice," said Benavides. "Gumbert will never get a separate gig going. We're going to have the Beer Barn Holiday Bazaar, as planned."

"Right," added the two Bills.

*****

Alice was still immersed in drafting liability releases for the bazaar at five when Silla stuck her head around her office door again. "Call your buddy M.A., over at the Tea Garden House," Silla said. "And I quote, 'Right away.'" Silla rolled her eyes.

Dutifully, Alice picked up the phone. Her friend and client M.A. was unstoppable, a force of nature. Retired from teaching high school biology, she was now one of the owners of a B&B just two blocks from Alice's office.

"Alice!" bellowed M.A. into the phone. "Stay right where you are. Clear the conference room. I'm bringing you a new client." Click.

Good grief. Alice sighed and picked up a clean legal pad. By the time she saved the draft releases on her computer, M.A. was marching up her sidewalk carrying a briefcase, followed more slowly by a straight-backed woman with silver hair and a cane.

Alice hurried to the front door and ushered them into the front hall.

"Alice!" bellowed M.A. "Meet Lacey Gunn. She needs your help."

Alice led them to the conference room and showed Lacey Gunn to a seat. M.A. placed the briefcase next to her. "Want me to stay, Lacey?" asked M.A.

Lacey smiled. "Sure. I'll shut you up if you talk too much." Lacey's face reflected years of sun and outdoor work. Her eyes were still clear and direct. She turned to Alice. "Thank you for seeing us on such short notice. M.A. has spoken highly of your work."

Then she opened the briefcase and unfolded a county topo map on Alice's conference room table. Alice leaned closer to see.

"Here's the north-south highway along Sister Creek, in Kerr County," Lacey said, pointing with a pencil. "See these pieces of property?" She indicated four properties outlined in pencil, abutting the west side of the highway. "On the north, this smallish parcel is Wilkins Ranch. Only two thousand acres." Alice blinked. Two thousand was "smallish"? That made her own one hundred acres...a flyspeck.

Lacey pointed her pencil again. "The next parcel, the biggest, is Gunn Ranch. That's mine. Seven thousand acres. Then comes the Dobbs Ranch. Eighteen hundred. After Dobbs comes the Rock Shelter Retreat and Church Camp." She glanced at Alice, then pointed at a blue line that began on Gunn Ranch, ran south through the Dobbs Ranch and Rock Shelter Camp, and continued south. "This is Sister Creek. The headwaters are on Gunn Ranch. Gunn Ranch has by far the longest creek frontage of these properties. You with me?"

Alice nodded.

"And you see there's no direct connection between the Wilkins Ranch and the Dobbs Ranch?"

"I see that."

"Some group wants to buy all three ranches—but only if they can get mine. Their agent's been hounding me. Calls three times a day. 'We've got big plans, Ms. Gunn. We need your land for this grand project.' Well, that ranch has been in my family over a century. I've told them—I'm not selling. But I'm worried."

"Why?" Alice asked.

"Because I'm afraid these people will wreck Sister Creek. My family has guarded Sister Creek for a century, but I'm the last of my generation. And if anything happens to me—" Her mouth was a grim line.

M.A. leaned forward. "Tell Alice about the creek."

Lacey nodded. "Most all the water in Sister Creek comes off our ranch. The springs there are famous. On the long bluff above the creek you can see hollow tunnels in the rock—right now they're dry, but when the aquifer's full they gush water. Plus there are springs in the creek bed—you can feel the cold water when it bubbles up."

A spring-fed Hill Country creek. Alice imagined the clear water, the limestone bed underfoot, the fish hiding along the banks.

M.A. said, "Tell Alice what you heard about this group."

Lacey took a deep breath and turned to Alice. "I've heard from the agent that whoever the buyers are, they're talking about combining the properties and building a big theme park, like Six Flags up by Dallas. The agent claims they got a big study by some amusement park developers showing that because of Sister Creek, they could include a water park along with the concessions, big rides, all that stuff a successful theme park needs. And the developers think it's accessible—they'll get thousands of tourists coming up I-10 from San Antonio and Fredericksburg and Kerrville."

"You're not interested?" Alice asked.

"Hell, no. I mean, I wouldn't be around to hear all the noise and smell all the car exhaust, right? See all these thousands of acres paved and draining crap into the creek? But look here." She pointed her pencil below the third parcel. "Down here, this is Rock Shelter land."

"Ah." Alice had heard of the Rock Shelter, a religious retreat center and church camp for kids. One friend who'd attended a "silent retreat" there had come back talking about its peaceful beauty.

"That's where I met Lacey," M.A. broke in. "She was my camp counselor. Later I was a counselor too." Alice grinned to herself, sure M.A. had never been a counselor at a silent retreat. Impossible.

Lacey looked at Alice. "Even if Dobbs and Wilkins were willing to sell, this group says they need my property for their theme park to work. I don't want them to be able to build anything that would hurt the Rock Shelter. I want to put some covenants on Gunn Ranch. Prohibit commercial use. Allow only ag use, like I have now."

"Who gets Gunn Ranch when you die?" Alice asked.

"I don't have children, so it goes to the kids of my sister and brother. But they all live out on the west coast—they're almost never in Texas. I expect they'd sell it eventually."

"Well," Alice said, "if you want to put covenants on your land to restrict its use, let's think about who can enforce those covenants, especially if your heirs sell the land. I don't suppose Rock Shelter could buy your ranch?"

"They don't have the money," Lacey said. "Maybe they'd manage to scrape up enough to buy Dobbs Ranch, which is next door to them. But probably not mine."

"You want to tell me what this group is offering?"

"For mine, fourteen thousand three hundred an acre. I've got the water, you see. Wilkins and Dobbs, those offers supposedly won't be made unless they get my land first. The Wilkins offer is more for the highway frontage acres, less for the rocky acres further west. Maybe a thousand an acre. Same for Dobbs."

Alice's jaw dropped. "Lacey, you're turning down over a *hundred million dollars*?"

"It means nothing. The ranch means everything to me. It's my life. The quiet, the beauty, the history. Arrowheads everywhere. People have been coming to those springs, depending on those springs, for more than twenty thousand years. I'm not going to be party to ruining my piece of the planet."

"But your neighbors—are they furious with you for not selling?"

"It's none of their business. Besides, they know how I feel about my land."

Alice thought for a minute. Silla brought in ice and bottled drinks. "I assume you don't want ever to move off your ranch. Is that true?"

Lacey's face hardened. "I'd rather die out there alone than get shipped off to a nursing home, if that's what you mean."

But, Alice thought, what if you wind up hospitalized, and need ongoing care, and have no one to stay with you...?

M.A. stirred in her chair. "Carlos and Sara Cortes will take care of you."

Lacey nodded. "They've lived in the bunkhouse apartment for years. And their parents before them." A long silence. "But I'm worried about them too. I don't want them to have to leave." Her face crumpled. She groped in her purse for a tissue.

M.A. leaned forward. "Lacey, you've got to tell Alice what's going on. Why you're worried. Tell her about these bastards! Tell her what happened yesterday!"

Lacey finished blowing her nose. "I'm a Gunn, through and through. Ever since my sisters and brother passed, I've lived alone out at the ranch—except for Carlos and Sara. I've always said I can take care of myself. The last few days the agent for this group drove me nuts, calling several times a day. I told him no and no and hell no, I would never sell. Finally, I started hanging up on him. Then yesterday afternoon, Sara and Carlos were up in the high pasture loading goats for market. I was alone. I heard a car come rolling down the drive. Then someone banged on my front door. I never used to lock it, but yesterday for some reason I had. Anyway, I opened the door, and there stood this big man, dark glasses, dark suntan, Hawaiian kind of shirt. I asked who he was. He shook his head and said, 'You don't need to know. Let's cut to the chase, Lacey. You're gonna sell this place. I've got papers in the car. Time for you to cooperate.' By then he was leaning his left hand on the outside of my door frame. Putting his hand on my property!

"I was furious. My blood pressure flew to the moon. 'Get your hands off my house and get the hell off my property before I call the sheriff,' I said. Well, I was still holding onto my front door, but I hadn't locked the screen door. He yanked open the screen door with his right hand and was grabbing my front door with his left. I slammed the front door on his fingers as hard as I could. Took all my strength. He yanked his hand away, yelling. I locked the front door and got my shotgun, which I keep in the closet by the door. I could hear him cussing, and it wasn't nice language. I went to the front window and tapped on it with the barrel of my shotgun."

"Loaded, of course," said M.A.

"What's the use, otherwise?" Lacey snapped. "He hustled back to his car—big black SUV, Florida plates. He was on his cell phone. He spun that car around and tore back up the drive. In fact, he ran right over my bed of canna lilies."

"So Lacey called me and I drove out and picked her up," M.A. said. "Thought she might like a night in town."

"This is worrying me to death," Lacey admitted. "I called Carlos and told him to watch out for this guy. Carlos is tough, but he's no spring chicken. So now I'm worried about Carlos and Sara..."

Alice sat, thinking. "If you want to make your property unusable for this project, or any similar project, you could impose a covenant precluding commercial use. That's a big decision as it would affect subsequent owners."

"It's mine now. I'm going to do exactly what I think is needed. I say forbid commercial use. Keep it in ag." Lacey's voice was firm and clear.

"You might also want to give a nearby non-owner the right to enforce that covenant. I'm thinking of the Rock Shelter. Do you currently let their campers, or the retreat folks, use your ranch?" Alice asked.

"Sure. I let them come hike. Sometimes they'll bring horses over in a trailer and ride. The kids look for fossils, identify birds, that kind of thing."

"And you always take them along the bluff to see those dinosaur footprints!" added M.A.

"Dinosaur footprints? Seriously?"

Lacey nodded. "Yep."

"Well, I want a tour," said Alice. "Here's an idea. What about granting the Rock Shelter, so long as it continues as a camp or retreat center, a limited recreational easement to use parts of your property? You'd basically put in writing what you're already allowing. You could exclude commercial uses, except for ag and ranching, and impose limits on what recreational activities are permitted. Prohibit anything that would harm creek flow or water quality. Specify that their use can't interfere with ranch operations or your heirs' use and enjoyment of the property. But the covenant will run with the land, so that even if your heirs sell the ranch, the covenants would still be in place." She thought for a moment. "Are you comfortable with excluding anything commercial? Seems a little drastic...what about allowing dude ranch operations? Hunting leases? Bed and breakfast? Geology and archeology talks?"

M.A. jumped in. "Sounds fun, Lacey. You know how you love showing people the ranch. And maybe that would interest your heirs and their kids."

Lacey gazed out the conference room window at the pecan tree in the back yard. The last yellow leaves littered the grass. Her eyes had a faraway look. "I like it. I like the thought of generations of kids getting to see the dinosaur tracks, getting to see the springs pour out. And I need to protect those springs." She looked at Alice, nodding. "Good. Let's do it."

"What's our deadline?" asked Alice.

"Yesterday!" barked M.A. "You didn't see her when I picked her up to bring her here, Alice. She was shaking."

Alice frowned, imagining what her own reaction would have been to Hawaiian Shirt Guy.

"I was scared," Lacey admitted. "I'm still scared. I want to get this done. Get these restrictions in place before something happens to me. It's better to have it on record, right? Give everyone notice?"

"Right," Alice said.

Lacey straightened her back. "Bring in your computer, Alice. Let's roll!"

The setting sun had turned the pecan tree orange. Silla stuck her head in the door. "I'm going to order dinner," she announced. "Shade Tree all right?"

"I'll go pick it up," M.A. offered.

Alice brought her laptop to the conference room. Lacey sat next to her, watching Alice spell out her wishes in a covenant limiting most commercial use and creating a recreational easement in favor of the Rock Shelter Retreat and Church Camp. Alice talked her through each paragraph. Lacey made suggestions on off-limits areas and activities.

"What about hunting or target practice under this recreational easement? I assume no?" asked Alice. "And let's talk fences and locks."

"Visitors can't cut fence or cut locks," Lacey said sternly. "No hunting, no fishing, no shooting—that's reserved for family. No activities during hunting season, period. And no swimming. Rock Shelter can use its own creek frontage."

"Do you want advance notice of entry?"

"At least twenty-four hours in advance of coming on the ranch. I'll give you phone numbers."

"Entry is at their own risk, right?" Alice said. "Rock Shelter should provide proper supervision for its campers and visitors and should indemnify you for any damage they cause and for any claim of personal injury or damage to their property."

"You're gonna scare them, and they'll quit coming," Lacey scolded.

"I would be remiss if I didn't insist," Alice said. "Any harassment of animals, wild or tame, is forbidden. No throwing rocks at the goats."

Silla arrived to finalize the draft, plugging in the legal description and survey of Gunn Ranch from the county records. She handed her usual impeccable document to Alice and Lacey, who pored over it.

Alice looked at Lacey's tired face. "Want to wait and re-read in the morning? This is a big step."

"No. I'm ready. Let's get it done."

Silla watched Lacey sign, then notarized her signature. "I'll get this to the Kerr County courthouse for filing at eight tomorrow morning," she promised.

"Barbecue!" called M.A., elbowing open the conference room door. "No rest for the weary or the wicked in this vale of tears, but barbecue for us tonight."

Lacey's description of Hawaiian Shirt Guy rose in Alice's mind. "Let's think a minute," she said. "As soon as this is filed tomorrow,

Lacey, do you want me to try to get the agent and hopefully Hawaiian Shirt Guy off your back? Send a letter saying commercial development is not available on your ranch? Because I don't want you going back to the ranch tonight."

Lacey looked relieved. "Yes. Please do that. I've got that agent's name somewhere."

"Totally agree," said M.A. "You've got to stay here another night, Lacey. You can supervise our table setting for that fancy ladies' lunch tomorrow at the Tea Garden. I'll drive you back to the ranch after that. Tonight we can play a few more hands of poker. Maybe I'll win back some money."

Alice grinned, imagining the silver-haired competitors slapping down the cards.

"I do believe there's beer in the office refrigerator," said Silla primly.

They cleared off the conference table and celebrated.

Afterward, driving home in the moonless dark, Alice was so tired she had to roll down her windows so the night air could keep her awake. But she couldn't keep her mind off that hundred million. Unimaginable! An outlandish amount, based on her knowledge of recent prices—although land prices were definitely trending higher. Still, what "group" could, or would, offer that much money for a Hill Country ranch that produced only goats...and water?

Chapter Sixteen

Pretty Cold

Friday morning, grinding coffee, she realized with a shock that just a week ago she'd been eating lunch with Nanette and Mischa. The next night Nanette was dead. She'd still heard nothing from Detective George Files about Nanette's murder, or the brown paper packet—an oversight on his part she intended to rectify.

While the espresso pot burbled to readiness she checked messages. Ann: "Grinding away at term papers." John: "A couple of interesting classes today. Glad I picked this place."

Not much, but better than nothing.

Fortified by ritual latte (espresso dribbled into hot milk foam) she called Files. No answer. She left a message.

At the office Alice plunged into organizing the critical path documents for the Beer Barn Bazaar. She needed to finalize the necessary city permits, vendor releases, band contracts, equipment rentals...Silla had already created her spreadsheet.

Silla swung in the front door at nine-thirty, waving a plastic folder. "Here they are. Time-stamped copies of the covenant, duly recorded this morning."

"Great." Alice still got a thrill from a freshly-recorded document, still amazed that her job allowed her to transform a piece of paper, a few words, and a proper signature into a new legal reality. She thought part of the genius of the rule of law was that it empowered ordinary citizens to imagine and create a document establishing their rights and needs going forward. Wills, deeds, contracts, covenants. Flimsy pieces of paper—yet powerful.

At eleven-fifteen, Alice threw down her pencil, desperate for a break. "I'll take Lacey's copy to the Tea Garden House," she told Silla. "Then I'll stop by the Sheriff's Annex." Files still hadn't called back.

M.A. and her friend Val had renovated the Tea Garden House, a Victorian beauty, and served dinner Thursday through Saturday, aided by high school students enrolled in their cooking class. Lunches were by reservation only, at the owners' whim. Walking the two blocks from her office, Alice wondered who'd persuaded M.A. to say yes to a "fancy lunch." She took her usual route, sneaking through the Tea Garden's side yard, with its herb garden, gazebo, and flower beds—mostly the blazing orange, bronze, and gold of chrysanthemums this late in the fall. She trotted up the steps from the garden into the dining room, glittering with china, silver, and crystal, and found Lacey reading in the parlor.

"Here it is! Recorded this morning." Alice handed Lacey the envelope containing the recorded covenant.

"Thank you," Lacey said. "It's official, right?"

"Right."

"So now you're going to write that agent? Tell him to quit calling?"

"Yes, and tell him to keep his criminal buddies off your property," Alice said.

Lacey reached into a pocket and handed Alice a scrap of paper. "Here's the address and phone number."

"Ted Lemmon, Grandee Properties," Alice read. An 800 number, an email, a post office box, but no address.

"Here they come!" warned M.A.'s voice from the dining room. "Cars arriving!"

"I can't believe M.A. does this on purpose," Lacey whispered to Alice. "She says I have to say hi to Mayor Betty Wilson—I know her from back when. And M.A. wants me to meet all those women the mayor invited!" She made an exasperated face.

"Are you missing Gunn Ranch?" Alice whispered back.

"Yes, indeed!" Lacey gripped her cane, leaned forward in her chair, then rose and marched toward the entry hall. Alice followed, entertained by the sight of chattering luncheon guests voicing their admiration for the Victorian restoration. All women, they ranged in age from forty to eighty. Mayor Betty Wilson caught Alice's eye and slipped deftly through the crowd toward Alice. The two had become allies after working together on Coffee Creek's first barbecue competition.

"Welcoming newcomers," Mayor Wilson said. She lowered her voice. "Bankers, wives of bankers, new lawyers, private equity something, et cetera."

"Private equity?"

But the mayor had rejoined the crowd and was greeting new arrivals.

Alice slipped out the front door. Outside, she took in the array of valuable autos parked along the curb, all looking new. She strolled past an Aston Martin, Porsche Cayenne, even a Bentley. But also a new red Ford 150 pickup. Well, someone had the Coffee Creek spirit.

She walked back to the office, deciding she'd write Lacey's letter first, then see Files. Back at her desk Alice hammered out a letter to Ted Lemmon: "This firm represents Lacey Gunn, owner of Gunn Ranch. Your agent trespassed on her property, threatened physical assault, and attempted forcible entry to her home demanding she should immediately sign a sales agreement. This alone warrants an action for damages, including punitive damages. You are placed on notice that (1) Ms. Gunn has no interest in selling her ranch to your clients, as she has repeatedly told you; (2) you must immediately cease your repeated phone calls which constitute harassment; (3) any further entry onto any part of Gunn Ranch by you or your agents or anyone acting for or on behalf of you constitutes willful trespass and will be prosecuted. You are further notified that Ms. Gunn has executed the attached covenant, which essentially precludes commercial use."

She noticed that as she drafted her shoulders had tightened, she'd clenched her jaw, and her fingers were pounding the keyboard. This always happened when she was drafting while angry, and, thinking of Ted Lemmon and his buddy, Hawaiian Shirt Guy, yep, she felt anger.

She handed the draft to Silla. "Have you ever heard of Grandee Properties? Lacey had email and phone and a post office box for this Ted Lemmon, but no street address."

"Whoo-ee! That's hot," said Silla, scanning the letter. "No, never heard of Grandee Properties."

"And is Ted Lemmon a licensed realtor?"

"Lemme look." She bent over the computer. In a moment she announced, "Nope. I'll get this out right away, copy to Lacey, of course."

Now for Files, and Nanette. Alice grabbed her jacket and walked the two blocks to Courthouse Square. She cut across the lawn to the Sheriff's Annex, marched into the entrance and asked the sergeant at the desk if Detective Files was available.

"He's in a meeting but should be out in about fifteen minutes," said the officer, putting down his phone and glancing up at the clock.

Alice sat where she could stare down the hall toward Files's office and waited, checking her phone. After twenty interminable minutes, he finally appeared in the hallway, making his way toward her, shoulders less erect than usual. He offered a small smile and tilted his head, indicating she should join him.

Alice settled herself on the truly penitential chair Files kept for visitors. "I've never found a comfortable position in this chair," she said, rearranging her legs.

He nodded, fiddling with a manila folder on his desk. "You want to know what happened to Nanette Ferris, right?"

"Yes. For starters." She watched him, noting the tired brown eyes—tireder than usual.

"According to the Travis County medical examiner, she sustained serious injury, including multiple broken bones and internal hemorrhage, as a result of being struck by a vehicle. You've been to Limestone Lodge, right? You remember if you enter from Kestrel Lane, the tenant spaces are on your right, along the landscaped area, not next to the building?"

Alice nodded.

"Looks like she'd parked her car and was walking across the parking lot toward the building when she was hit. Then she was dragged under some shrubbery at the site. She died sometime later. It might've been more than an hour."

"Around three or four a.m.?"

"Possibly."

"You can tell from her injuries how she was hit?"

He stared down at the papers in the folder. "Yes. More on her left side. Fractured left hip and femur, left humerus. Broken left elbow. Punctured lung."

Alice shut her eyes, stared at her lap for a moment, then looked up. "So where are we, George?"

He looked more deeply weary than she'd ever seen him. "She was hit by the front of a large vehicle, probably the right front fender. But the ME says the impact left some marks from the edge of the front grille on her body."

"Grille marks?"

"Yeah."

"What kind of car was it?"

He shook his head. "You'd think all those fancy silver grilles would be as distinctive as fingerprints. But some are pretty similar. And they're mainly plastic these days, so the marks may not be as distinct."

Alice was surprised. "I thought they were metal."

"That was then, this is now. Plastic parts. Also, the marks they left on the victim's skin? They're harder to read because of the bruising."

Alice sat, remembering Nanette. "She was very slender."

Files nodded. "And was hit very hard. But didn't die immediately." He picked up what appeared to be a photo in the packet. "Meaning her heart kept beating long enough for bruising to occur. The pattern of bruises on her torso and hip show what looks like the edges of some grille marks."

Alice swallowed, imagining the bruises, the grille marks, the slim body flung across the asphalt. Finally, she said, "You talked to Michael Greene, right? His apartment is down the hall from hers."

"Yeah. He seems pretty broken up."

"He told you he'd seen a white SUV that night?"

"Yes, but he couldn't tell the make, didn't get the plate, couldn't see who was driving."

"No other witness?"

He shook his head again. "No. Very frustrating. We did get one tire print just outside the parking lot. Not sure if it's related. We're checking for others."

Alice thought for a moment. "She was dragged under the shrubbery, right?"

Files nodded. "Yes. She sustained some bruising from being dragged, mainly on her ankles."

"Is there any way to get fingerprints? DNA?"

Files nodded. "Yeah. If a victim's dragged, it's usually by wrist or ankle. We used that superglue fume technique and got a couple of prints."

"Superglue?"

"Well, cyanoacrylate. You use heated fumes under a plastic tent or from a special nozzle. The heated fumes attach to the print. Then you whiff on some black powder, like Amido Black. Joske did that before they took the body off to the Austin medical examiner."

"Does that mean whoever dragged her under the hedge didn't

wear gloves?"

"Yes." He gave a short laugh. "You wouldn't believe how many murderers don't use gloves. They haven't planned that far ahead."

"But whose are the prints?"

He shook his head. "We found no matches in our database."

Maybe an amateur, Alice thought. "What do you think about the body being dragged under the shrubbery?"

"Seems like a delaying tactic. Someone wanted to buy time but didn't feel a need to dispose of the body. Or couldn't figure out where or how to do so."

"Which is different from your typical hit-and-run, right?"

He lifted an eyebrow. "Yeah."

Alice thought for a moment. "Did the body get dragged right after she was hit?"

"Apparently. According to the pathologist, lividity was fixed. In other words, she probably died under the hedge, and no one moved her after that. Lividity stains matched her body position under the hedge."

But it still didn't make sense to Alice. "I could imagine hitting someone—then speeding out of the parking lot without stopping. I'd be panicked," Alice said. "But hitting someone, then stopping to drag the body under a hedge, throw her bag under there..." She looked up. "That's pretty cold."

Files nodded.

Alice sat still for a moment, grieving at the thought of Nanette dying alone under the shrubbery. "Nanette was working late. She texted me that she planned to leave a letter on her boss's desk saying that she was leaving the firm."

"Isn't that the text you showed Joske on your phone?" asked Files. "He did follow up with Pat Simpson. Simpson denies that she left any such letter."

"I could see why he'd say that," Alice said. "She emailed the letter to me. Simpson wouldn't want any imputation that Nanette left because she was dismayed by the deal he was having her do."

"She didn't by chance send you a picture of the letter sitting on his desk, did she?" asked Files, his voice dry.

Alice took a deep breath, let it out. She had no proof. "No, and that wouldn't be enough, would it? You still wouldn't know he actually got it." This is why lawyers sent particular documents by certified mail, return receipt requested. That way you at least had proof of sending. Alice also realized she had no way of knowing whether the draft Nanette had emailed her was composed on her office or personal laptop. "Nanette told us she always carried her own laptop in that orange bag. But you didn't find it, Joske said."

"Right."

"Didn't she have an office laptop too?"

Files frowned. "Not sure. I'll check the file on that."

Alice wondered if Nanette had actually cleaned out her desk on Saturday night, after working all day and having some sort of 'discussion' with her boss. Wouldn't she have been exhausted? She'd need to carry home framed diplomas and photos, her private law books, continuing legal ed notebooks, plus her private papers. Surely she intended to come back and load her personal belongings the next morning, Sunday. "I assume she hadn't packed up her car with personal stuff from her office?"

Files shook his head. "Not according to the report."

"Was the Simpson's security guy still on duty when she left that night? Anton, I think?"

Files looked up from the folder on his desk. "Joske talked to him. He claims he didn't see her leave."

"I thought that building had video cameras everywhere," Alice said.

"Well, so far we've got nada." His phone rang repeatedly, then stopped. "I've gotta make a call," he said.

"And I've got to pick up Nanette's personal belongings at the Simpson office, on behalf of her parents. They're her executors. Okay if Silla and I do that? You're through looking at her office?"

Files picked up his phone. "Yeah, Joske sent someone out there earlier. Go ahead."

Alice escaped from the penitential chair and gave Files a half-hearted wave as she left. She wanted justice for Nanette. At the moment, the prospects were uncertain.

She decided to detour past the Tea Garden House. The luncheon was just ending; the last cars were departing. Ahead a white Land Rover SUV had pulled out. It sped away, paper tag flapping, before she could grab her phone and get a picture. No way to know whether it was the same one she'd seen at the H-E-B carwash or how many white Land Rovers were in Coffee Creek, what with new people moving in every day.

Alice found M.A. inside, clearing china and silver from the dining room table.

"After I get these dishes clean, I'm going to run Lacey back out to the ranch," M.A. announced. "In case you're worried, I'm spending the night there. I'd enjoy an encounter with Hawaiian Shirt Guy."

"I'll bet." The first time Alice met M.A., M.A. was pointing a shotgun at Alice while warning, "You're on my property."

"But listen, M.A. Who came to your luncheon in that white Land Rover SUV?"

"No idea. I'm not the valet," M.A. grunted. "Here, look through the place cards."

Alice picked up fourteen place cards, in calligraphic handwriting. Mayor Wilson, then the newcomers, including "Suzanne Simpson" and "Carlotta Simpson."

"How about the Simpson ladies?" she asked M.A., who was snatching up linen napkins from the place mats.

M.A. wiped one of the napkins across her forehead. "Hate this scut work," she said. "Maybe we'll move to paper plates and picnic tables. Okay, the Simpson ladies. Lah di dah."

"What do you mean?"

"Way too highfalutin' for Coffee Creek. They kept looking for a flaw. Had I set the table right? Were the dessert forks in the right place? Were there stray fingerprints on the crystal water glasses? I saw one of 'em hold my clean Waterford right up to the light! Tchah!" She snorted.

Alice pressed on. "Is one married to Ron Simpson? And the other to Pat Simpson?"

"They did say they married brothers."

"Well, which married which?"

M.A. gave an exasperated sigh. "How the hell do I know?" She paused. "One has a big blonde pompadour and wears pearls. The other had short black hair, a little bit of gray in it, kind of Italian looking—tousled, but chic?"

Alice loved this from M.A., who'd worn her hair in the same braided coronet for fifty years. "Which was Carlotta and which was Suzanne?"

"I don't know. The dark-haired one was definitely wearing Italian stuff. Maybe from Wear Art Thou up on Burnet Road in Austin."

Alice raised her eyebrows, impressed at M.A.'s fashion smarts, particularly since she'd never seen M.A. in anything but chinos and flowered blouses. "Neither happened to mention which brother she'd married? One's a lawyer, one manages the hedge fund."

M.A. put her hands on her hips. "Wait a sec. Blonde pompadour kept talking about Ron. 'Ron says this, Ron says that.'"

"Aha. But who drove the Land Rover?"

"I told you, I don't do valet parking."

Lacey appeared from the hall. "The Simpson with short dark hair drove up in a white convertible. I heard her say it was a Lamborghini."

Alice felt a wave of disapproval. What was a Lamborghini doing in Coffee Creek? What was it intended to communicate? Perhaps what the beloved Texas satirist Molly Ivins would call "wretched excess." But stick to the point, Alice, she told herself. The question is, who drives the Land Rover?

There might be zero connection between the Land Rover and Nanette's death. Yet Alice felt a strong urge to check out the fancy cars at the Simpson building. The afternoon was young.

Chapter Seventeen

Here We Go!

At three o'clock Alice and Silla turned off the Old Hays Road at the stone monument engraved with a giant S. A smaller metal sign announced Simpson Strategic Assets.

"You emailed Pat Simpson to say we were coming out to collect Nanette's personal belongings, right?" Silla asked.

"Yep. He never answered." Alice slowed as the driveway curved past manicured flowerbeds. "He's probably hoping we won't come or that if we do, we can't get in. But Mischa gave me the gate code."

A stone guardhouse next to a sliding metal entrance gate blocked their access to the parking lot. No one was in the guardhouse. Alice punched in the code. With a creak the metal gate slowly opened.

Alice grinned at Silla. "Here we go!" She parked close to the entrance. She and Silla each grabbed an empty banker's box.

As they reached the steps leading to the front door, around the side of the building rolled a Gator driven by a burly dark-haired man in a short-sleeved gray shirt. As he leaned out, Alice noted the bulging muscles in his left arm. "Hey! Where are you two going?" he demanded. He consulted the clipboard on his dashboard. "No visitors are scheduled."

"We're going to Nanette Ferris's office." Alice climbed the front steps, pulled open the front door and started in.

The man jumped out of the Gator and elbowed past Alice into a small marble lobby, then turned to face her. She smelled sweat and aggression. "Anton" read the name embroidered on his shirt.

"Hold on, lady," he said. "I've got to call Mr. Simpson first."

"That won't be necessary, Anton," Alice said coldly. "I represent the parents of Nanette Ferris. We're here to pick up her personal belongings. Second floor?"

Anton nodded. "But—"

She moved around him and pushed the button for the elevator.

"I wouldn't mess with her," Silla advised. "She's pretty cut up about Nanette's death. Hey, I guess you knew Nanette?"

A pause. "Yeah. She was a hard worker. Worked late a lot."

"We'll collect her personal stuff and get out of your hair." Silla joined Alice at the elevator.

When the doors opened, Alice thought for a moment Anton would push his way onto the elevator. He contented himself with glaring at

Alice. As the doors closed, she noticed his left hand was bandaged, with white gauze peeking out from under the Ace bandage strapped around his hand.

Alice and Silla exited on the second floor into more marble, white with a black inlay. A young woman sat at a rosewood reception desk. It was so big she looked lost. "May I help you?"

"Point us to Nanette Ferris's office, please," Alice said. "I represent her parents, who are her executors. We need to box up any personal belongings."

The receptionist had a deer-in-the-headlights look. This wasn't in her script, Alice decided.

"Just point us to her office, please. Shouldn't take us long." Alice lifted the box, ready to walk.

"Um, I believe one of our lawyers, Brett Bradley, is now in her office."

"Oh, we've met Brett. We won't bother him."

The reception phone rang. The receptionist looked at it, then at Alice and Silla. Silla smiled beatifically. "We'll find our own way. You need to get that call."

The hallway behind the reception desk held several large partner offices with big views of the Hill Country. On the interior side of the hall were smaller offices with glass doors but no windows. "Can't be too many," Alice muttered.

They spotted Brett Bradley standing outside the third office, removing the name plate from the slot by the door—"Nanette Ferris." He was sliding in his own nameplate. He gave it a pat, then looked up, startled, at the two women.

"Hi, Brett," Alice said. "Moving in?"

"Um, I've got to take over Nanette's work," he said. His eyes darted from Alice and Silla to the banker's boxes and back. "What are you, um...?"

"I represent Nanette's parents, who are her executors. We just need to clear out her belongings. Won't take a moment," Alice said. She smiled at him and slid past him into the office. "Maybe you could help us get down the diplomas, Brett?"

"Oh, um, of course." With Silla's encouragement, he lifted down the UT diploma, an "Order of the Coif" certificate for high marks, certificates of admission to federal district and appellate courts and the Texas Supreme Court, and a framed watercolor landscape titled *Rain over the Pecos.* Silla worked at the rolling wooden file cabinet, collecting Nanette's private papers—firm health care and insurance policies, personal letters, 401k documents, state bar materials, and other bar committee documents. Nanette's office files were as tidy as her apartment drawers. Alice folded up the raincoat hanging on the back of Nanette's door and added it to the box. She watched Silla make a final careful survey of the bottoms of the drawers—perhaps watching for a loose thumb drive, a folded piece of paper?

She turned her attention to Brett. Ignoring the two women, he was already working at a document on the big monitor—looked like a trust document.

"Firm laptop?" Alice said, pointing at his Dell laptop on his desk.

"Yeah," he said. "We use PCs. This is mine."

"So you've already removed Nanette's PC?"

"I think it's in the IT room."

"That's on this floor?"

"Yeah," Brett said. "We have one IT guy, who runs the systems for both the hedge fund guys and the law department. His office is just down the hall. But listen—I've got to—"

"I need to be sure," Alice said, "that the company laptop Nanette was using has been turned in." (Well, that wasn't strictly true.) "Could you just let me peek to be sure it's there? We didn't find it in her apartment." (Well, that was true.) "Where's the IT guy's office?" She marched down the hallway, Brett behind her, protesting. She pulled open the door marked "IT."

The IT guy's desk and chair were empty. "He may be over in the hedge fund area," Brett blurted. "We shouldn't be in here."

The IT office shelves were full of computer equipment. Above the IT guy's desk she spotted a short stack of black Dell PCs like the one Brett was using. Alice's old Austin office had held just such a stack, waiting for repair or assignment.

"Could you just check to see if Nanette's PC is over there?" Alice asked, pointing. "Over on that shelf, above the IT guy's desk?" She herself could see, very clearly, a silver laptop stuck behind a monitor on the shelf next to the door where she stood. Split-second decision. Witness needed? She grabbed a tissue from her pocket and stood poised.

Brett blew an exasperated sigh but walked over to the desk and examined the black laptops on the shelf above, picking up each one and checking the serial number against a list taped to the shelf.

"I think this one's hers," Brett said, holding up the third laptop. He slid it back into the stack and turned to Alice, his face reflecting anxiety and irritation. "Listen, do you need anything else?" He glanced at the wall clock. "I've got to finalize this deal Nanette was working on, and it's a booger. A jillion documents and now the deal's in trouble. I'm under the gun. If I don't close this deal, we don't get the rest."

Alice filed that last line for later discussion. "Oh, look. I'm sure this is Nanette's personal laptop." Palming the tissue, she picked up the laptop by its edges and slid it into her shoulder bag, saying, "She told us that the little boy she tutors gave her the sticker on the cover."

Alice spun on her heels and was out the door, ignoring Brett's "But wait—"

"What do you mean, the deal's in trouble?" she asked.

"I mean, closing's scheduled for Monday, all the docs are ready to go, but now one owner's screwing us on the PSA."

Alice translated that as "purchase and sale agreement."

"Messing up the entire deal," Brett went on. "We have to rescind a stupid document."

Rescind? That was unusual—pulling back an already-signed document. "Did your seller sign the wrong draft, or what?" she asked.

Brett glanced at her, then averted his eyes. He was checking emails on his phone as he speed-walked toward his office. "I've got to finish drafting right now."

"Life in the fast lane," Alice said, trying to keep up with him. "Where's the property?"

"Nowhere," Brett said. "Out in the boonies. Kimble, Kendall, Kinney County? One of those. I've gotta have this draft done by five," he said. "Or else..."

Silla stood at his office door, the two banker's boxes at her feet. "All done here, I think," she told Brett. "If you find anything else of

Nanette's, could you call me? Here's my number." She handed him a yellow sticky accompanied by her irresistible smile.

Alice heard footsteps. She turned to see Pat Simpson glowering at her. "What are you doing here?" Not a friendly tone.

"As I said in my email to you, we represent the Ferrises, Nanette's parents. They're her executors," Alice said. "We're collecting Nanette's personal property." She pointed at the boxes. "Diplomas, private papers, et cetera."

He bent and grabbed the top off one of the boxes. Nanette's Order of the Coif certificate stared up at him.

"As you know, executors must account for and inventory all the decedent's property. Happy to send you a copy of the inventory when we finish," Alice said. "It's public, of course." In case he'd skipped trusts and estates in law school...

Simpson's face was red. "Let me remind you that doesn't include firm documents. Or work product!"

Alice lifted an eyebrow. "We've collected her personal documents, Pat. Again, we'll be happy to provide a copy of the inventory, if you're at all worried." She glared at him, appalled that he'd said not a word of concern about Nanette's death, not a word of sympathy for Nanette's parents.

Belatedly, he appeared to remember his manners. "This must be hard for them. Sorry, we're under a great deal of pressure, trying to finish this project."

Alice lifted one of the banker's boxes. Silla picked up the other. "We're done. Thanks for your help, Brett." Deliberately, she excluded Pat Simpson. She marched back down the hall without a goodbye.

Alice held her breath until they were out of the building and had stowed the banker's boxes in the car. Anton followed them out of the building lobby, silent, glowering. Alice glanced in the rear-view mirror as she waited for the gate to open. He'd pulled a snub-nosed pistol from his pocket and was fondling it ostentatiously, staring at the Discovery. Alice did not like the brooding face, the angry eyes. In her hurry to exit, she almost hit the sliding gate and sighed in relief as it clanged shut behind them.

Silla was still staring at the side mirror on the passenger door. "Not anybody I'd care to meet again," she announced.

Alice drove back to the office, hoping she hadn't committed grand larceny. As they turned onto Live Oak, she pointed at her shoulder bag, which sat by Silla's feet on the passenger side.

"There's a laptop in there."

"From the IT office?"

"Yes. Looks like the one Nanette showed us at the Beer Barn."

"The one we didn't find in her apartment?" guessed Silla.

"Right. The one that Joske couldn't find at the crime scene. But if I'm wrong"—she shuddered at the prospect: what if Nanette used her home laptop for work? Alice routinely drafted at home and emailed work documents to her office computer. By grabbing Nanette's laptop, had Alice snitched work product from Simpson? How long would it take Pat Simpson to learn she'd taken the laptop?

Would he care?

She suspected he would.

When would that shoe drop?

But maybe Nanette had left her laptop in her office, along with her diplomas and personal papers. That could explain how it wound up on the shelf in the IT guy's office. Maybe Joske's team couldn't find it because Nanette didn't have it when she drove home to Limestone Lodge.

Alice consoled herself that in any event it was Nanette's personal property. She was fully justified in collecting it. Right?

Chapter Eighteen

An Unusual Welcome

Back at her desk just after five, Alice called Files. No answer. She left a message: "Got Nanette's laptop from the Simpson's IT guy's office."

She locked the laptop in the massive safe. Oppressed by general uneasiness after the confrontation with Pat Simpson, she took refuge in wordsmithing proposed releases for the Beer Barn Holiday Bazaar. She glanced out her office window as a car pulled up in front. Black, official-looking.

A man in a trench coat—not the usual Coffee Creek male garb—emerged from the driver's side, stared at her office for a moment, and strode to the entrance.

Silla moved fast to the front door, closing Alice's office door as she passed.

Alice heard Silla. "Yes? May I help you?"

A deep voice, a smooth British accent. "I'm Edwin Davies, from the British Consulate General in Houston. I'd like to speak to Alice Greer."

"May I see your identification, please?"

A pause, then a rustle.

"One moment," Silla said. "Hold still, please."

A small snort, then the deep voice again, slightly cooler: "Well, this is an unusual welcome, having my credentials photographed. Is this adequate? Will this do?"

"For the moment," Silla said. "I'll see if Alice is available. What do you need to talk with her about?"

Alice couldn't quite hear the answer. Passport application?

She heard footsteps receding down the hall. Clever Silla, she'd trapped the man in the conference room. Her office door opened. Silla.

"He's very London Fog, very Brit," she said. "About a passport application?"

Alice couldn't imagine any earthly reason this man would need to talk to her. "Nice move, asking for his ID," she commented.

"Plus the photo—my new trick of the week. Gives us a record, at least." Silla handed her phone to Alice, adding, "Of course I wouldn't know a fake Consulate ID if I saw it, but it's fairly convincing."

The photo showed an erect head, thinning brown hair, focused blue eyes. Alice hit "save" on her draft liability release and walked down the hall to the conference room.

Edwin Davies stood at the window, gazing at the office back yard with its big pecan tree and picnic table. He turned, extended a hand. She took a long look at his face before extending hers.

"May I?" The tall man gestured at her conference table.

"Please sit down." Alice took the seat at the head of the table, by the door. "You drove all the way from Houston about a passport application?" She didn't hide the doubt in her voice.

"It sounds odd, I know. Your name was used as a reference on a passport application submitted to Her Majesty's government at our Hong Kong Consulate."

"Hong Kong?" Alice's mind raced. Couldn't be John, he had his American passport, so—who?

"Yes." He paused. "Your son is John"—he glanced down at a small notebook—"John MacDonald Greer?"

"My son is named John MacDonald Greer."

"We're merely checking the background of the applicant, who gave his name as Jameson Jeffrey Greer. A young man called John Greer accompanied this Jameson Greer to the Hong Kong Consulate. The applicant listed his name, and yours, as references."

Jimmie. Jimmie was in Hong Kong. And John apparently accompanied him to the British Consulate. She struggled to keep her face calm. Why hadn't John called to alert her? Why had Jimmie used her name as a reference? Why wouldn't he have listed as a reference Gran—his own aunt, and a British citizen to boot? Maybe the person needed to be available, in Hong Kong...

Davies leaned forward. "Ms. Greer, do you know Jameson Jeffrey Greer?"

"If your Jameson Jeffrey Greer is the same man I've met, he was my husband's first cousin."

"When did you see him last?"

"At my wedding. Over twenty years ago."

"Can you tell me anything about him?"

"Assuming this is indeed my husband's cousin, can you tell me why you're asking?"

"He reported losing his passport. We don't want to issue a passport in Jameson Greer's name to the—the wrong person."

That sounded fairly reasonable. "What specifically do you want to know?"

"His education, job, whether he's married..."

"I know nothing about his current status. I recall he trained as a geologist with a specialty in seabed geology." Should she tell him about Emma? About no word from Jimmie for a couple of years? Was this Consulate guy for real?

Alice stood. "I'd like some coffee. Would you prefer coffee or tea?"

"Coffee's fine."

"I'll be right back." She needed to think.

On her way to the kitchen, she spied Silla outside in the street taking pictures of the car and its tags. She scribbled a note on Silla's desk—"Call Houston Consulate and find out if this guy's legit."

Alice loaded a tray with cream, sugar, and two cups of coffee and carried it back to the conference room. Davies was jotting in his notebook.

She handed him his coffee and took a sip of her own—strong, with cream, no sugar. Bracing. Armed and reinforced, she said, "You began by asking about my son. I'd like to understand why."

"His name was given as a reference, as was yours. We simply need to know whether we're issuing a passport to the correct person," Davies answered, frowning. "When someone loses a passport, or claims to have lost a passport, our procedures are necessarily more cautious."

That made sense. And didn't Alice want Jimmie to have a passport? Yes. But she didn't like John's involvement. Was this the real Jimmie or a plant, trying to pass himself off as Jimmie?

"Can you show me his photo? Jameson Jeffrey Greer's photo?"

Davies looked up. "I wondered if you'd ask." He passed across a folded sheet of paper. She unfolded it to see a small color print of a passport photo.

Suddenly it was her wedding day, two decades ago. Jordie stood waiting at the altar, his best man next to him, both men in kilts. Jimmie was jaunty, cocky even, with dark hair, color high on his cheeks, and merry blue eyes as he glanced up at Jordie. She remembered some hero-worship in his face, and mischief too. And something tough in the tilt of his jaw.

But the blue eyes of the man in the passport picture were wide and wary. His dark hair was now streaked with gray. His leathery cheeks were creased with deep frown lines. His face still held that grittiness she remembered.

"I think that's Jimmie," she heard herself say. "But I can't be absolutely sure."

She hoped she was right. But she wondered—if it was Jimmie—how he'd convinced John to vouch for him?

"Is this all you needed?" she asked. "When will you issue the passport?"

Davies sat for a moment, looking at the photo. "I can't say for sure," he said, pulling it toward him and folding it back in his notebook. "Hopefully, quite soon."

He stood, thanked her, shook hands, and left.

Silla was hanging up the phone. "Can't get an answer from the Consulate."

Back in her office, Alice watched Davies drive away, then tried John's phone. No answer.

She called Ann's phone. No answer. "Call me."

She closed her eyes in total frustration. The last thing she wanted, given the increasingly tight controls on Hong Kong (including foreign visitors), was for John to get sideways with the authorities—whether local or otherwise.

She started a fierce text to John—"Imagine my surprise to get a visit from someone claiming to be from the British Consulate about my name being used as a reference for someone purporting to be Jimmie..."

Then she thought about the fact that use of VPN to evade electronic scrutiny was not permitted in China, about the increasingly tight controls on electronic information, on telephones, texts, apps. Her heart pounded. She deleted the text as ill-advised.

But what the hell was going on over there?

*****

Kinsear picked her up at six-thirty. "We're going to dinner at Jobell's in

Wimberley," he announced. "I'm in need of a vegetable."

A new restaurant. That sounded fun. Alice slid her arm around his neck, massaged the muscles. "That's distracting," he said, maneuvering an S-curve. "Don't stop."

She watched the cedar-covered hills whirl past.

"Thinking?"

She sighed. "I had a weird visit from a guy at the British Consulate in Houston this afternoon. Trench coat, black car, the whole shebang."

"Why were you favored with this attention?" The words were light, his tone was sharp.

"My son John gave his name—and my name—as references for someone who may be Jordie's cousin. Who apparently lost his British passport and was applying for another."

"What does John say about this?"

"Not a damn thing!"

He frowned. "That doesn't sound like John."

"He's not answering emails, phone calls. An occasional pro forma text—'Everything's fine. I like my classes.' Ann just tells me not to worry."

She watched Kinsear's strong profile—the black curls touched with gray, the laugh lines at his eyes, the humorous mouth. No smile at the moment, though.

"Hong Kong, right?"

"Yep."

"Maybe he doesn't want the authorities reading his communications."

"Seriously?" She felt another chill down her spine.

Raindrops battered the windshield as Kinsear turned his old Land Cruiser into the restaurant parking lot. He grabbed an umbrella from the back seat. "Hang on. Let's get inside."

*****

Alice felt her usual excitement when arriving at a new restaurant, taking a seat, investigating a new menu. "Ooh," she said, as two tall beaded glasses of prosecco arrived. She found the bubbles extremely cheering.

"So," Kinsear said, leaning forward, his eyes on hers. "Did Mr. Trench Coat show you his ID?"

"Silla made him. She even took a picture of it."

"Smart girl."

"Then she called the British Consulate in Houston to double-check, but no one's called her back."

"Probably checking her out first."

"Good grief." Alice sipped her prosecco, grateful for every bubble. She tried to relax her shoulders, her neck.

"Remind me about Jordie's cousin. I assume John met him in Hong Kong. How'd that happen?"

Alice sighed. "His mother should know, right? But I have no idea. John's got a cheap room in a combination Zen monastery/men's hostel—he always lands on his feet. But he hasn't mentioned a single word about Jimmie. I don't know where, when, or how they met." Another sip. "I just hope that whoever he's volunteered me as a reference for—is really Jimmie." She thought about that for a moment. These days, what did she really know about Jimmie?

Nothing.

She checked her phone in her lap. No message from John. She closed her eyes, frustrated.

"It'll be okay," Kinsear said. "John's got good sense."

Does he? Alice was beginning to wonder. She shivered, watching rain lash the restaurant windows.

"Look, here come my crab cakes." Kinsear lifted his fork in salute to his plate. "And your seared tuna."

*****

Partway through dinner Kinsear put down his fork—sign of a serious discussion. "I've been wondering about something. Okay if I ask you about that trip to Aberdeen?"

Surprised, Alice nodded. Since her return from Scotland, he'd tactfully left that topic untouched.

"The doc at the mortuary gave you only a few of Jordie's possessions, right?"

It felt strange to hear Jordie's name on Kinsear's lips. Alice thought of the skimpy plastic bag with its pitifully few contents and Jordie's jacket. "That was all. What was found in his pockets or...nearby."

"No backpack, no carry-on bag, no briefcase?"

"No. It...it sounds like they recovered only what he was wearing."

"She didn't mention anything else?"

"No. It's funny, that Coastguard guy asked me the same thing. Ian Blane." She jumped at a crack of thunder outside. The rain redoubled in volume. "He promised me the forensics report on the chopper and everything else. So far, all he's sent is a short summary of the pilot's only transmission. And a contract, and a letter from the company about the hiring of GGI, geology consultants." She looked at Kinsear, feeling again her anger at the Coastguard's stonewalling. "Ian Blane hasn't answered my last couple of emails, either."

"What exactly did he say his role was? For the Coastguard?"

Suddenly she was back in cold gray Aberdeen, in the grim mortuary waiting room, looking at the uniformed man waiting in the corner. His role?

"Ben, I don't know. He was already there. I had both kids with me...I'd never been to a mortuary before. He told me he'd be my contact."

"What was his rank?" He was staring hard at her, one questioning eyebrow lifted.

"Ah," she said. "You know, I didn't ask to see his ID."

A wave of apprehension washed over her. "He—he presented himself as our liaison. Said he wanted to ask a few questions. Acted like he knew his way around the mortuary." But did he? The image popped into her head: Blane opening the waiting room door, peering down the empty hall, then taking Alice and the kids to the conference room. As if he was authorized to do so. But was he? He'd double-checked the conference room, hadn't he? And perhaps he hadn't wanted to be seen?

"What if tomorrow you call Coastguard headquarters?" suggested Kinsear. "See if someone else is assigned to the chopper investigation besides Blane?"

Alice nodded. Aberdeen was six hours ahead. She'd make coffee and call Aberdeen as soon as she got up.

"Good," Kinsear said. "Now let's get serious about dessert. Here's what I'm thinking..."

*****

Kinsear still had an hour's drive back to Fredericksburg after they reached Alice's office. He walked her to her car.

She kissed him. A tiptoe stretch to get up there, but very satisfying.

"If the front porch light were on, and my dad were standing there, silhouetted against the light, waiting for me to come in from a date, I'd be seventeen again," she said into his chest. "He always waited up. With very high visibility. Drove me and my sister nuts."

Kinsear kissed her back. "Call me if you want company tomorrow. Call me anyway. I'm curious what you'll find out about Blane." Actually, he looked worried, not curious.

"I wish you could stay," she said.

"Wish I could too. But Carrie's driving out tonight from town, just for the night." His younger daughter was a freshman at UT Austin. "Gotta be there."

Alice nodded, holding up her face for another kiss. Warm, comforting, definite, and positive. Unlike the situation with Ian Blane, the unsettling visit from the British Consulate, and the evidentiary gaps in Nanette's murder.

Not to mention the failure of her children to communicate in any meaningful way.

The Land Cruiser disappeared, rolling toward Fredericksburg. Alice drove home, feeling suddenly very alone.

Chapter Nineteen

That's Not The Man

In pre-dawn darkness the next morning, clutching her first cup of coffee, she dialed Ian Blane's cell. No answer. She tried again. Still no answer. Next, the Scottish Coastguard, Aberdeen headquarters.

"Alice Greer here. Widow of Jordan Greer, whose body was recovered last month from the *Grampian*, a helicopter crash."

Short pause, then, "Of course, madam. How may we help?"

"I'm trying to reach Ian Blane. He's supposed to be keeping me posted as Coastguard liaison. But he's not answering."

"Let me just check." A longer pause, then the voice returned. "Madam? You say Ian Blane has been in touch with you? About the—the helicopter recovered last month?"

"Yes." Impatiently.

"But madam, there seems to be some mistake. Officer Ian Blane has been home on sick leave for three months. He's recovering from a serious accident and not expected back at work for another two weeks. Are you sure there's not a mistake about the name of the person you spoke with?"

"I didn't just speak with him!" Alice snapped. "He met me and my two children at the Aberdeen Mortuary. In uniform. He was waiting when we arrived."

"And you were there to—to—"

"To identify my husband's body. Yes."

"He identified himself as Ian Blane?"

"Exactly."

A polite cough. "Madam, may I ask—did he offer to show you any identification?"

"He did not." How had I not noticed this before? she wondered. The scene replayed in her mind. Blane there waiting, apparently ignored by the woman at the glass window, who merely took Alice's name. Blane didn't approach her, and no one questioned his presence.

Alice went on. "He took us out of the waiting room into the conference room next door. He asked what items were found with my husband's body, in the wreck."

"Madam, I've put you on speakerphone. My commanding officer has joined us. He'll take over."

A new voice. "Mrs. Greer, I'm Captain Donald Hartung. I'm concerned about this—this inquiry about Ian Blane, because we here at the Coastguard are still conducting our forensic investigation of the crash. I've asked that a photograph of our officer Ian Blane be emailed to you. While we're waiting, I have a question. You say the man who called himself Ian Blane asked what was found with your husband's body. Did you show him anything?"

"No." She paused. "Did the Coastguard look at his belongings when you—when you found the wreck?"

"We did. I've got the list here: small waterproof bag. Ring, medic alert bracelet, notebook and pen, wallet, keys, phone. And a jacket. I understand those were returned to you."

"Yes."

Her email pinged. Email from the Scottish Coastguard with attachment—"Ensign Ian Blane." Curly red hair; freckles; eyes that looked wiser than his age. "The picture's here," she said into the phone. "That's not the man who met us at the mortuary."

"You're sure?"

"I'm sure. Look, I told Blane—or whoever he was—I want all the information on why that flight crashed. I asked for copies of the forensics investigation, maintenance records on the chopper, any transcripts between the pilot and the rig or the airfield. He told me a geologist was supposed to make that flight, but didn't, and said the forensics investigation still hasn't ruled out maintenance issues or sabotage. If Blane's a fraud, I'm repeating those requests to you. I'm entitled to know what happened to my husband!" Alice felt her heart starting to thud and took a deep breath.

"Yes, you are," Hartung said. "I'm quite surprised that this person claiming to be Blane suggested the possibility of sabotage. I can see how that possibility would be quite upsetting. But that's the first I've heard of it." He paused, then went on. "Of course weather's always crucial, particular if low visibility raises the possibility of pilot vertigo. And we always scrutinize maintenance. Can you email me copies of what this person sent you? And I commit to send you our investigation papers to date, including anything not classified."

Alice started to argue—why shouldn't she get classified information?—but decided to defer that fight. "If I send you what Blane sent me, will you send me those reports today?"

"Yes, as soon as I can. Of course I realize—it wasn't exactly a photo op at the mortuary."

"Hardly." But she appreciated that dry comment. Of course she had no photo of the man who'd been waiting for them there. Alice hung up and forwarded the "Blane" emails to Hartung. Kinsear's instincts were right, asking whether she trusted Blane. And so were hers, but she hadn't followed through. What a waste of valuable time. She could hardly bear it. Five years gone...and still nothing! She hoped Hartung was right about sabotage. If he was wrong...she'd have no peace. She'd live with fury forever.

She made a second mug of coffee, comforting herself with vigorously frothed milk atop the espresso, and called Kinsear. "Your instincts were right." She described the back-and-forth with the Coastguard.

Her phone beeped: a text from John. "Wait a sec." She scanned the text, sat speechless for a moment, then read it aloud to Kinsear: "Scheduled on direct flight Hong Kong to DFW, arrive Austin four p.m. Saturday. Please pick us up! Love, John."

"Who is 'us'?" Kinsear asked.

"No idea." No, maybe she did have an idea. Her fingers flew, texting John. The message wiggled, then she saw the red "undelivered" response. "He must already be on board."

"He was coming home for Christmas, right?"

"Yes! But not this soon. What in the world?!" She stood up from the breakfast table. "Gotta go. I'm going to call Ann."

*****

"Ann?"

"Mom! What's up?" Ann's voice was hurried.

"Do you know anything about John flying home?"

Alice heard someone in the background yelling, "Ann! Taxi's here!"

"What did you say, Mom? Can't talk right now. Taxi's waiting. I'll call you as soon as I can. Love you!" Ann's usual cheery goodbye.

What was going on? Ann seemed unworried. Maybe she too had no idea about John, though that seemed unlikely. Her kids seemed almost telepathic sometimes. Well, if Ann wasn't worried, maybe she shouldn't be. But why was he leaving Hong Kong now? And with whom?

She called Kinsear back. "I got nowhere with either of my kids. I have no idea what I'll find at the airport."

"Want me to..." he paused.

She could tell he was going to ask if he should come with her. She was tempted, but for goodness' sake, she was John's mother. "I'll be okay."

"But you'll fill me in."

*****

Alice poured herself more coffee. It was barely seven. John must already be somewhere over the Aleutian Islands, his airplane curving across the Pacific toward DFW.

Her cell pinged. Voicemail, from Ann's number. "Mom! Listen, I just boarded the flight from Boston! I'll be in around four! Can you pick me up? Love you!"

Immediately, she redialed Ann's cell, which went straight to voicemail. She must've turned it off. What was going on? What were her kids up to, ignoring her calls and texts, leaving her in the dark and then abruptly flying home?

She didn't think of herself as a helicopter mom. She tried not to invade their privacy, tried to let them solve their own problems, work out their own love lives. She did beg them to take their vitamin C and to get enough sleep. But this deliberate collusive silence? Yes, it felt collusive. Conspiratorial.

Maybe John was bringing home that girl he'd met, the one Ann sniffed about? But why now?

Well, damn. At least there were clean sheets on the kids' beds. Also in the small guestroom...but for whom?

*****

Late Saturday afternoon, Alice parked in the new airport parking garage and made her way to the second floor of the terminal, on the bridge above baggage claim. She always waited there for her kids so she could hug them the moment they exited the concourse. Usually they texted her: "Landed!"

Today she alternated between joy—both children here, under her roof!—and rage over their conspiracy of silence. Why? What was the reason?

She paced back and forth from the security guard's desk to the flight announcement monitor. Finally—Boston flight, a bit early. John's connection from DFW, on time. She took her traditional position, peering out through the glass, watching for John's head above the crowd.

And there he was, walking fast through the door—pale, tired, but smiling. With a man directly behind him—shorter, older, dark hair turning gray. Worn clothes, wary face, but familiar bones, very like John's, and Jordie's. Alice caught her breath, started forward.

John didn't stop. "Mom. It's Jimmie. Let's keep moving. Hug downstairs." Ignoring the escalators, John plunged down the stairs toward the ground floor, Jimmie following, Alice hurrying behind. What was wrong with taking the escalator?

At the bottom of the stairs she paused, expecting a wait for baggage. John lifted his carry-on. "I'm waiting for one bag. Jimmie, none. Otherwise, this is it."

"Ping!" from her phone. "Landed and exiting plane." Ann.

"Ann should be here in five minutes!" Alice said. "John, did you know she was coming?"

John nodded, glancing at his phone. "I made her promise not to tell you. I'm sorry, Mom. I'll explain later. You can go meet her like you always do. We'll wait here."

Alice raced back up the stairs. Ann was on Southwest—those gates were close to the exit. And there she was—glossy brown hair, big smile, warm kiss.

"Surprised?" Ann hugged Alice hard, then looked into her eyes. "Mom, John's here, right? I'm sorry I couldn't talk. But now we're here!"

Alice felt tears rise, blinked them back. She loved her children, loved them more than life itself, but they'd kept her in the dark. Why?

Watching her mother, Ann wrinkled her nose and hugged her again. "We'll explain."

John had found his suitcase. He quick-marched them to the garage. As they arranged themselves in Alice's car, Ann begged from the passenger seat, "We've got to stop at Maudie's! Boston can't do Tex-Mex. I need a fix."

Maudie's was the kids' traditional demand after flying home—immediate recourse to Tex-Mex.

A pause. John said, "Let's call in an order. We need to get Jimmie out to Coffee Creek."

Ann was already on her phone. "Pan of Josie's enchiladas. Four tacos al pastor, four fish tacos. One sol diablo, one large guacamole. Thanks." She hung up. "Beans, rice, chips, and salsa included. Okay, Mom. Now you can ask questions."

"I do have a few," Alice said, one eyebrow lifted. She didn't smile. She shot a glance at Ann. "So glad your phone actually works."

Ann gave her the 'uh-oh' look she'd perfected in middle school. The car was silent—none of the usual 'how was your flight?' chatter. As they left Maudie's, with the car full of the fragrance of Tex-Mex, Alice glanced in the rear-view mirror. Jimmie had fallen asleep—head lolled over, eyes shut.

From the back seat John whispered, "He hasn't slept for weeks."

Chapter Twenty

How Did He Escape?

Jimmie stirred as Alice's Discovery bounced over the cattleguard at her gate. He looked around. "Looks a bit like Australia," he muttered.

Alice showed him to the guestroom. "We'll have a late lunch, then you can nap," she said.

He offered a small, tired smile. "Thank you, Alice." He looked out the sliding doors at the hillside and creek below. "Lovely. I can't believe I'm here."

Ann and John had arranged their take-out dishes from Maudie's on the kitchen island.

"I'll get Jimmie," John said, walking back toward the bedrooms.

He returned almost immediately. "Dead to the world already. Poor guy." He and Ann loaded their plates and installed themselves on stools around the island.

Alice did the same. But she couldn't eat yet. She could feel her blood pressure rising. "Okay, you two. You've got some explaining to do. Tell me how you met Jimmie, how he got a passport, how you got him out of Hong Kong. What was he doing there? And why didn't you tell me what was going on, for heaven's sake!"

"Hang on a sec," John said. He took two more bites of cheese enchilada, closing his eyes in appreciation. Alice's blood pressure soared. "Sorry, Mom. Okay. Here's the tale. I'd installed myself at the monastery—tiny room, just a monk's cell, on the second floor. You may remember Dad talked about the monastery—he stayed there a while on his big post-grad trek."

Alice remembered. She'd envied Jordie that trip, which sounded so exotic. He'd shown her some faded photos—Nepal, Macao, Bali, Australia...and Hong Kong.

John went on. "It turns out Jimmie joined him for part of that stay in the monastery. I hadn't met the guy in the room next to mine. Unlike the rest of us, he hadn't put a name-card on his door. Now you have to know—the monks don't let in strangers. There's a desk at the front door, and we leave our keys at the desk. The monk on duty puts the keys in the same small pigeonholes where our mail goes. I'd been there several days when I got a letter from Gran—she'd printed my name in big capitals on the blue airmail envelope, as if people in Hong Kong might be weak on English. The envelope stuck halfway out of the pigeonhole. Easy to see. That afternoon after class I stopped at the desk, got my mail and my room key, and started upstairs."

He stopped for a bite of fish taco. "Lord, I've missed this," he mumbled. "Hold on."

Alice sat riveted at the counter, imagining Gran's blue airmail letter sticking out of a wooden pigeonhole. Growing up, John and Ann had gotten just such envelopes from Gran at least monthly. Another reason they loved their Gran...

"I think he was waiting for me," John said. "As soon as I stuck my key in the door, he popped out of his room. Barefoot—you couldn't hear him. He came close and whispered, 'Are you related to Kathy Greer who lives in Broadview, Scotland?' He pointed at the letter in my hand. 'Couldn't help but see the return address.' I said yes. He looked nervously up and down the hall, so I invited him into my room. Because it had occurred to me, from his question, and from his face..."

"That it was Jimmie?" Alice asked.

John nodded. "I suddenly thought of that Antwerp woman and her postcard. Plus he looks so much like Dad. But he was so thin, so nervous. After he came in, he looked back at the door. I thought, he's afraid someone will see him. So I locked the door. By then I knew—he was in deep trouble.

"He asked if I knew anything about his situation." John paused, remembering. "But first I wanted solid confirmation that he was really Dad's Jimmie. I said, before we go further, can you show me your passport? Or ID?"

"But did he have one?" Alice breathed.

"Nope. Neither one. You remember Ann and I met him in Scotland when I was ten and she was eight? I asked if he remembered what he and I did on that visit. He said, 'I took you fishing. You caught a sea trout, a big one. You fell out of the boat when we tried to land the fish. Your dad had to haul you out of the water.' Then he added, 'Gran fixed your fish for dinner.'

"That was every bit true. So I asked where he'd been for the last couple of years. It was a crazy story, but it matched what Emma Linden said. He'd been studying seabed geology in the Pacific. He wouldn't say why, but he was mapping and sampling seamounts, sediments, and some really deep plains. But get this, Mom."

She waited.

"The last couple of years, he couldn't leave."

"What do you mean, he couldn't leave? Wasn't he working with GGI?"

"Not for the last two years. You'll have to ask him. He refuses to name names to me, says it's too dangerous. He saw his bosses only rarely, but their henchmen—that's what he calls them—wouldn't let him go. Took his passport, ID, credit cards, followed him everywhere, posted a guard outside his cabin. He threatened to go on strike; they said fine, go ahead and starve."

"So how did he escape?"

"The night the ship docked in Kowloon, across the harbor from Hong Kong, he squeezed out a porthole—that's how thin he was, after his hunger strike—and slid down a nearby hawser. He hid under the dock, moved over to the next pier, and so on. He heard them looking, but he stayed on the ocean side of a nearby garbage scow. Powerful stink, he said."

"Then what?" Ann asked. "With no ID, no money?"

Aha, Ann didn't know everything, Alice thought. But what was Ann's role in this shindig?

"I don't know the whole saga, how he escaped his captors," John answered. "Slept under an abandoned tarp in the dockyard. Then, amazing, and I wish I'd done it—he somehow dodged the harbor police and stowed away on one of the Star Ferries docked overnight in Kowloon. The next morning, it turned out that was the first morning ferry to Hong Kong. He says he was lucky—it left before dawn, and the crew was still yawning."

"Where did he hide?" Ann demanded.

"Behind a lifeboat, he claims. Ask him. No one stopped him disembarking on the Hong Kong side. He headed to the monastery, where he'd stayed years before. One of the older monks remembered him.

"So there I was in the Hong Kong monastery with my dad's cousin Jimmie. He said, 'All I want is to get home to Scotland. But I need a passport. I'm afraid those guys may still be after me. I've seen a couple of people nosing around, watching the monastery. I can't get to the Consulate. If I could just get in the door...' Well, I thought, what would Dad do? And the answer came, get your cousin to the Consulate. Then I thought, what would Mom do? And the answer was the same. I knew you'd figure out a way. So I came up with a plan, except I couldn't tell you."

John looked at Ann.

"That's when John called me," said Ann. "Middle of the night, my bro calls. 'Ann, remind me how *back in the day* you dressed up for that high school play where you were the mean old lady. What did you wear? Didn't you have to do a quick change, onstage, to go from old lady to old man?' Of course I was never in any such play. But '*back in the day*' is our code for 'just help me out here and don't ask questions.' Comes in handy. So I made suggestions on a disguise for a man visiting the British Consulate. Hat with wig. Long skirt. Cane. Bathroom visit."

"But why didn't you two tell me?" Alice broke out. "I've been worried sick by your radio silence!"

"I made Ann promise," John said, "*Nothing to See or Hear.* That's our code for no text, no phone."

Ann nodded. "I had to promise."

"Besides, Mom," John went on. "What's the first thing you'd have done if you'd known I was going to try to help Jimmie get a new passport? The very first thing?"

"I would've"—She stopped.

"You'd have jumped on the first plane to Hong Kong. You'd have emailed, texted, and called repeatedly," John said. "But Jimmie begged me—no text, no phone. After all he'd been through, I had to honor his fears. And suppose, despite his warning, I'd told you? There I'd be, a male student in a Zen monastery with strict rules, with my mama standing out on the Hong Kong sidewalk texting and calling me, beating on the door..."

Ann interrupted. "But worst of all, we'd have put our own beloved mother in mortal danger. How do you think Dad would've felt about that?"

For once Alice was speechless. Her children, her precious, perilous children. Thinking about the risk they'd run, she felt so frightened...and simultaneously so proud of them.

"But wait a minute." Alice looked at Ann, then John. "Ann, were you actually worried someone was listening to your phone conversation?" Alice turned to John. "Surely no one in Hong Kong's interested in your call to your sister in the U.S.?"

John lifted an eyebrow. "Maybe not. But Jimmie was so worried, so sure he was at risk, I couldn't take the chance. Anyway, it took me a while to corral what we needed. I had to buy a third- or fourth-hand ordinary suit. A long skirt, elastic waist. Gray wig, pinned into a sunhat."

"Can we show you?" grinned Ann. She hopped down from the counter stool and pranced into the middle of the kitchen, fluttering her eyelashes, taking a small bow.

"First," announced John, "the old lady puts on a small man's shirt and her old-man suit. Plain gray, quite ordinary."

Ann slipped her arms into invisible sleeves, lifted her eyes and chin to the ceiling, and buttoned invisible buttons.

"Then she puts on her long skirt over the pants, pulled up to her waist but with the suit coat hanging out. Many old Hong Kong ladies wear coats like that. The skirt covers her tennis shoes. Lots of old men wear tennis shoes with a suit."

Ann's face crinkled with the difficulty of pulling the invisible skirt up to her waist. She ducked her head and pulled up the front of her invisible skirt to peek at her shoes.

John proceeded. "Then she puts on her hat-wig." Ann complied, fluffing the invisible gray curls. "And her big black sunglasses with side panels like you wear after cataract surgery." Ann adjusted the invisible earpieces. "Then, of course, she puts on her little white mask, because someone out on the street may be infectious."

Ann raised her eyebrows in horror at the thought of infectious passersby. She adjusted the loops on her invisible mask.

"She brings along an old shopping bag, because she might find decent vegetables at the market." Ann adjusted the bag. "She picks up her cane, takes the arm of the young man who's helping her, and sets out for the British Consulate." Ann, shoulders hunched, eyes lifted, shuffled over to John and took his arm. "On the way she twitches her cane vigorously back and forth toward anyone who might bother her."

Alice held her breath, imagining the scene. "You, of course, are the helpful young man."

"Right. I should mention that under her mask our old lady has grown a short new mustache."

Ann lifted one corner of her invisible mask and fondled the new growth.

Alice heard a sound from the hall. Jimmie stood there, eyes wide, face amazed. How long had he been watching?

"And you two waltzed right into the Consulate?" Alice asked.

John and Ann waltzed around the kitchen island, box-stepping. Jimmie collapsed in laughter. His laugh was rusty, like he hadn't used it in a long while.

John continued his tale. "Once inside, my companion made a quick trip to the ladies' restroom, stashed hat, wig, skirt, and mask in the shopping bag, which he then left outside on a chair, with the cane." Ann tottered through an invisible door, and ripped off her disguises, stuffed them in a bag, and exited, dropping the shopping bag and cane on an invisible chair. With manly strides she entered the invisible passport office.

"Success!" John declared. "It took a few tense hours to get that new application approved, believe me."

Alice glanced at Jimmie. "You used John's name, and mine. As references." She stared at each of the three. "Do you have any idea what could have happened if you were caught entering the Consulate in disguise? And wound up in the slammer, in Hong Kong?"

Jimmie nodded slowly. "I'm sorry I dragged you into it. But the officer kept asking if anyone could vouch for me..."

Alice still felt narrow-eyed about Jimmie's inclusion of John but kept her face still. "Okay, how did you get back to the monastery?"

John recited, "Man with short mustache retrieved bag and entered restroom, then emerged, transformed into confused masked old lady who'd gone in wrong restroom door."

Ann leaped back into old-lady character. Flurried, she rearranged her mask and tapped her cane.

"Question," Alice said. "What did the monastery think about John stashing this old lady in his room?"

"Oh," Jimmie said. "The old lady just disappeared into the garden shed outside. For costume changes, we used the garden shed by the monastery koi pond. There's a hook in the shed where I keep a gardener's outfit and one of those big hats with a hood and visor and mask that all the street cleaners use. I can wear it in the monastery if I have to." He looked at their puzzled faces, then went on. "I'd had the feeling someone was watching me. You know, odd men—a woman, too—hanging around the monastery. Made me afraid to leave my room. I even stooped to asking John to bring me food. A couple of times when a new guy showed up at the hostel, I've disappeared into the garden shed." He paused, remembering. "I worked out my rent by hoeing the flower beds, raking the path. It's meditative. I miss that hat."

Alice noticed Jimmie staring longingly at the lunch containers.

"Hey, let's get you a plate!" She looked at his face, his eyes traveling across the tacos, the chips, the chili con queso, the guacamole. "Aren't you starving?"

His face grew puzzled. "Hard to know. When you don't have food, you try to ignore hunger. By God, that smells good." He glanced at Ann. "And you made me laugh. I don't know the last time I heard myself laugh out loud." He shook his head. "Unbelievable. From hiding in Hong Kong to laughing somewhere in Texas—it's a miracle. A dream. Thank you, all of you."

After they finished the last chip, the last ooze of queso, the last splash of salsa on the last bite of enchilada, Alice put another log on the fire in the fireplace and pointed at the sofa. Jimmie sat.

"I've got more questions," Alice announced.

He nodded, eyes wary. Ann and John sidled over and sat with Jimmie. Alice couldn't tell if they were offering him moral support or getting ready to stop her from cross-examining him.

"Why were those 'henchmen,' you called them, so determined to keep you captive? Where were you, and what kind of seabed geology were you doing?"

She waited.

"Back before I saw Jordie out on the Lucky Strike, I'd been in Myanmar, up in the mountains. Didn't like it. The new company I got the offer from, GGI, seemed like a geologist's dream. GGI had contracts in the Pacific. I was hired to look at volcanic seamounts, abyssal plains, and Pacific sediments near certain land masses. My job was bringing their operations up to cutting edge with the latest sampling and mapping techniques. And being at sea! I love the ocean. It holds so many secrets."

"But what were you sampling for? What were you mapping?"

"Metals, mainly. Some of them pretty rare..."

"Rare earths?" she asked. His head jerked up.

"You've heard of them?"

"Sure," interrupted Ann. "Critical for electric cars."

"Critical for Asian economic policies," John added. "Keep asking questions, Mom. He wouldn't tell me what he was up to in the Pacific. Didn't want to endanger me."

Alice stared at Jimmie's thin face, the deep lines at eyes and mouth, the sunburned hands, rough with hard labor. "You've been underwater or—or out of pocket for a couple of years, right? Didn't the henchmen let you read the news?"

"Well, after I got kidnapped in Jakarta, I got access to only a couple of scientific journals and technical reviews. They limited my computer access. No phone."

"Who was involved? Why were they keeping you captive?"

He shook his head.

"Does that mean you can't tell us? Or won't?"

"Strictly need to know. That's what the Consulate..." Jimmie stopped.

"Aha," John said. "I wondered about that. Don't know how many skinny men in gray suits with new mustaches get their new passport hand-delivered in a plain wrapper addressed to the head monk. Or get picked up for the ride to Central and the train for the airport by a Hong Kong taxi driven by a guy we met at the Consulate."

Jimmie's eyes darted to Alice, then back to John. Ann's eyes were on John. Alice stood motionless.

After a moment she said, "Anyone want to feed the burros with me?" She had some questions for whoever said yes.

"Sure." John grabbed his jacket and followed her out the door.

*****

Carrots in hand, Alice and John walked toward three waiting burros. Queenie jostled Big Boy, who swung his head at her. "Plenty for everyone," John said, leaning toward Big Boy, holding out a carrot. Alice fed Queenie, then Princess.

"What does this mean, this special delivery of Jimmie's passport?"

John's eyes met hers. "They were helping him, um, get on the first available plane."

"Why Texas? Why not Scotland?"

John just looked at her, waiting.

"Ah. So he'd be harder to find? Or at least harder to follow?"

He nodded.

She thought of the visit from the black sedan. "Is he going to talk to that guy from the Consulate who came and quizzed me?"

"Sorry about that, Mom. I don't know."

"So what's the deal? Is there a plan? Aren't you going back to Edinburgh to finish your paper?"

"No, I can finish it right here. I'll go back after Christmas."

"What about Ann?"

"She'll fly back Monday for finals."

"Did you tell him we'd met Emma? Tell him about her visit to Broadview?"

John nodded.

"What did he say?"

"Direct quote: 'I don't want her anywhere near this mess.'"

A huge gulf of uncertainty opened ahead of Alice. What was she supposed to do with her visitor?

"So—what about Jimmie? What's the plan?"

"We've got to keep him safe. At least until the Brits take him in hand."

Alice felt terror—for her children. And anger—what possessed Jimmie to involve her kids?

And how was she supposed to keep him safe? Alice looked around at the open pastures, the burros, her ranch house, the live oaks. She had nothing with which to protect Jimmie—nothing but fence with three strands of barbed wire and a gate anyone could open. And her flare gun.

What the hell was going on?

Chapter Twenty-One

The Last Photo

That night, with all houseguests safely in bed, Alice stole out to the treehouse with a blanket, settled herself on the bench where she could look out through the branches at the stars, and called Kinsear.

"Been thinking about you," he said. "What did you find at the airport?"

"John, Ann, and Jimmie. Jimmie was on that Hong Kong flight."

"Mmm. Interesting. So, now what?"

"They're all asleep. Ann flies back to finish exams on Monday. John says we need to keep Jimmie 'safe.' So Jimmie's staying here."

"Good lord, Alice." She listened to him breathing. Then he said, "You know, you could stow him out here at my ranch. He'd be safe. Javier's always around." Javier was foreman at Kinsear's Fredericksburg ranch. "And if Isabel's here tomorrow, she could get him situated. I can't imagine anyone would look for Jimmie out here."

Alice was fond of Kinsear's daughter Isabel, a UT senior. She and Isabel had grown close during a Santa Fe adventure in June.

"I like the idea of your ranch," Alice said. "Particularly since I had a run-in with Nanette's boss on Friday afternoon. But I don't want your kids or mine mixed up in whatever's going on with the Simpson crew." She told him about her expedition with Silla to pick up Nanette's personal belongings. "That place is weird," she finished. "Big partner offices, big conference room, nasty security guard—and only one clueless young associate, who's desperately trying to close on Monday the big deal Nanette had been working on."

"Is he the one you saw at the Beer Barn? Second-year associate, hiding behind the bar?"

"Yeah. I can't tell if he had a crush on Nanette or was spying on her—or both."

Kinsear was silent for a moment. "You're right. Sounds way understaffed for a hedge fund operation. Maybe they're just cherry-picking a few deals...but still."

"Well, at least we snagged Nanette's personal laptop. Someone" (she did wonder who) "stashed it in the IT room." Maybe she'd spend Sunday morning scrolling through it so it could be properly inventoried. There was a pause.

"Miss you," Kinsear said, finally.

Typical Kinsear, offering sanctuary to Jimmie in that casual way of his, never making it a big deal. Yet Alice had immediately felt the weight lift from her shoulders.

"I miss you even more."

*****

Sunday morning at seven, Alice found the jet-lagged males already in the kitchen, peering hopefully into the refrigerator.

She got them started with coffee (John) and tea (Jimmie), then toast and eggs for both. John kissed her, gobbled his breakfast, and headed back to his bedroom.

Time to quiz Jimmie. He looked more relaxed this morning. He took a second cup of tea out onto the deck and stood looking at the valley. A few Spanish oaks still had their red leaves. The creek below glistened gold in the morning sun.

She waited, curious.

He came back inside. "What incredible peace."

"For the moment."

He gave her a wry smile.

"Let's talk about who might be following you, Jimmie."

He nodded. "You're right. I need to leave. This isn't fair to you or your kids."

"I want to keep you safe. But to do that, I need to know who was hanging around in Hong Kong, why you flew here instead of Scotland, why this is safer. Who's after you?"

His face was pained. "It's better you don't know. That's why I can't answer all John's questions."

She sat, imagining the monastery, the streets and sidewalks outside, the hastily delivered passport. "A Consulate guy from Houston visited me—before your passport was issued. So presumably the Brits want you safe. Safe from whom?"

He didn't answer, just looked upset.

Impatiently, she slid off the counter stool, hands on hips. "Jimmie, my children are involved. You owe some simple answers to some simple questions. Who was watching you in Hong Kong?"

"One was a woman. She called herself Rose Chu. She tried to get into the monastery, supposedly for a school project, but the head monk barred her."

Alice remembered that name—the same woman, per Ann, who kept popping up on John's bus, in John's classes.

"I saw another guy hanging around outside in one of those sun-shield caps, you know, big brim in front and a neck flap in back. I hoped he wasn't the same guy who nabbed me in Jakarta and locked me up on the *Seabass*. But we'd docked in Kowloon, so...who knows."

Alice started to ask if he had pictures, then realized he had no phone. Then Emma Linden's face rose before her, showing Gran the picture sent by Jimmie.

"You sent a picture to Emma Linden. Of the man on the street in Jakarta."

Before Jimmie could respond Alice was tapping her phone, emailing Emma Linden: "Can you forward to me the picture Jimmie sent you of the man he thought was following him?" She hit send, then turned to Jimmie.

"Don't you want to get in touch with Emma? Tell her you're alive?" She wondered if John had told him about Emma's visit to Scotland. Did Jimmie have any idea that Emma had traveled all that way to Broadview to ask Gran if she'd seen Jimmie? "We could call her now."

His eyes lit up, then darkened. His shoulders sagged. "No. I wish—but no. What have I got to offer her? No home, no job, nothing. And it's not safe to drag her into this."

"You gave her address to Jordie. He left it at Gran's—hidden. Why?"

"Because I asked him to protect it. She was my refuge. I needed Jordie to know how to reach her if something happened to me, but I didn't want her name, her contact information, disclosed—Internet, phone, whatever. And I sure didn't want Gran worried. Anyway, my understanding is that in a few days they'll let me get home to Scotland."

"Your understanding from the British Consulate? How in the world does that make you more secure?" Alice demanded. "Look, Jimmie, I'm not just going to sit here. I've got to be able to assess how safe you and John are."

"It's the people involved," Jimmie said. "They're bad news, Alice. I don't want them anywhere near you. Or John. Or Ann. Or Emma. Or Gran. I don't want them even to know you know their names."

Alice checked her email. Nothing yet from Emma. When she looked up, Jimmie had vanished. She heard the guestroom door close.

Well, damn. She decided to give him a little space before pressing for more answers.

Ann was on the six a.m. flight back to Boston tomorrow. Might as well spend time with her precious children for the rest of Sunday. She heard Ann's voice down the bedroom corridor and couldn't repress a smile—Ann always had that effect. Ann could make her smile just by sticking her head around the door. As she was currently doing.

"Coffee, puh-leeze!" sang Ann.

Alice hugged her. "What shall we do today? Apparently, we need to hunker down."

"Let's go climb Enchanted Rock. Nobody'll look for us out there. Jimmie'll like it. Pure geology."

*****

And he did. "Granite! The strong foundation!" he said two hours later, sitting atop the legendary pink granite dome known as Enchanted Rock. He, John, Ann, and Alice had made their way to the top and had found some comfortable depressions in which to sit. They gazed out at the Hill Country landscape, five hundred feet below, while unwrapping picnic sandwiches.

Jimmie ran his hand across the pink surface of the mountain, stroking it gently. "A powerful pink granite bulge in the earth's crust."

"It's a billion years old," Ann told him. "Part of the Llano Uplift. The Tonkawa and Comanche revered this place."

"It glitters in moonlight after it rains," John added. "And it creaks and groans as it cools off. The Tonkawa said they saw ghost fires on top. Whether or not it's haunted, as some people claim, this part of the Hill Country does feel special."

Alice thought of the German immigrants who settled nearby Fredericksburg beginning in 1846, building their Easter bonfires on the surrounding hills. So close to Enchanted Rock. Yes, there were legends in these hills.

Despite Alice's paranoia, the rest of the day passed smoothly. When they returned in mid-afternoon, John sat down at his laptop, sheafs of paper stacked around him. "I'm in scholar mode. Got to finish this paper. Call me for dinner."

Jimmie borrowed some waders and headed down to the creek. Alice, spying from the deck, watched him slowly hiking upstream, picking up stones, gazing at the water. When he returned, his face looked more relaxed. "You've got some nice trout," he said. "I found a fossil." He offered Alice the white heart shape of a clam fossil. "Cretaceous, right? More than a hundred million years old?"

Alice nodded. She and Ann were sitting together at the kitchen island, looking online at possibilities for Christmas presents. Alice was trying, for one peaceful Sunday afternoon, not to think of Nanette's murder, the perfidy of the fake Ian Blane, or the peril surrounding Jimmie—Jordie's favorite cousin. She vowed that tomorrow, after she got Ann on the early morning flight to Boston, she'd call the British Consulate in Houston. Surely they owed her some help, some guidance.

Ping! Email from Emma Linden. With attachment. It must be nearly midnight in Antwerp, Alice realized. With Ann leaning over her shoulder, Alice opened the photograph, apparently taken from a window on an upper floor, with one edge framed by curtain fabric. The picture showed a man in a narrow busy street, staring up at the building holding Jimmie and his camera. The man on the street was significantly taller than the Asian passersby. The upper part of his face was shaded by a cap.

"It's Ian Blane!" breathed Ann. "Don't you agree, Mom?"

John and Jimmie hurried over.

"You're right," John said. "He sure looked different in Aberdeen, wearing that Coastguard outfit, but see that jutting jaw? That's the man."

Jimmie stared at them blankly. "You know this guy?"

John explained their visit to the Aberdeen Mortuary. "He wanted Mom to tell him which of Dad's belongings were returned to her. Whether they showed anything Dad should report. Anything of concern."

Jimmie's eyes raced to Alice. "What did you say?"

"Nothing!" Alice said. "It was none of his business."

Ann abruptly left the kitchen. Alice could hear her pulling storage baskets off the shelves in the study. What was the child doing?

In a few minutes Ann returned, face determined, holding a canvas storage basket. She placed it on the kitchen island. Alice recognized the basket in which she kept all the letters she and the children received after Jordie's helicopter disappeared. Whenever Alice decided to attack the clutter in her study, vowing to clear away old correspondence, whenever she picked up that basket and read a note or two, she found herself sticking the basket back on the shelf. Too soon. She'd wondered when she'd feel free to let it go.

"Look." Ann held up an envelope. "This is the note we got from the engineer Dad worked with on the Lucky Strike. Remember? They knew each other from Houston days."

Ann reached into the envelope and pulled out a snapshot.

"Remember this, Mom? He'd taken it on the rig!"

Yes, there was Jordie, wearing the yellow rain jacket with his name on the label. Next to him stood Jimmie, also in a yellow jacket. The two men were on the rig deck, wind blowing their hair, big gray clouds looming in the background. Same foreheads, same strong jawlines, same challenging eyes on each man. Cousins. Both men grinned at the photographer. Behind them, a man glanced at the camera. He was hunched over, slipping behind them, holding a container.

Alice gasped. Ian Blane. Rather, the man calling himself Ian Blane.

"When I saw the photo Emma sent, I knew I'd seen that face somewhere, long ago," Ann said. "It came to me that it was something to do with the Lucky Strike. And I remembered Dad's friend had sent us this picture. You remember his note, Mom? He wrote that it might be the last photo taken of our dad, and he wanted us to have it."

Alice had forgotten. Or repressed the memory, not wanting to think of the "last photo."

The four stood silent. Jimmie finally heaved a sigh. "I don't remember seeing him on the rig. But there he is."

"He's the same man who followed you later?" Alice asked.

"Yes. But here's the deal. I was pretty sure I recognized the man who followed me in Jakarta. I saw him outside my hotel. I'd seen him many times at the mine in Myanmar."

"What's his real name?" Alice asked.

"Who knows? But in Myanmar he went by 'Dickie Manners.' He monitored the mine's computer system. He was muscle for a retired general there, Shwe Sone."

Alice's eyes opened wide at that name.

Jimmie went on, "I got crosswise with Manners about the radioactive exposure levels the company was reporting for its miners and mining waste. I thought they were under-reporting. Rare earth mines can release radioactive waste, including from thorium."

Alice felt sick, thinking of the mine workers.

"Manners threatened me, said he'd brought me to the attention of General Sone, and that I was a problem," Jimmie added. "Apparently Sone kept me at the mine only because of my rare earths knowledge. But I didn't know Manners was also on the Lucky Strike."

Alice hoped this guy had never made it to Hong Kong. "John, you don't recognize him, do you?" Her anxiety level was rising.

"Nope. I think Aberdeen's the only time I've seen him."

"Jimmie?" She'd crossed her fingers, mentally.

Jimmie looked up, eyes thoughtful. "I don't think I saw him in Hong Kong."

Ann, John, and Alice looked at each other. "So what was he doing at the Aberdeen Mortuary?" Ann asked.

"And where is he now?" John echoed.

Chapter Twenty-Two

Let's Take A Peek

Alice studied the snapshot for a moment, then found her phone and shot photos of it, including a blow-up of the figure behind Jordie and Jimmie. She emailed those photos plus the one Emma had sent to Donald Hartung of the Scottish Coastguard: "These appear to show the same man who posed in a Coastguard uniform at the Aberdeen Mortuary and called himself 'Ian Blane.' One photo shows him on the rig behind my husband Jordie and his cousin Jimmie, before the helicopter leaving the Lucky Strike went down. Earlier, at a mining operation in Myanmar, this man used the name 'Dickie Manners.' The same man appears in the later photo taken in Jakarta." She thought a moment, then added to her email: "Some questions. Do you know what name this man was using on the rig or what he was doing there? How did he know when my children and I would be at the Aberdeen Mortuary? How did he come by the uniform he was wearing when he met us?" She hit "send."

Then she thought of her visitor from the British Consulate. Should she forward the photos to Edwin Davies? He'd seemed coldly polite, the opposite of warm and fuzzy. He'd only demanded information and provided none. He'd conveyed no interest in Jimmie's safety, much less in hers or John's. What was his motivation, where were his loyalties? Be fair, Alice; while she'd been vetting him, he was vetting her. He might have information *she* could use, information that could protect her family. She emailed him the photos and the information she'd sent the Coastguard.

*****

At five a.m. on Monday, Alice was up, making coffee in go-cups, and whispering "hurry" to Ann. Silently as cats, they left the house and tried to close the Discovery doors without making noise. Stars were out; the sun wouldn't be up for hours. Thank God for coffee, Alice thought, taking another sip. A high-speed drive down Highway 71 to the Austin airport, then she'd have to say goodbye again to Ann. She hated these hurried goodbyes, hated watching her child disappear into the maw of the airport, far from her mother's arms.

"I'll be back in a month, Mom." Ann, the mind-reader. "Just have to get through these finals. Okay, here we are. By the time I get back, Jimmie will be back in Scotland, and life at the ranch will be back to normal!" She hugged her mother, grabbed her backpack, climbed out of the car, and raced into the airport.

Normal? Driving west again, Alice realized she'd told John and Ann nothing about Nanette's death or the Simpson brothers. They often complained their mother was over-protective. Maybe she'd call Files this morning, ask if he'd identified a suspect yet.

Nanette's face flashed before her, blushing when Mischa twitted her about a boyfriend.

Nanette shouldn't have died.

But even Files wasn't in the office at five a.m.

Kinsear would be up, however.

"I'm on my second cup of coffee," he said. "All alone. Both girls are back in Austin on campus. Listen, I meant what I said about getting John and Jimmie out here. Let Jimmie see more of the Hill Country? He could ride, read, fish, whatever. Or just sit. Give you a break from babysitting. John doesn't have to come along unless he wants to. Isn't he trying to finish his big paper? Chinese economic policy?"

"He is." She felt a wave of relief. Jimmie would be out of John's hair, and John might be out of reach of whatever danger Jimmie carried with him. She could take them to Kinsear's around lunchtime. "Thanks, Ben. That'll be great. What if we pick up some Shade Tree on the way out?" Kinsear, a barbecue maven and general foodie, deeply cherished Shade Tree barbecue.

She wanted to talk to Files. But first she needed—admit it, at least *wanted*—to find out what Nanette kept on that little piece of paper, the one she'd hidden in a box of very old-fashioned ink cartridges. Before returning to the ranch to tell John and Jimmie the new plan, Alice decided she'd stop at the office.

*****

Live Oak Street was quiet at six-fifteen in the morning. She unlocked the office and headed for the coffee maker. When it began the soothing burbling noise that promised caffeine, she unlocked the double doors to the conference room closet. On the floor sat the boxes of Nanette's personal belongings from her apartment and from Pat Simpson's law firm. But Alice had stashed the little box of cartridges in the huge black safe.

Alice worked the combination, took out the box of cartridges, and relocked the safe. She stopped in the kitchen for coffee. She wanted Silla here before she peeked at the paper.

She heard Silla in the office entry, saw her smiling face pop around Alice's office door.

"How was the weekend?"

Alice filled her in on the sudden appearance at the Austin airport of her kids—and Jimmie.

Silence for a moment. Then Silla said, "This ties into that guy from the British Consulate who paid us a call, right?" You couldn't hide anything from Silla. Alice took a deep breath before explaining that Jimmie was Jordie's cousin, last seen on the oil rig before Jordie's chopper went down, then later reportedly held hostage by unknown baddies in the Pacific until he escaped. What kind of explanation was that?

"Whoo-ee," Silla said. "So you're gonna hide this guy out at Kinsear's?"

"At least for a day or two," Alice answered.

"I like it."

"Before the day starts, let's take a peek at that rolled-up paper of Nanette's."

She picked up the box of cartridges, pulled out the cylinder of paper, and unfolded it. Silla peered over her shoulder.

It was a printout, on one sheet of copy paper, of an email from Ron Simpson to his brother Pat: "Okay, bro. We've hit the big time. The Miami investor group I visited? They're on. We get three potential deals. A big investment with decent fees for us on the first, another deal with bigger fees on the second, and a very significant investment with very significant fees on the third. They've imposed conditions: no redrafting the docs, no reinventing the wheel. Get your girl to use the same docs attached here. Tell her no due diligence crap! Like, none. These investors are extremely private. A deep dive could screw the whole deal. First deal absolutely must close on time, no screwups, no delays. Word is, these guys dislike failure. Keep me posted."

Alice double-checked. Nanette was not copied on the email.

"You know what?" Alice muttered. "I'll bet Pat or his secretary printed this email, probably like she usually does for his file, and Nanette saw it on the printer. And made a copy."

"Because...?" Silla asked.

"Maybe to use in case she got fired, or quit? Evidence of what she was having to push back against? Evidence she was instructed by her boss to do no due diligence?"

If she hadn't feared she'd need this paper, Alice thought, Nanette wouldn't have hidden it so carefully. What to do with it?

Alice grabbed her iPhone and took a picture of the printout. AML, KYC, Alice thought, re-folding the paper and sticking it back in the small box of cartridges. Had Pat done as their new client asked? What would Nanette think about those instructions to Pat's "girl"? Instructions not to investigate investors, not to re-draft documents—even if required by her best judgment? And AML, KYC regs? Alice re-locked the cartridge box in the safe.

Could she show it to Files? Was it work product? She stewed over that for a moment. Her first reaction was—no. This email wasn't created in anticipation of trial or litigation. And even if the Simpsons did claim work-product privilege, she thought the document could be admitted as evidence under the crime-fraud exception for work-product documents. The Simpsons were legally responsible for adequate due diligence.

She'd think this through again. Her instinct was Files should see it, but she'd talk to him first.

Now she really wanted to take a look at what was in Nanette's own laptop, which she carried wherever she went. Alice could ask Boy Genius, a computer maven she'd hired before. Or—what about Michael Greene?

She dug his card from her bag. Just past seven-thirty. She called him, holding her breath, and heard a flat "hello."

"Michael. Alice Greer. Sorry to call this early. I'm the lawyer for Nanette's parents."

A pause. She waited, fingers crossed.

"I remember. How can I help you?"

"I'm trying to be sure we have a complete inventory of Nanette's property for her parents. Including documents on her laptop."

"Is that normal? Her private documents?"

Tell the truth, Alice. "Executors need an inventory. But also, I want to be sure the police won't miss anything that might help find her killer. I think her parents would agree."

After a moment Greene said, "I've got a meeting in Austin this morning. But if you're in your office, I could stop by right now. Does that work?"

"Yes," Alice said in relief. She just needed the password. "Thanks."

She found Silla. "Remember Michael Greene? Nanette's friend? He's coming by. We need the password to Nanette's laptop."

*****

Michael Greene looked thinner and paler than when she'd met him at Limestone Lodge. Grief could do that. Or maybe an encounter with a Coffee Creek detective?

Silla offered coffee; he said no. Alice ushered him into her office and pulled up another chair next to hers.

"Listen, thanks for coming this early. I'm curious: did George Files contact you?"

He nodded. "We've met. Don't worry, I'm apparently not a suspect," he said, a bitter edge to his voice. "Although they did ask for my fingerprints. Happy to comply. So far, they don't seem to have any idea who—who killed her. But I want to know."

"So do I," Alice said. "And Nanette's parents. So, I've got Nanette's laptop. Ready to take a look?"

He lifted an eyebrow. "Feels kind of invasive..." He glanced at his watch, then back at Alice. "But you and her folks should have the right."

If he could tell her the password, that was all she'd need.

Back to the safe. But first she grabbed some of the disposable gloves Silla kept in her worktable drawer. Alice pulled them on before carefully toting the laptop to her desk.

Michael looked quizzically at the gloves, then at her face.

"It wasn't found at the scene," Alice said. "It was in the IT office at

Simpson Strategic Assets. Maybe she left it in her office, and someone moved it. But if someone took it from the scene—we don't want to spoil any prints." She handed him a pair of gloves.

"Got it." He pulled them on.

She opened the laptop. The screen sprang to life—a vivid coral reef with striped angelfish and a lurking eel.

"You know her password?"

He nodded. She watched him type PecosRiverNM. Alice scribbled the password onto her legal pad. The screen popped open, the home page showing a river canyon with red rock walls. "Her parents live in the Pecos River Valley," Michael said. He looked at the screen for a moment, then began typing.

Predictably, Nanette's documents were in folders. Family. Finance. Employment. Photos. Music. The Family folder held letters she'd sent her parents, neatly dated. Alice didn't read any beyond the first line, "Dearest Mom and Dad..." The Ferrises planned to arrive after Thanksgiving to meet Alice and learn whatever they could about Nanette's death. Alice clenched her jaw, dreading the meeting, knowing she'd feel not just their grief, but the shiver of unbearable grief any parent felt when hearing of another parent's loss. As in—what if something happened to John or Ann? She shook her head, trying to erase the thought, and blinked at the screen.

The next-to-last folder was titled Forms. Any lawyer kept a forms folder: versions of specific agreements or pleadings that seemed useful enough to qualify as a go-by or starting point for some future deal. Alice had amassed her own forms file; Silla made sure that useful forms were snatched from Alice's computer and filed in the Forms folder. Alice assumed Nanette had just assembled the best documents she'd encountered, whether at her old firm or Simpson, as an insurance policy against having to start from scratch every time she needed a purchase and sale agreement.

Alice remained conscious of Pat Simpson's sneer, "No work product!" She wasn't after any work product. But she scanned the titles of the documents in Nanette's Forms folder: sample purchase and sale agreements, sample deeds, sample partnership agreements, sample LLC filings, blank corporate minutes, stock options, etc. A panoply of corporate transactions. Nothing surprising. Most were dated years earlier, when Nanette was learning her trade.

Buried at the end of the document list in Forms was another folder, titled Ocean. She clicked her mouse. A box popped open: insert password. She tried clicking again. Nope, said Nanette's ghost.

Michael was staring at the screen. He glanced at her. A very small smile reached one corner of his mouth. "That Nanette. Okay, it's our joke. We're—we were planning a diving trip. You can hide anything in the ocean. So let's see how she passworded this sucker."

Alice watched as he tried variations of "scuba," "tank," "reef," and then she left for the kitchen to get more coffee. Michael looked up when she walked back to her desk. "I'm in," he said. "Abyss."

Alice shivered, thinking of unsafe depths.

On the screen she saw a short list of documents. Greene scrolled down, then down further. "So, what are these?" he muttered.

"First, the proposed investors have to become limited partners," Alice said, "in the hedge fund involved."

"You drive," Michael said, handing Alice the mouse. He watched as she clicked through the document titles. "Form of limited partnership agreement." "Form private placement memorandum." "Form subscription agreement." These too were full of blanks, just forms to be filled out, possibly the same forms she used at Betts. But when do I cross the line? When am I trespassing into Simpson's work product? What she really wanted to see: actual investor names, actual proposed projects, actual dollars to be invested.

Nanette certainly hadn't included the deal documents here.

After the few blank forms, Alice saw only screenshots and Internet printouts. First came two she'd seen earlier: the blurry photo of General Sone on the prow of the yacht and the photo of the two racehorse owners celebrating at Hialeah Racetrack. Next came printouts of what looked like Internet research connecting the named investors to Dmitri Novikov and Tino Vitale, as well as the British Virgin Islands documents Nanette had mentioned during their lunch at the Beer Barn. Then she found pages of Internet data on current ranch prices in the Hill Country. This must be where Nanette stashed the documentation of her due diligence, Alice guessed. Documentation she wasn't supposed to have. And was afraid to put on her firm laptop.

She exited the Abyss folder and turned to Michael Greene. "You said Nanette was worried about this closing."

He leaned back in his chair, frowning. "Very worried. She was always closemouthed about her work, but she didn't like this deal. She told me she'd found data on people, possibly relatives of investors, indicating they weren't what you'd call squeaky clean."

"What about the project itself?"

He nodded. "A real worry. She was afraid the purchase prices for the land parcels were so high it might mean money laundering. She intended to talk to her boss about it. Another thing—she was getting a bad feeling about the stability of Simpson Strategic Assets. She'd seen the September financials they must send out to investors, and they didn't look good. But she said she shouldn't have told me that."

"When did you have this talk?"

His face turned pink. "Our last call..." Abruptly he turned away from Alice, facing the window into her office's back yard. He pulled a tissue from his pocket, blew his nose, cleared his throat. "I talked to her around four on Saturday. She said she wouldn't be home until late. That wasn't unusual—it was just over a week until the scheduled closing. I'd seen her pull all-nighters before some closings."

Alice waited.

"She promised me we'd go hiking at Big Bend the first weekend in December. I made reservations."

Big Bend. For Alice, Big Bend meant romance. After she re-encountered Kinsear one afternoon in Fredericksburg, years after his wife had died and Jordie's chopper had disappeared, they'd rekindled their law school affair. She'd gone hiking with him again at Big Bend: vast skies, brilliant starry nights, and breathless climbs to views far across the Rio Grande into Mexico. She gazed out the window, remembering.

Then she looked at Michael Greene's bleak face.

"But she didn't say anything about leaving Simpson? When you talked to her Saturday afternoon?"

"No."

"I wonder when she created this folder?"

"Not sure. But she downloaded some of the files on her last Saturday at the office," Greene said, voice flat. "See the dates and times?"

Alice nodded.

Were these documents evidence? Work product? Or both? Could Pat Simpson call them "firm work product" where he'd forbidden due diligence? Maybe they'd fall under the exception for documents relevant to a lawyer's breach of duty. Meaning Pat Simpson's breach...and his possible motives.

She'd have to decide, but not now. Michael had an appointment; she needed to grab Jimmie and head for Fredericksburg.

One thing she did know: everything on the laptop needed to be preserved.

"Thank you, Michael."

He stood, pulled off the gloves, dropped them on Alice's desk. "Let me know what else I can do." His face tightened. "Please."

And he was gone.

She found Silla, explained the disposable gloves, said she didn't want to forward or upload any documents from Nanette's laptop at this point. But they needed to be preserved. Could Silla work her magic? Inventory the documents, only name and type. "We can't look at any actual Simpson deal documents, Simpson work product. I still don't know what the land deal is, or what development costs the investor's obligated to pay." Because that went to whether the purchase price was reasonable—or indicated money laundering. She thought for a moment about the Abyss documents, those reflecting Nanette's anxiety about criminal connections and excessive purchase prices. What if, despite Alice's best efforts, those disappeared? Shouldn't she preserve evidence of possible motives for murder? "Let's at least take screenshots of the Abyss documents. Then stash the laptop back in the safe. I've got to get Jimmie out to Kinsear's. With barbecue."

"Hey. Not my first rodeo," Silla said. "This'll be fun. I'll get my own gloves. You be careful."

Chapter Twenty-Three

What's Up?

Finding herself needing a little burro therapy, waiting for Jimmie and John to finish packing for the sojourn at Kinsear's ranch, Alice stood in her driveway surrounded by the three animals. At the moment, she was brushing Big Boy. He leaned solidly against her; the warmth felt good in the late morning chill. Those long eyelashes, those soft ears, Alice thought. No wonder Titania fell in love with Bottom. "All done, Big Boy. It's Queenie's turn."

He didn't budge, but leaned in.

"Okay. Just a little bit more." She ran the brush down his neck, down his back, along the side of his belly. Queenie, four feet away, inched closer. "Queenie's turn," Alice announced, moving toward the waiting burro. Queenie had papers; Queenie had lovely conformation; Queenie never dropped her dignity. But Big Boy—knock-kneed, pudgy, chipmunk-cheeked, shorter than both Queenie and her daughter, Princess—remained Alice's favorite. While reliably kind to children, he firmly believed the ranch was his to protect and that coyotes (or any stray dogs) were his sworn enemies. When he laid his ears back and lowered his head—get out of his way.

Alice leaned over Queenie and began brushing her other side. Queenie leaned back against Alice. Alice found her own breath slowing. Burro therapy at work.

Jimmie and John emerged from the house. To her surprise, John had announced he'd join Jimmie. "I'll mostly be working, but Jimmie might want company."

Alice studied Jimmie for a moment. Was he turning back into his old self? The haunted look was fading. Today the lines around his mouth didn't look as deeply scored, and his blue eyes weren't flicking back and forth, checking the surroundings.

Maybe one day Jimmie would actually answer her questions.

"Jimmie, you sit in front, by Mom," John ordered. "I get the back." He popped open the rear of the Discovery, threw in his backpack and Jimmie's, then stopped, noisily inhaling. "Mom," he said. "you don't seriously expect us to wait until we get to Fredericksburg before we get some of this barbecue?"

"Nope," she said. She pulled two greasy paper bags out of the wooden box in the rear of the Discovery where she'd loaded her purchases from Shade Tree. She handed one to Jimmie and one to her son. "You each get a snack pack for the trip. One chopped barbecue sandwich apiece. Don't you mess with the brisket or sides, you hear? Let's go."

Alice backed out of the carport, checking to be sure the burros were out of the way. She heard John's paper bag rustle, then the sound of exploratory chewing from the back seat. Next to her, in the front seat, Jimmie slowly unwrapped his sandwich and took a bite.

"Lord, this tastes amazing!" Jimmie said. Another sign of life, Alice thought.

And they were off.

*****

Though he had a house in Fredericksburg, Kinsear spent most nights at the ranch outside town. He'd shown Alice around, but by tacit agreement, though he often spent the night at her place, she declined to spend the night at his. That might still be too soon for his girls, she thought, still grieving the death of their mother, who'd been thrown while jumping her horse. Just another reason why Alice felt her own fear of horses was entirely rational.

Kinsear had moved home to Fredericksburg after a successful tenure as general counsel to a New York hedge fund. His former employer still occasionally demanded his services, but he stayed busy in Fredericksburg. He'd opened a small bookshop, The Real Story, and also spent time on strenuous projects at the ranch with his foreman, Javier—installing new fencing, repairing windmills, mowing hay. "I like messing with dirt and water," Kinsear explained to Alice.

Alice understood completely.

The ranch lay in the hilly territory north of Fredericksburg. In mid-November the hills were still green, covered in live oak and cedar, with the taller Spanish oaks waving the last of their red leaves. Jimmie sat up, showing some interest as Alice left the pastures along the creek and wound up the steep caliche drive. "Tell me about the trees. These evergreens."

"Ashe juniper, but we call them cedar," Alice said.

"And live oaks, mixed in?"

"Yes." The live oaks kept their leaves all winter, flinging them down in a sudden whoosh in April, then revealing their new baby leaves and chartreuse-colored catkins.

"And they're so short because...?"

Alice resented his calling them short. Though they were.

John spoke from the back seat. "They're growing in rocky limestone. Old Cretaceous seabed. Just imagine what that was like, when this was all ocean, full of thrashing whateversaurs."

They rounded the last uphill curve and saw the house—also limestone, a traditional old ranch house, shaded by live oaks and facing south to catch the prevailing breezes.

Kinsear stood waiting by the pole barn. John was first out of the car. Kinsear greeted him with a smile, putting one arm lightly around his shoulders for a nanosecond. Watching, Alice felt her heart melt at his tact, his warmth. Kinsear would never invade Jordie's space, but he'd offer John friendship, man to man. Kinsear shook hands with Jimmie and gave Alice a sideways hug, then peered hopefully at the Discovery.

Grinning, Alice popped open the rear door.

"What a woman you are," Kinsear said, picking up the wooden box of barbecue. "It's warm enough I think we can eat on the screened porch. But first let me show these guys their rooms."

He disappeared into the house, saying, "Mi casa es su casa. All yours."

Later, they sat on the porch looking out at the pastures below, satisfied and greasy-fingered after plates of brisket, meltingly tender under its dark crust, and the smoked sausage made by John at Shade Tree using his old Czech recipe. Kinsear brought out apples for dessert.

"You guys can stay as long as you want," he said. "No plans, no deadlines. Maybe John can get his big paper done." He turned to Jimmie. "You'll meet Javier later. You can rest, loll in the hammock, go riding—whatever you want. Watch out for Javier, though. He's liable to have you mending fence or taking hay out to the cows."

"Will I get to drive that pickup truck?" Jimmie asked. He pointed toward the ancient Toyota under the pole barn. "If so, I'm on." He gave a one-sided smile.

Was Jimmie showing signs of interest?

Kinsear grinned. "Try it out. It's stick shift, six gears." He scooped up the lunch detritus and headed for the kitchen, Alice following.

"I can stay until about six," she said.

"Hmmph. I knew you wouldn't stay under my roof tonight, with those guys here."

They hugged. He kissed her. Alice considered revisiting her decision to leave. But again she saw those bones, the cracked skull...Jordie's son, Jordie's cousin. So, not tonight.

Her cell phone rang.

The navigation screen said "call from M.A. Ellison."

"M.A.? What's up?"

A hoarse whisper: "Need help."

Chapter Twenty-Four

Drop The Knife Now

"What's wrong? Where are you?"

"Lacey's. Listen, there's a"—Alice heard a muffled scream, a thump, then nothing. She redialed. The phone went to voicemail. Alice found Lacey's number, dialed it. Voicemail.

She looked up at Kinsear. "Something bad's happened to M.A. She's at Lacey's. Neither one's answering the phone."

He frowned. "Let's go. It's what, thirty minutes?" He was already grabbing a jacket, heading outside. "I'll drive. You'll have to navigate."

Alice raced to the Discovery and dug under the front seat before joining Kinsear in his ancient Land Cruiser. In less than a minute, they were hurtling down the drive. Alice texted John, explaining their hasty exit: "M.A. is at Lacey Gunn's ranch. Not sure what happened. Will call. Kinsear says there's lasagna in the fridge."

*****

They braked at a red light in Fredericksburg. "Do you have armament?" Alice asked.

"Oh, we've got armament, Alice. But probably unnecessary, given what you're carrying."

Alice looked at him. "I brought all I had."

He grinned. "I'm not worried, so long as you've got that flare gun. You ever been to Lacey's?" he asked, maneuvering south across Fredericksburg's Main Street onto the highway to Kerrville.

"No. I just have the damned legal description, from working on the covenant she wanted." Alice found it in her email. "But it's upstream from the Rock Shelter Retreat Center. Looks like we go through Hunt, then find Wildcat Road, then Narrow Way."

"I like that. The narrow way. Story of my life," Kinsear said. "About thirty minutes?"

"Less, if you don't get a ticket. I didn't know the Land Cruiser could go this fast."

"Listen, we've got to save M.A. She still hasn't given me her pimento cheese recipe. She always balks at telling me her secret ingredient."

"If there is one," Alice said. "She's cagey."

But she was worried, worried sick. M.A. was one of her first friends in Coffee Creek. Sharp-eyed, sharp-tongued, and soft-hearted. But she'd sounded truly scared. Alice was furious at whoever had scared M.A. And why didn't Lacey answer her phone?

South of Fredericksburg, they passed the Gillespie County fairgrounds, passed the pecan and peach stands, closed for winter. Over Wolf Creek; now onto I-10, off at the next exit. They sped through Kerrville, along the is-it-green-or-is-it-blue of the Guadalupe River, then slowed at Hunt, looking for Wildcat Road. They found it the second time they drove past the old limestone gas station and shot out of town heading northwest. The sweet narrow blacktop they'd driven into Hunt turned into a single-laner, asphalt faded to gray, no center stripe. Almost immediately Wildcat Road rose up onto the rocky plateau above the Guadalupe, crisscrossed by narrow curved valleys that created a vast maze—a maze with water at the bottom. Water from springs, from wet-weather creeks, water that came and went whenever and wherever it chose. Not when or where humans chose.

Alice bent over her phone, looking for Narrow Way. "About three miles ahead," she said.

Narrow Way was older, grayer, its cracked asphalt not recently patched. It looked less used than Wildcat Road. Here atop the plateau there were big views of folded hills, south and west. "This is gorgeous country," Kinsear said. "How come I've never seen it?"

"Looks like it's mostly ranches."

They hadn't passed any RV parks, any shops. "Thank goodness you had a full tank," Alice said.

"First commandment at the ranch," Kinsear answered. "Keep it on full, because..."

"...you never know," Alice finished.

He pointed to the right. "Wilkins Ranch." The ranch gate was welded black iron with a center medallion showing a cowboy on a bucking horse.

"The next ranch is Lacey's." Alice leaned forward, watching for an entrance.

Half a mile later they reached a turnoff. "Here." Alice unhooked her seatbelt. "I'll get the gate." The gate, faded green ironwork, was closed only by a chain looped through a slot. Alice held it open, thought for a minute while the Land Cruiser rolled through, and shut it again, looping the chain twice around the post before feeding it into the slot. Because, she thought, if someone's menacing my friends, and we wind up chasing the bad guy, I want him to have to stop for a moment while we catch up.

Lacey's ranch drive was basically an ungraded white streak of caliche, in spots as steep as a luge run, with sporadic heaps of river rock that made it more, not less, slippery. Kinsear put the Land Cruiser in low gear. They edged up through the live oak and cedar. Then the nose of the Land Cruiser turned down. Before them, the drive snaked down a steep bluff, with switchback turns. Sister Creek sparkled below.

"The creek gets its water from springs on Lacey's ranch. Then it runs on past the next ranch and past the Rock Shelter Camp, where it rounds a bend and flows into the Guadalupe," Alice said.

Kinsear was concentrating on the road. "How many acres?"

"Seven thousand."

He raised his eyebrows.

"She doesn't want to sell. Whatever group wanted to buy it—they offered a hundred million."

Kinsear frowned. Alice suddenly realized she hadn't told him about this. "The group made an offer for her ranch and also the ranch upstream and downstream of hers. She said no, and whoever this group is sent some goon out to threaten her. M.A. brought her to me. She wants the ranch to stay a ranch. She was worried about the retreat center, too."

"Why?"

"The investor group wants to build a huge project, like Six Flags in Dallas, but in the Hill Country. Lacey's the sole owner of Gunn Ranch. She has no kids and doesn't think her nephews care about the place. She wanted a covenant requiring that it not be used for commercial purposes. In her words, she doesn't want to be responsible for screwing up her little piece of the planet."

"And you did it?"

"Yep. It's signed, sealed, and recorded. Then I notified the agent for the group of that fact so his clients would get off Lacey's back."

"Uh-oh. What if they try to make her rescind?"

"Rescind?" And into her mind popped her memory of the feckless associate, Brett: "Messing up the entire deal. We have to rescind a stupid document."

And Michael Greene, saying Nanette worried that "the prices seemed ridiculous."

Could Gunn Ranch be the Simpson target?

But Brett said "Kimble, Kinney, Kendall." They were in Kerr County.

They'd slowed on the last switchback, just above the narrow low-water bridge that crossed the stream, when Kinsear pulled to a stop. "See the house, through the trees?"

"Yes." Alice saw M.A.'s antique gold Cadillac station wagon parked in front. Next to it, a black SUV.

"I'm wondering if we can find a back door." He pointed again. "See the dirt road that goes to that barn?"

"Let's do it. Maybe no one will notice."

He snorted. They crossed the bridge, then Kinsear slowed down, reducing their noise on the dirt road toward the barn. The road from the barn ran toward the back of Lacey's house. Alice tugged Jordie's flare gun from beneath her seat, inserting a flare. As they slid to a stop behind the house and got out, Kinsear motioned to Alice—don't close the car doors. He retrieved his shotgun from the floorboards in back.

Lacey lived in the original two-story wooden ranch house, yellow with green shutters flanking tall windows. A wide back porch held a porch swing and an old metal glider with flowered cushions. Lacey's geraniums were still blooming—no hard freeze yet. Through the window on the right at the back of the porch, Alice could see into the kitchen, but not beyond. Next to the window was a doorway. The screen door was closed, but the main door stood open to the interior.

The house was essentially a dog-trot downstairs, with a wide central hall running from the front door all the way to the back door. Down the hall, with its ancient Turkish carpet, they could see the front entry. Its carved oak front door was ajar; it didn't hang quite straight. A brass chandelier, its graceful arms somewhat tarnished, hung from the entry ceiling. Voices echoed down the hall, seeming to come from the right. Dining room, Alice guessed, next to the kitchen. Living room would be on the left.

"Sign it, damn it! Sign it now!"

The harsh voice was somehow familiar.

"Don't listen, Lacey!" M.A.'s voice—but high, strained.

Kinsear opened the screen door and started down the hall, shotgun raised. Alice followed, flare gun in her right hand.

"Sign it, or your friend gets a new airway!" The harsh voice again.

Kinsear sped up, then skidded to a stop in the front entry, facing right. He racked the gun. Alice was unprepared for the shock of that unmistakable sound in a closed space. Kinsear moved forward. "Drop the knife."

Sneaking up behind Kinsear from what Alice guessed was the living room came a whey-faced young man, blue blazer, wrinkled gray pants, hefting in both hands a large ceramic planter.

Alice yelled "Hey!" and lifted the flare gun. The newcomer swerved toward Alice, one foot tangled in the hall rug, heaving the planter at her face.

She dodged and fired.

The blast echoed.

With a solid loud thump, the brass chandelier fell from its moorings on the shattered ceiling and landed on the young man's head. He collapsed onto the floor, head encircled by the brass arms of the chandelier.

Alice loaded another flare, then stepped across bits of broken ceramic, waving away the red smoke in the air. She peered at the still figure, lying on his belly, face turned toward her. His nose had taken a hit, and the top of his head was bleeding.

Alice hoped that meant he probably wasn't dead. Didn't you stop bleeding after death? Maybe he was just severely bruised, possibly with a broken nose?

He groaned.

"Thanks for shedding some light on the subject," Kinsear said. He didn't turn her way, still pointing his shotgun toward the dining room.

Alice ignored his little joke. She was transfixed by what she saw.

"Anton!" she breathed.

Anton, the security guard, held a switchblade knife to M.A.'s throat. With his free hand he yanked her up from the dining room chair, holding her in front of him. He kicked away the chair. Alice realized M.A.'s hands were tied behind her.

Lacey sat across the dining room table, ball point pen in hand. "I won't sign," she said.

"You're going to," Anton snarled. He glared at Kinsear, then Alice. "She signs it, I leave, everything's fine. She doesn't sign it"— he yanked M.A.'s head back, exposing her throat to the knife—"this old bag dies. You fire at me, she dies. That one signs the papers"—he nodded toward Lacey—"I leave, and we're all copacetic. Your choice."

Alice moved slowly around the edge of the table toward Lacey, one step at a time.

"Nope, it's your choice," Kinsear said, voice level. "Shotgun blast in your gut, or a flare gun in your face. Drop the knife now." He moved a step closer.

Anton's eyes were on Kinsear. Alice tugged her phone from her pocket, using her left hand, glanced down. Camera. She lifted it and took pictures of Anton, knife at M.A.'s throat.

"Can't wait to show these pictures to the Simpson boys," she said. Then she raised the flare gun.

"Drop the knife now. Back against the wall," Kinsear ordered. "Let go of M.A."

Anton's eyes flickered at Alice, then back at Kinsear. He showed signs of thinking about his next move. Kinsear took a step forward, gun raised. Anton dropped the knife and put his back to the dining room wall.

M.A. dodged away from him, her hands still tied.

"Don't move a muscle," Kinsear ordered Anton, moving a step closer.

"You have no idea who you're messing with," Anton hissed. He flicked his eyes toward the knife on the floor, then back at Kinsear. "When my friends get hold of you"—

A sudden blast; the air filled with sound and smoke. Kinsear had fired into the floor, a scant foot from Anton's shoes. "Kick that knife away. Now." Kinsear racked the gun again. "Next time, it's your knees." Anton sullenly kicked the knife toward the kitchen door.

Lacey got up from the table and kicked the knife all the way into the kitchen. Then she marched to the coat closet by the door and emerged with her twenty-gauge. She walked back around the table, shotgun trained on Anton's head.

"Now we've got buckshot and birdshot," Kinsear said. "Anton, face the wall. Alice, shove that chair up behind Anton here."

Alice did so with gusto. Anton had no choice but to sit, facing the wall.

In the entry Young Wheyface—Alice assumed he was Ted Lemmon of Grandee Properties—lay snorting, trying to lift his head. He might need attention.

Alice followed M.A. to the kitchen, found the kitchen shears and sawed through the rope on M.A.'s wrists. M.A. rubbed her chafed wrists. Alice returned to the entry with the cut rope, knelt by the wriggling young man, roughly maneuvered his hands behind his back while kneeling on one of his arms, then used the same rope to tie his wrists tightly. "Recycling," M.A. said. She'd reappeared from the kitchen with a length of clothesline. Alice used that to tie his elbows together. His head had quit bleeding, his nose was a mess. He'd live.

Kinsear grinned. "Now for Anton," he said.

A drawer slammed in the kitchen.

M.A. returned like the goddess of wrath, holding a spool of picture wire and a pair of needle-nose pliers. She grabbed Anton's right wrist, bending his forearm up behind him. He yelped. M.A. yanked harder, wrapping the wire tightly around and around one hairy wrist, then grabbed the other wrist and bent it up, wrapping the whole time. "Pliers," she growled. "Cut the wire."

Alice obeyed, then watched M.A. twisting, knotting, and retwisting the wire until she was satisfied.

"That's too tight!" The man stank of sweat and aftershave. And now fear.

"Thanks, M.A.," Kinsear said.

"Need any more?" M.A. asked.

"We're good," Kinsear said.

"Let's talk," Alice said to the back of Anton's head.

"You don't know who you're messing with. Just let me go."

"Scooch that chair around, Anton. Now." Kinsear waved the

barrel at the side of Anton's face. "I'll be happy to blast your knees if you don't."

Exuding hate, Anton lurched around in the chair until he faced the table.

Alice picked up the papers on the table in front of Lacey. "Rescission of Covenant," she read. "Purchase and Sale Agreement. Deed. Who gave you these, Anton?"

He scowled at her.

"I assume it was someone at Simpson Strategic Assets?" Now she was photographing each page of each document.

He just stared.

"Brett Bradley?"

He snorted. "Yeah."

"Did Brett Bradley tell you to put a knife to her throat?" Alice tilted her head at M.A., who stood glaring by the table.

"I can't get up! Someone help me!" bleated a voice from the entry floor.

Alice thought about that. If you were lying on your belly with your hands tied behind you, standing up could be a challenge. What if you rolled sideways and got to your knees? Was there a yoga move that could help? She tried to picture one, but failed.

On the other hand, why did the kid need to stand up? He was safe where he was. On the floor.

"The old bag's an idiot," Anton blurted. "Buyer's offering her a hundred million for this dump! Out here in this godforsaken state! She shoulda just signed the deed!"

"Godforsaken?" bristled Alice. "Remind me—aren't you from Florida?" Florida plates. "Wait a minute. Who exactly sent you out here? The Simpson boys? Or someone else?"

She watched his face close tight. "You don't get another word from me. You're not law. You got no right to hold me."

"What about me?" groaned the entry floor.

Kinsear looked at Alice. "Let's call the sheriff. Agree, Lacey? These guys shoved their way in, threatened you, threatened M.A. with grievous bodily harm, trespassed. What else?"

"Ran over my canna lily bed," Lacey said, indignant. "Knocked my front door off its hinges. Shoved me aside—that's why I couldn't get my snake gun out of the front closet. And pissed me off." Lacey stood up, leaned on the dining room table, and said, straight into Anton's face, "You're a disgusting human being. I'm prosecuting you to the full extent of the law. Not just criminal charges. Civil charges. You picked the wrong county for this, buster."

Well! Alice lifted an eyebrow at Kinsear, who was smiling at Lacey.

Lacey pushed her chair back and stalked over to the agent, still groaning on her entry floor. She bent over, shaking her finger in his face. "You too, buddy boy. I'm suing you and everyone who hired you! I'm bringing criminal charges for aiding and abetting this piece of criminal scum. Furthermore"— now she stood up—"I'm going to call your parents. I'm going to post the picture of you, lying there with a chandelier on your head, on social media. You'll be unemployed. And a laughingstock."

"He made me!" whined Young Wheyface, barely lifting his head from the floor. "He—he threatened me!"

"Right, and you were tippy-toeing across the floor trying to brain Mr. Kinsear with my best Chinese planter! Real estate agent, indeed! There's no Ted Lemmon listed with the licensing board. You have no license, and if I have anything to do with it, which I will, you'll never get one."

"Add fraud to the mix," Alice said. She knelt by him, patted his pockets, and pulled out a felt bag with a drawstring. "Got someone's notary seal in your pocket? Were you going to, ah, notarize Lacey's signatures and forge the notary's signature?" She took a picture of the seal, including the notary's name and contact information.

"I—I'm sitting for the real estate exam," he blurted from the floor.

"Interesting," Kinsear said. "Admission of fraud. Okay, Lacey, where's your phone? I believe you know the sheriff. Personally, yes?"

"Yep," Lacey said. She peered at her screen, dialed, then demanded an instant connection to the county sheriff. And got it. "We have the two men cornered, Sheriff. And restrained. My friends are here. Are you on your way? Oh, already? Thank you, Sheriff."

Chapter Twenty-Five

The Gunn Ranch Gang

The sheriff left a rooster tail of dust as he and a deputy roared down Lacey's drive in a Kerr County SUV, followed by a patrol car with two other deputies.

Lacey met them on the front porch, with M.A. close behind her. The front door stood open, hanging from one hinge.

Alice waited in the front entry, watching. The sheriff was burly, gray-haired, suntanned, sixty-ish. Straight from central casting, Alice thought.

"What've you been up to, Lacey?"

"Catching rascals. Sheriff Oates, meet my friend, M.A. Ellison, from Coffee Creek."

"Ma'am," said the Sheriff, touching his hat. "This is Deputy Denton." Denton nodded, eyes moving back and forth from the two silver-haired seventy-plus ladies to the damaged front door.

"That's his car?" asked Denton, thumb aimed at Anton's black SUV. "Florida guy?"

"Yes. That man showed up last week with this supposed real estate agent, the one lying on the floor in there, wanting me to sell my ranch. I refused. That man tried to shove his way in my front door, wanting me to sign the sales contract. I had to slam his hand in the door and get my snake gun out of the closet and wave it at him from my picture window before he left. Just take a look—that hand's still got a bruise.

"Anyway, I have no intention of selling. They say they want to build some theme park. That'll wreck the springs. I got Alice here to help me draft a covenant to keep the ranch in ag. Keep it a ranch."

The sheriff nodded. "Makes sense."

"But then today"—Lacey's eyebrows rose dramatically—"today that man came back with that same dippy little guy. See what they did to my front door? They wanted me to undo my covenant, wanted me to sign some paper saying I didn't mean it, and sign a sales contract and a deed. I said no, I wouldn't. Then the big lug grabbed a knife out of his pocket and threatened to cut M.A.'s throat if I didn't sign."

The sheriff looked bemused. "Where'd you put him?"

"Oh, our friends are guarding him and that agent. They're inside."

The sheriff and his deputy carefully maneuvered past the unsteady door. Alice, standing in the entry, introduced herself. "Alice Greer, Coffee Creek. Lacey's lawyer. This is Ben Kinsear, from Fredericksburg."

Kinsear, still holding his shotgun, nodded at the two men, who nodded back.

"That's Anton, don't know his last name," Alice said, pointing toward Anton, parked in the dining room chair. "He works security for a Coffee Creek outfit." She pointed at Anton's accomplice, now uncomfortably propped against the piano bench in the living room, hands still bound behind his back. "They wanted Lacey to sign the papers on the table."

"How'd you two get here?" asked the sheriff, eyes moving from Kinsear to Alice and back.

"M.A. called us just after lunch, but we couldn't tell what was wrong. When we tried to call back, M.A. didn't answer, and we couldn't get Lacey either. We got here as fast as we could." Alice pointed at Anton. "He'd tied up M.A. and was holding a knife to her throat." She pointed again. "The knife's in there, on the kitchen floor."

"Said if Lacey didn't sign the papers, he'd give me a new airway!" M.A. burst out.

The sheriff looked up at the blasted and singed ceiling, broken wires dangling where the chandelier had hung. "Someone tried swinging from the rafters?"

"That's my fault," Alice said. "At least it didn't catch fire." She glanced at a smoke detector on the dining room wall. "So far."

Kinsear added, "She only had a flare gun, Sheriff, and Mr. Secret Agent was trying to brain me with that." Kinsear indicated the shattered ceramic bowl on the floor. "Alice stopped him."

Alice looked at Lacey. "I'll get that ceiling fixed, Lacey."

"Don't you worry about it, hon. You two saved our bacon. Besides, Carlos can fix anything. And don't worry about the floor. I'll put a brass historical plaque on it, with today's date."

"We don't want you here alone, with a busted front door," Alice said.

"I'm staying," M.A. huffed. "This time no one's taking me by surprise."

"And Carlos and Sara should be back tonight," Lacey added. "They're visiting relatives in San Antonio."

The sheriff looked hard at Lacey.

"I'll be fine."

"I'll send a patrol by tonight, just to check," he said. "But these bozos will be staying in jail...at least overnight."

"I'll post bail," Anton grunted. "My bosses will."

"Not after I email these pictures, they won't," Alice retorted, waving her phone. "You with a knife at M.A.'s neck."

"Get his ID, Denton," the sheriff said. Denton reached, not gently, into Anton's pockets. He extracted a wallet, and three phones.

"That pink phone's mine, Deputy." M.A. announced. "The white one's Lacey's."

"Don't touch them till they get finger-printed, please," the sheriff warned. "Crime scene team's on the way right now." He looked at Alice. "Please forward me those photos."

"Anton Ivanov?" Denton looked up from his scrutiny of the wallet. "Miami." He disappeared out the front door, talking on his phone.

The sheriff made the young man roll sideways, extracted his wallet, then went to the front door. Alice heard him tell Denton, "Call this in too. Bennie Vitale. Also Miami."

When Sheriff Oates and Deputy Denton returned, Denton handcuffed the young man, now snotnosed and red-eyed. "Don't move," he said.

"Wait a sec. Your real name is Bennie Vitale?" Alice asked. "So who's Ted Lemmon?"

She explained to Denton and the sheriff that Lacey's harassing phone calls came from someone calling himself "Ted Lemmon" at "Grandee Properties."

The sheriff glared at Bennie Vitale. "Let me guess. You're Ted Lemmon?"

The young man's eyes shifted left, then right, then to the floor.

"I get it. There's no Ted Lemmon—you just called yourself that?"

"Yeah," muttered the young man.

Meanwhile Deputy Denton handcuffed Anton, then took the pliers and clipped through the wire. "Effective, though," he muttered. He and the sheriff marched the two prisoners outside.

Alice watched as two other deputies, waiting on the porch, grabbed the prisoners and maneuvered them toward the driveway, where not one but two county SUVs were pulling up, followed by a Ford pickup. Out of the pickup jumped a middle-aged couple, faces alarmed. Sara and Carlos Cortes, Alice thought.

The sheriff walked back inside. "Those names rang some bells in Florida. We'll see. Remind me who this Anton guy works for in Coffee Creek?"

"Simpson Strategic Assets," Alice said.

He made a note, then glanced at Lacey and M.A., Alice and Kinsear. "The Gunn Ranch Gang, huh? Be sure those guns are on safety, and put them away. The crime scene team's here now. Get out of their way, and don't touch anything. Now, Miss Lacey, you're going to have to come down and fill out a complaint. Can you do that right now? Then you can get back home before dark. We'll be sure you two have your phones back by then."

"I'll come," she said. "M.A., you'll come too?"

"Without a doubt."

Alice gazed admiringly at the pair. Both women were nearing eighty—maybe Lacey was already there? M.A.'s hair, braided in her usual coronet, was mussed. Lacey's eyes looked tired. But they'd risen up against bullies. Alice hoped she'd have been even half as brave as they were.

Lacey gave Alice a big hug. "Thank you," she whispered. She grabbed Kinsear's shoulders. He leaned down and she kissed his cheek. "You saved us."

The two women followed the sheriff outside.

"Remember, you can't stay here alone tonight," Alice called.

"No worries." Lacey waved at Sara and Carlos Cortes, wide-eyed in the driveway, watching two county vehicles depart with Anton and his sidekick.

Inside, the crime scene team got to work.

*****

Kinsear and Alice took the Corteses aside and recounted what had happened. Carlos Cortes fingered the front door. "I'll get this fixed tonight."

Kinsear gave them his card. "Anything happens, don't wait. Call me."

He and Alice climbed back in the Land Cruiser and looked at each other.

"Good lord," Alice said.

"If M.A. hadn't phoned you—" Kinsear's mouth tightened as he cleared the low-water bridge and started uphill.

In the west the sky was pink and apricot, with heavy gray stratus layers to the north. "We're due for another norther," he said. "Sure you don't want to spend the night at the ranch?"

Alice stared down at her phone, thumbing the messages. "I can't," she said. "Silla's finished looking at the documents Nanette had copied onto her laptop. She's trying to figure out who's behind the money for this deal."

"I think you mean whose money's getting laundered," Kinsear said. "That very high price? You did hear what Sheriff Oates said about the south Florida mafia?"

"Yeah. Did you know the Russian mafia was also in Miami?"

"Of course. Are we talking Russian money too?"

"Maybe."

"Sounds like my days back in the Big Apple," said Kinsear. They'd reached the top of the ridge. Alice unlocked the gate; he drove through, and she hung the heavy chain back on the gatepost and hoisted herself back up into the Land Cruiser. "But if someone's laundering dirty money, what made it dirty?"

"You might ask Jimmie about that. He won't talk details with me or John, says he's trying to protect us."

"From?"

"He won't say. But if you ask me, I particularly want my family protected from the man who called himself Ian Blane."

She told Kinsear how Ann had located the five-year-old photo of Jimmie and Jordie on the rig, with a dead ringer for "Ian Blane" visible in the background. "I sent his picture to the Scottish Coastguard and the British Consulate in Houston, along with a picture Jimmie took earlier in Jakarta."

"What do they say?"

"I'm waiting to hear from Hartung. And getting tired of the silent treatment."

It was full dark as Kinsear sped north out of Kerrville toward Fredericksburg. Alice looked at his face in the dim light from the dashboard. He'd offered to keep Jimmie and John at the ranch. Then, without a moment's hesitation, he'd ridden to the rescue, saving Lacey from being forced to sell the ranch she loved, saving M.A. too.

Kinsear glanced at her. "What?"

"Just admiring your profile." She leaned toward him, kissed his cheek. "You're—you're a man to ride the river with."

"What about you? I didn't know you could aim that flare gun so precisely it'd drop a chandelier on that guy's head."

Should she admit she'd almost tripped on the rug? That she was trying to hit the ceramic jug before the faux agent whacked Kinsear with it?

On mature reflection, not necessary. Suddenly she burst out laughing, thinking of Kinsear's comment on her flare gun shot. "'Shedding some light on the subject,'" she repeated, then convulsed into giggles.

Kinsear started chuckling himself. But Alice couldn't stop. She leaned back on the seat, eyes closed, laughing until the tears came.

He glanced at her, his face quizzical. "Are you okay? I've never seen you laugh so hard."

She just shook her head, still laughing. "Hysterical afternoon." But it was more than that. Some sort of dam had broken, some breach of the tight restraints she always imposed on herself. She felt...lighter.

They were nearly to his ranch gate when Kinsear said, in a different tone, "I'm worried that Jimmie seems so worried. So I'm gonna quiz him tomorrow."

"Good."

"But listen, I'm more worried about the reaction of these Simpson brothers."

"Well, assuming Lacey's ranch was key to the transaction, their deal probably didn't close today. When we went to the Simpson building to pick up Nanette's belongings, Brett kept muttering that he had to get it done today, Monday."

"Losing this deal may be a serious financial hit," Kinsear said.

"Michael Greene—Nanette's boyfriend—said she'd told him the

hedge fund's September financials looked bad."

"Whoa. They'll be deeply pissed. They may need this deal to stay afloat. They'll be scared existing investors will pull out."

"Hmm."

"Well, stay out of their way," Kinsear said. "I mean it. Anton—he's bad news, and they can find more where they got him."

That sent a chill down her spine.

They slowed to a stop in front of the ranch house and climbed out. Alice retrieved her flare gun from beneath the seat. "Don't point that thing at me," Kinsear said, enveloping her in a hug. He kissed her. She kissed him back. A cool breeze made her hug him tighter. He wrapped his canvas coat around her, and they stood together, feeling the wind increase, watching the moon appear and disappear behind fast-moving clouds. "I wish you would stay."

She thought about it. He caught her glancing at the pole barn. She didn't see Isabel's car.

"I told you. The girls aren't here. It's cold. Come inside. You can leave at five in the morning if you want. You'll be at your office by six."

Alice was tempted. She could feel the wind getting stronger; she needed to check the burros; and most of all, she wasn't sure her first night at the ranch should include her son and his dead father's cousin. "If I'm not here, maybe you can get some information out of Jimmie."

Chapter Twenty-Six

Show Me Whatcha Got

Tuesday morning. Alice buttoned her jacket against the chilly wind and headed for the barn. Kinsear's predicted norther had arrived overnight, with fast-moving gray stratus clouds and blasts of wind rattling the live oak leaves. The burros had retreated to their shed, protected from the north wind. Alice rolled and kicked a bale of hay out of the barn and into the pen. The burros gathered around her and were eating before she managed to cut the string on the bale. Pale gold and green stalks spilled onto the ground. She sneezed at the smell of grass—stored sunshine, she thought—as Big Boy edged past her, nose to the hay. She rolled another bale into the pen and cut the string. Her purpose was to make an adequate bed for the burros in the shed, but she knew they'd have eaten their bed by lunchtime.

On her way into Coffee Creek, she rewarded herself with hot breakfast tacos from the Flores take-out shop, filling the car with the breakfasty smell of egg and chorizo. She bought two more, migas with green sauce, for Silla.

Her Live Oak Street office was quiet. Inside she found sticky notes from Silla on her desk: "Call Captain Hartung, Scotland. Call Edwin Davies, British Consulate, Houston. Call Louie Gumbert, 'highly irritated you weren't available; how does she keep clients if she's not in the office?'" She'd included their numbers. Another sticky: "Remember Ferrises will arrive the Friday after Thanksgiving. Have made reservations at M.A.'s B&B." Also on the desk, a stack of paper titled "Ferris Inventory: Laptop Contents," tightly clipped. Looked like Silla had created a spreadsheet of Nanette's folders and the contents of each (photos, emails, etc.), and a stack of screenshots from the passworded "Abyss" list. Alice wouldn't touch those yet.

First, coffee. She started the coffee-maker in the office kitchen, waited for the precious dark liquid to finish filling the pot, then filled her cup and poured the remaining coffee into the thermos. Not ready to be at her desk yet, she took her coffee to the antique tea table by the window that overlooked the back yard, watching a squirrel descend the pecan tree trunk. How clever, the claws that let the squirrel stay upside down, tail twitching, whiskers twitching, waiting for—revelation? For clues to another pecan, hidden under the leaves?

Okay, what to tackle next? Gumbert? Scottish Coastguard? Houston Consulate? And she must deal with the nagging obligation to get Nanette's laptop to Files so he could dust it for prints. How much could she tell him? That she'd purloined it off the IT guy's shelf? That she didn't know when it left Nanette's possession—whether she'd left it at the office, or taken it with her that Saturday night before she was killed? Well, it was definitely Nanette's personal laptop, so no harm, no foul. What about the unidentified fingerprints on Nanette's body? The thought of someone dragging Nanette's battered body under a hedge—broken, but still alive—sent a wave of rage through Alice, making her set down her coffee.

She wondered if Files, confronted with unidentified fingerprints in a murder case, felt the same fury. She'd never seen him lose his composure. Did he discipline his rage with patience? "Don't make assumptions," he repeated. Maybe that kept him from blowing up.

But she could tell Files that Anton, security for the Simpson brothers, was currently in a county jail after threatening to cut M.A.'s throat to force Lacey Gunn to sign away her ranch. At least she hoped he was still in jail; she'd better double-check with Sheriff Oates.

What about Anton? Would he, did he, murder Nanette? He drove a black SUV, not a white one, but Nanette had said he liked to drive other peoples' cars, the costlier the better. He hadn't shown guilt or been evasive when she'd asked about Nanette at the Simpson office. Called her a "hard worker," hadn't he. On the other hand, he'd held a knife to M.A.'s throat.

First, she'd deal with Louie Gumbert. If she was lucky, he'd be away from his phone.

"H'lo?"

Damn, the man was audibly eating breakfast. With his phone on speaker.

"You could call me back, Louie, since you're apparently eating."

"No pro'lem." He swallowed.

Alice rolled her eyes.

"Listen, Alice, about this bazaar business. Doesn't make sense to have two festivals, right? Wasted effort. So how about you just send over all your documents, you know, all that liability stuff? We'll combine forces. More efficient."

"I'm not sure what you mean."

"We won't duplicate effort. We'll call this shindig the Coffee Creek Holiday Bazaar. You send me what we need, insurance, all that stuff, and I'll get the mayor to open the Bazaar. Over at City Park."

"Oh, you're planning your, what, Weihnachtsmarkt? A Christmas market in the park? That will be a nice addition, Louie. But the Beer Barn's already way down the road with the Beer Barn Holiday Bazaar." She emphasized "Beer Barn." "We've got everything in place except the microphones for the band."

"You're just duplicating my work here, stealing my concept."

"That's ridiculous. Your concept was tents in the park. Fine. But the Beer Barn owners came up first with their own plan, and it's going to happen."

He adopted a wheedling tone. "Now, Alice, don't be that way. You don't want me wasting my time and effort on the little stuff."

"What do you mean?"

"Well, you said you were doing all these liability releases, contracts with music people and stuff, toilets, I don't know."

"Right. We've got it all handled. For the Beer Barn venue."

"So why should I reinvent the wheel? Just add our folks' names to everything you've done and we're good!"

"Louie," Alice said, "that's a problem. The Beer Barn will be covered by its own insurance. Our insurer won't cover your activities."

"No problem. The City'll be immune from liability, right? You know, governmental immunity."

Alice heard the front door open. Silla's red head popped around her door. Alice put Louie on speakerphone.

Louie slurped something, then said, "Just get your girl to convert your documents to include the City booths and contests." Silla rolled her eyes in disgust.

"Actually, Silla's a grown woman. Might also be wise for you to do some research on the scope of immunity. Listen, I've got to run."

He harrumphed. "I'm taking this to the mayor."

"Taking what?"

"Your lack of cooperation. Lack of civic-mindedness."

"Louie, I'm not authorized to draft documents for whatever

you're planning for the City. We're going to keep the Beer Barn Holiday Bazaar on track. That's been our plan from the get-go. But keep me posted, will you?"

He harrumphed again. "You're gonna regret this. Tell your clients I'm gonna stop their little shindig if you don't cooperate."

"How do you plan to do that, Louie? Are you threatening my clients?"

"Hide and watch, little lady. I know my way around a courthouse." He hung up.

Alice looked at Silla.

"What a jerk," Silla announced. "You know what Jennie says? You know, Jennie Wilmot. Mayor Wilson's secretary. She says the mayor just rolls her eyes over Gumbert, says he's off on a frolic of his own, has no commitment whatsoever from the City." She tossed her head, the red ponytail bouncing, mouth set. "If Louie Gumbert thinks he's getting his hands on my Bazaar spreadsheet, he's nuts."

"I can't figure out what he thinks he's doing," Alice said. "Miranda claims the Chamber hasn't voted on his holiday notions, much less on any joint proposal with the City."

"Oh, come on, Alice. Gumbert plans to run for City Council. He wants to make a big announcement during this mythical Christmas deal. Probably dressed up as Santa Claus. I know that's true, because I heard it at the Camellia Diner." She laughed and disappeared into the kitchen. "Hey! Are these breakfast tacos for me?"

"Yep!"

"Whoo-ee!"

At her desk, Alice could just hear in the distance a steady bass drumbeat: the high school band practicing for its half-time show at the regional playoffs. Coffee Creek's football team this year was small but feisty. What about her own team? Any holes in the offensive line? Defensive line? She called up Silla's spreadsheet on her computer, looking at the division of labor: the Beer Barn's list of to-do's, and her law firm's list of to-do's. She called Jorgé Benavides at the Beer Barn.

"You've already sent out some invitations to the Beer Barn Holiday Bazaar, right? To some bands, or dance groups?"

"Yes, indeed. We've sent some letters, some emails. Got some acceptances right away from businesses wanting a booth. Our first ad's coming out today in the Coffee Creek ad rag. Sun Radio called to schedule an interview about the Bazaar."

"Are you thinking of a special draft beer for the event?"

"How'd you guess? Yes."

"You're using 'Beer Barn Holiday Bazaar' on your letters and emails?"

"Yes. Anything wrong with that?"

"No. You're using it in commerce. Let's register the service mark."

"Fine." He paused. "Sounds like you're in a hurry. Why?"

"I don't trust Louie Gumbert."

Jorgé was silent for a few seconds. "Aha. That's as good a reason as any."

They hung up. Alice found Silla. "Let's file the service mark application today." Then she emailed the Beer Barn guys: "Please send us a copy of everything you're using with 'Beer Barn Holiday Bazaar' on it including posters, flyers, ads, plus tickets, press releases, tweets, emails, anything public. Can you send those over?"

"Sure," came the response.

Offense and defense looked stronger.

*****

Okay, she'd dealt with Gumbert for the moment. She called Captain Donald Hartung in Aberdeen. "Did you get the photographs I sent? The one of Jordie Greer and his cousin Jimmie Greer, and the man calling himself 'Ian Blane' in the background?" she asked. "Where is he? Why was he on the oil rig five years ago?"

"Unfortunately, we don't yet know where he is. As to the rig, NorthOil recognized the man in your photo and tells us he used the name 'Alec Dunning.' NorthOil hired him as a computer assistant through an Aberdeen personnel company a couple of weeks before your husband's helicopter went down. Their regular employee was in hospital after being mugged in Aberdeen."

Yikes, Alice thought. Rough town. "When did Dunning leave the rig?"

"He left on the offshore crew boat two days before the helicopter crash. He was scheduled to return after the break. NorthOil says he was reasonably competent with their computer system, but he never came back. However, this may explain one puzzle. You sent me three documents that the so-called Ian Blane had sent you. But they weren't from Coastguard investigation files—they weren't in proper format. We think they were downloaded directly from NorthOil. Presumably a computer assistant would have access.

"Now, you also mentioned the name 'Dickie Manners.'"

"Yes?"

"A man from Aberdeen named Richard Manners was dishonorably discharged from the Scottish Coastguard six years ago. His mother still lives in Aberdeen. She's retired, but, interestingly, she once worked at the personnel agency that sent 'Alec Dunning' to the rig. She claims not to have seen her son since his discharge. As I say, we're still looking for him."

"But he sent me that transcript from the helicopter pilot's radio transmission. That happened after he'd already left the rig," Alice pointed out. "Did he hack the NorthOil computer system later? What was his motive? It's very worrying."

"Understood. NorthOil took steps to block access after he failed to report. Meanwhile, I'd like to share with you the preliminary report on the likely cause of the fatal crash of *Grampian*, the helicopter carrying Jordan Greer." He waited.

She took a breath. "Yes?"

"Based on all the available weather data at the time, including fast-moving storm clouds, we currently believe the likeliest cause of the crash was pilot vertigo." He paused, waiting, then went on. "You'll remember the pilot radioed that if the weather started closing in, he'd try for Peterhead. He was using visual flight rules. It appears the weather closed in so quickly that he didn't realize in time the need to focus on his instrumentation. If that happens, even an able pilot can experience vertigo and become disoriented. The helicopter can start to spin; the pilot loses control."

And hitting the water's like hitting cement, the pathologist had told her.

"You've ruled out sabotage? Mechanical failure? Poor maintenance?"

"We've found no evidence of any of those."

Alice's mind filled with the image of the helicopter, spinning. "Captain, have you personally known pilots who got vertigo?"

"Unfortunately, I have. It was also part of my training. All I can say is, if a pilot's surrounded by clouds and doesn't check instruments quickly enough, loss of control can happen unexpectedly fast."

Again he waited. Alice appreciated the silence, letting her have a moment to respond. Finally, she said, "I don't like imagining what it was like. For Jordie."

"I understand."

Now it was her turn to wait.

"It was probably very fast," he said. "I'm sorry."

Alice thanked him.

"You'll get the written report when we finalize it. Meanwhile, if I learn the whereabouts of Richard Manners, you'll be my first call."

Maybe the Consulate had more information. She called and asked for Edwin Davies.

"Ma'am, he'll have to return your call. He's not available."

Damn again.

Next stop: George Files. She called. Yes, he was in the office. She told him about the laptop.

"Come on over," he grunted.

She unlocked the safe, slipped on disposable gloves, and laid the laptop in a box lined with extra disposable gloves. Amateurish but, she hoped, effective. She drove slowly down Live Oak Street to Courthouse Square and parked by the Sheriff's Annex. Carrying the box, trying to keep the laptop from sliding around, she marched to the entry desk. "I'm here to see Detective Files."

Sitting in the hard plastic seat where she could look down the hall, she waited, speculating about the journey Nanette's laptop had made to the IT guy's office. She saw Files emerge from his office and walk down the hall to fetch her.

"I've got just a few minutes, then a meeting," he said. He stacked some folders on his desk, making space. "Show me whatcha got."

She opened the box. "The day Mischa and Nanette and I had lunch at the Beer Barn, she showed us her personal laptop. The little boy she tutored at the elementary school gave her the Mario Brothers sticker on the lid. She said she always kept the laptop with her, after she found Brett Bradley snooping in her office."

"I remember," Files said. "I also remember the laptop wasn't at the crime scene. So tell me again how you got hold of it?"

"I represent Nanette's parents. They're her executors. They have to file an inventory of her property with the probate court."

Files nodded.

"Silla and I inventoried her apartment—no laptop there, as you already know. Then we went to the Simpson Building last Friday to pick up the personal stuff from Nanette's office. Remember, I told you we would."

"Yes."

"When we got there, Brett was already camped out at Nanette's desk. I saw no sign of her laptop, so I asked him to take me to their IT guy's office."

Files frowned. "Why?"

"At my old firm, that's where all the old, new, borrowed, or broken laptops wound up."

"Surely not personal ones?"

"True. But hers was there, half-hidden behind a monitor. So I grabbed it."

"Meaning your prints will be all over it."

"I hope not. I used a tissue and stuck it in my shoulder bag."

He was still frowning. "Our team had already checked her office."

"So you told me."

His eyes held hers. "You ask anyone how it got to the IT guy's office?"

"No." She felt her face turning pink. "Pat Simpson got mad when he saw us in the hall. He opened one of our boxes to check on us. No trust in his fellow lawyers."

"And you didn't mention the laptop in your shoulder bag." He gave her that one-sided smile.

"It needed to be in the inventory," she said.

A mild snort. He leaned back.

"Look," she said. "When Nanette came home, presumably late Saturday night, wouldn't she have brought her own laptop with her? But Joske said it wasn't found at the scene."

"So maybe she left it in her office, and the IT guy or someone moved it out when Brett moved in."

"Hard to imagine Nanette leaving it there," Alice said.

"If someone took it from the crime scene, why would it wind up stuffed behind a monitor in the IT room?"

"Maybe someone was curious about what's on it. Or worried. Someone who didn't have her password and needed help getting into the laptop. For some reason."

His eyes bored into hers. "Somehow I feel sure you already know what's on it."

"Here's the password. And the second password for the encrypted folder in her Forms file. The one called Abyss." She passed a scrap of paper to him. "Michael Greene helped. I didn't alter anything. I did open some of the Internet documents she'd downloaded."

He frowned. "Nanette's a homicide victim. Her laptop's evidence. I know why I'm interested in it. But why are you, other than as part of an inventory?"

Momentarily, she was at a loss for words, then realized he didn't yet know about Anton, M.A., and the shootout at Gunn Ranch. She took a deep breath. "This deal Nanette was working on, that she worried about? The one Brett Bradley was trying to close yesterday?"

"Yeah?"

"Apparently it involves the ranch of my client Lacey Gunn. Lacey doesn't want to sell. Sheriff Oates locked up Anton, the Simpsons' security guard, in Kerr County jail last night for threatening her. When Kinsear and I got to the ranch, Anton had a knife to M.A. Ellison's throat. You know M.A.? And Sheriff Oates?"

Files stared at her, then picked up his phone. Someone answered and he said, "I'll need ten more minutes."

He sighed, picked up his pen. "Start at the beginning."

Alice began with M.A.'s call last week demanding that Alice help Lacey Gunn, and Lacey's story of the burly man with Florida plates who bullied her, tried to make her sign a sales contract, and then tried to muscle his way into her house. "Lacey heard the buyers were planning a huge theme park. Lacey's afraid it'll ruin the springs that flow into Sister Creek. She wanted to put a covenant on the land to protect it. I drafted it, she signed it, and we recorded it and sent a copy to the sales agent who was harassing her. I thought that would put an end to the problem. I didn't know, nor did she, who was in the 'group' of buyers. Nor did I know the identity of the burly man who bullied her."

"Then what?"

She recounted yesterday's desperate call from M.A., the subsequent inability to reach M.A. or Lacey Gunn, and the mad drive with Kinsear from Fredericksburg to Gunn Ranch.

"And that's where we found Anton—last name Ivanov, apparently—in Lacey's dining room, holding a switchblade knife to M.A.'s throat. He's the security guard at Simpson Strategic Assets. He wanted Lacey to rescind the covenant, sign a purchase agreement, and then sign the deed selling her ranch. I've got pictures of the documents. Anton didn't deny they were Simpson docs. He and his sidekick, an unlicensed sales agent with a borrowed notary stamp, were supposed to get this done so Simpson could close the hedge fund deal Nanette had been so worried about." Alice leaned back in her chair, waiting.

Files grinned, shaking his head. "Mind telling me how this turned out? Or do I have to call my friends in Kerr County?"

"We disarmed Anton and his little buddy and tied them up for Sheriff Oates and Deputy Denton."

"Tied them up?"

"M.A. tied up Anton's wrists with picture wire. We tied up his buddy with the rope they'd used on M.A. I emailed Sheriff Oates my pictures of Anton with the knife."

"Show me the pictures."

Alice passed her phone to him.

"Anton Ivanov, you said?"

"Yes. Sheriff Oates asked Denton to run both guys' names. They're from Miami."

"So what are they doing buying Texas ranch land?"

"And offering very high prices. Michael Greene said the prices—suspiciously high—worried Nanette." She watched his eyes narrow, then went on. "But the two guys that threatened Lacey aren't the buyers. They're just the muscle."

Files nodded. "I'm beginning to get the picture. Okay, Nanette's laptop. We still haven't identified the prints on her body, the ones we got with the Superglue technique. It'd be interesting if there's any match for those prints on the laptop. But my first rule—"

"I know. Don't make assumptions," Alice said. "But Sheriff Oates has the documents Anton wanted signed. There might be prints on those too. Brett Bradley's or Pat Simpson's. Also, the purchase agreement has the sales amount. Shows a pretty high price." She paused. "Do you have prints yet from either of the Simpsons?"

He shook his head no. "Their office says they're both out of town. But Alice, explain their motive, assuming she quit? They could still use Brett Bradley to close these deals. Anyway, what did you and Michael Greene find on this laptop?"

"I don't think she has the deal documents, though you sure may want to see those. But you will see some of the due diligence she did on the investors."

"Why would Nanette put them on her personal laptop?"

"Various possibilities. Maybe she was afraid to put those documents on her office laptop. Maybe she didn't want her work destroyed. Maybe she wanted backup for a decision to leave Simpson. Maybe she'd found a smoking gun and planned to alert the authorities. Maybe she feared she'd be a witness if the state or the feds started investigating Simpson Strategic Assets. I know she wanted to be scrupulous about compliance with securities requirements. For sure, she never wanted to be a defendant.

"But we found one document Nanette did have, hidden at her apartment. It's important but the Simpsons will claim it's confidential." She took a breath. "I think maybe Nanette saw this document on an office printer—probably Pat Simpson's secretary prints out his emails for him—and made a copy and hid it."

"Why?"

She described the email Ron Simpson had sent his brother. "Nanette told Mischa and me that she was told—ordered—not to do due diligence on this deal, contrary to her obligations under state and federal securities law. She's—she was too good a lawyer to obey that instruction.

If this deal went south and the Simpsons were investigated, Nanette probably wanted evidence that her boss told her not to perform the required due diligence. Pat Simpson would never admit that. He'd deny he gave any such instruction. He'd probably claim she was negligent and lay the blame for any securities violation on her. Anyway, she carefully hid this at her apartment."

"Do you think it's privileged?"

"I think it's probably admissible under the crime-fraud exception. Obviously, you'll need your own ruling." She paused. "The Simpsons seriously needed to close the first deal yesterday. Nanette's resignation letter shows she refused to play along."

"As does the brown packet," Files said. "She wouldn't have sent that to you otherwise. But remember, Pat Simpson denies he got that letter."

"Right. But with Nanette out of the way, the Simpsons could still get Brett to try to close by yesterday's deadline." And they needed her out of the way so she couldn't ever testify, which gave them a motive for murder, she thought. "By the way," she added, "You've probably thought about checking the financial status of Simpson Strategic Assets. Also, Brett told me Nanette's firm laptop is on the shelf in the IT guy's room." She watched his face for a reaction.

Files nodded slowly, then stood, face grim. "Send me that picture of the paper the victim hid. What's the name of the kid who gave her the Mario Brothers sticker?"

"Benjy Patch. Fourth grade at Coffee Creek Elementary. He drew the screensaver. You'll see he signed it 'love, Benjy.'"

She felt her eyes sting with tears and hurriedly wiped her eyes.

Files leaned across the desk and held out a box of tissues. His tired brown eyes watched as she blew her nose.

As she walked back down the hall, Alice wondered about the tissues. Maybe allergies weren't the reason Files kept them on his desk.

Chapter Twenty-Seven

Not Fingerprinted?

"Who's that guy parked across the street?" Silla demanded, marching into Alice's office after lunch.

Alice looked up, startled, wresting her mind away from a difficult will provision. "Where?" She stared out her office window at the street.

"He's gone now. Some guy in a white sedan—looked like a rental. I swear he was taking pictures of the office. I think he saw me watching him, watching us."

"Huh. What'd he look like?"

"I couldn't see much. Ball cap pulled down low, short hair, maybe blond. White guy."

"Hang on," Alice said. She pulled up her emails to the Coastguard and to the British Consulate in Houston with the snapshots showing "Ian Blane." She'd told Silla about Jimmie's forced labor on the *Seabass*. "I just want to be sure the driver didn't look like this guy, the one Jimmie thought was following him in Jakarta and who kept him imprisoned out in the Pacific."

Silla studied the screen. "I can't say the driver wasn't this guy. But I can't say he was, either. Jimmie's out at Kinsear's with John, right?"

Alice nodded.

"That means you're by yourself? I dunno, Alice. Sounds risky."

Alice glanced back at the computer screen, then at Silla. "Tell me if you see that guy again."

"I'll get his license plate too. Hey, remember we're going to the Madrone Bank cocktail party. Starts at 4:30."

"Oh, yeah."

Alice tried to remember the clever solution for the will she'd come up with just as Silla came in. She got coffee, then finally captured the lost thought and wrestled the provision into shape.

Okay, enough of this radio silence. She dialed the British Consulate in Houston. "Edwin Davies, please."

A faraway "Let me check, madam." A pause. "I am so sorry, he seems to be out of the office. May I leave a message?"

"Call Alice Greer at your very earliest inconvenience." She left her number, swore under her breath, and called Kinsear.

*****

"How are the boys?" she asked. "Has John been writing? Is Jimmie on a horse, fixing fence, wading in the creek?"

"Yes to all the above. I bet you didn't call about that, though."

"Right. Remember the guy who followed Jimmie in Jakarta? Who was stationed at the mine in Myanmar? The fake Ian Blane?"

"Yes. Is he here?"

She was stunned. "How did you guess? Silla spotted a possible candidate for the Ian Blane look-alike contest on Live Oak Street just now. Taking pictures of our office."

"I've been waiting for him to show up. Last night I leaned pretty hard on Jimmie, and he finally told me a small part of the story. This is a hell of a mess, Alice."

She knew that. Her gut had ached for days, thinking of the reasons, none of them good, that her visit to the Aberdeen Mortuary had produced the fake Ian Blane in the first place.

"Well, damn. Why wouldn't he answer my questions?"

"He's trying to protect you and John. Can you come for dinner, spend the night? If you're going to be Miss Priss, you can have Isabel's bedroom. You can hear Jimmie's story and ask questions. And make me happy because I'll at least know you're safer out here."

The thought of joining the boys at Kinsear's sounded much more appealing than a solitary supper, followed by checking all the locks on the doors—twice—and lying awake diagnosing every nightbird call, every rustle of the wind. She closed her eyes in relief. Plus she could dig into the mystery behind Jimmie's silence.

"Sounds great. I'll finish this draft will, then head your way."

Alice finished the document and emailed it to Silla, who immediately popped her head into Alice's office. "Have you even touched that stack there?" She pointed to the corner of Alice's desk. "From that Abyss folder on Nanette's laptop?"

"Not yet. What did you find?"

"Just Internet printouts. There may be some answers there," Silla said, "but it's hard to identify the human beings involved, given the upstream private limited companies and LLCs."

Under Texas law the initial LLC filing required only the name of the LLC registered agent, the organizer, and, if member-managed or manager-managed, the name of the initial member(s) or manager(s). Other states and other countries made even less information public.

"What we've got so far from Nanette are the computer printouts in the brown envelope, the little folded paper, and what you wanted from the encrypted folder on her laptop. Is there anything else?" Silla asked.

"Nope," Alice said. "I expect she kept the deal documents and emails in her firm laptop. This stack may be the research she'd found by her last day at the office." She was still deciding whether the work product rules meant she shouldn't read them. Was Nanette's research "in anticipation of litigation"? "My copies, right?"

Silla rolled her eyes. "When's the last time I gave you an original?" Silla insulated Alice from any originals, making sure she got only copies. Originals were carefully maintained in Silla's files. One of the secrets of a happy working relationship, Silla said.

*****

At four-thirty Silla and Alice barreled into the parking lot of the new French restaurant on Highway 290. Alice had eaten there with her book group (including Miranda) just after it opened. They'd all liked the menu. Miranda, tall and blonde, in heels and a red suit, greeted them at the door, then pointed them to the table where they picked up their name tags. A smiling young woman in a crisp apron handed them champagne in tall flutes.

The restaurant was clean-lined and high-ceilinged, modern in feel, with tall windows and interesting lighting. A long bar dominated one wall. "Hey," Silla said. "I know those guys. The bartenders. Got to say hi."

Alice watched Silla's red pony-tail bob its way to the bar. She smiled to herself as she watched people smiling back at the irresistible Silla. Time for her to do her own mingling. She spied her friend Jane Ann, title company president, holding court across the room, and went to join her.

Alice typically could put up with a meet-and-greet for about nineteen minutes. At minute twenty, she usually felt an overpowering (and usually irresistible) urge to leave. But at minute twenty she froze, watching the front doors, as Ron and Pat Simpson entered.

Out of town?

A stab of anger in her gut. She could understand Files's caution about ascribing motive to either Simpson. But either, or both, might have felt Nanette was a problem needing a solution. Alice slipped away from Jane Ann's entourage and found Silla at the end of the bar, surrounded by a laughing group. She moved next to Silla and tilted her head, waggling her eyebrows.

"You already want to leave?" Silla scolded. "You could be working the room!"

"No! Check out the Simpsons," Alice whispered. "Picking up name tags."

Silla looked across the crowd toward the two brothers, now sporting name tags and holding champagne flutes, then back at Alice.

"Files says they haven't been fingerprinted yet," Alice whispered. "Their office told Files they were out of town."

"Out of town?" Silla's eyes narrowed. "Not fingerprinted?" She paused. "Oh. The laptop." Then she said, "Wait a sec. Give me your scarf."

"What are you thinking?" But Alice unwound the scarf from her neck.

Silla detached herself and made her way to the bar. After a brief conversation with the bartender, she vanished into the kitchen, then emerged wearing an apron, her distinctive hair entirely hidden by Alice's scarf. She glared at her watching friends, finger to her lips, signaling silence, as she picked up from the bar a tray of flutes of champagne. Alice watched in admiration as Silla, with her big smile, waylaid the Simpsons, relieved them of their nearly empty champagne flutes and provided replacements. Ron and Pat Simpson both grinned down at her and lifted their new glasses in salute. Silla grinned back, turned, and disappeared into the kitchen.

"Holy cow," Alice said to herself. "Never mess with Silla..."

Alice greeted several acquaintances on her way to the front door. She saw Silla outside, red hair still hidden under the scarf, trotting toward Alice's car, carrying two brown paper bags.

From the front door, Alice glanced back at the Simpsons. Pat Simpson was staring at her, a slightly baffled look on his face. She watched him turn suddenly to his brother, ask a question. Ron Simpson's eyes moved to her. "Gotta roll," she told herself, and hurried outside.

Silla was already in the passenger seat. "Bartenders there are the best. They sent me out the kitchen door," she said. She smirked at the two paper bags in her lap. "I enjoyed that. Pat Simpson seriously got on my nerves when we went to his office."

At the Sheriff's Annex Alice and Silla informed the desk officer they were delivering fingerprinted glasses to Detective George Files. "Don't mix them up!" Silla ordered. "The bags are labeled!"

"Huh! Out of town!" Silla muttered, as Alice dropped her off at her car in the office driveway. "I call bullshit on that."

"I hope Pat Simpson didn't recognize you," Alice said, remembering his face.

Silla tossed her head. "Bring it on."

"Maybe not. We need to steer clear of those guys."

*****

Big Boy brayed his traditional welcome as Alice drove through her gate at sunset. She grabbed the burros' carrots from the workshop fridge and dealt them out—first Big Boy (smallest, oldest, sure he was the boss), then elegant Queenie, then slightly skittish Princess, who had to stand in line behind her mother. The norther was gone, defeated by the steady prevailing southeast wind from the Gulf; tonight would be warmer. Alice raced back inside to pack an overnight bag, then locked the house and drove west toward the darkening gold of a November sunset.

She sped through the dusk up Kinsear's ranch drive, relishing the uphill curves ending at the long, low house beneath the live oaks. Kinsear stood outside by the barbecue grill on the patio, doing something with tongs. Orange sparks drifted up in the evening air.

As she parked, Alice felt a rush of joy. A homecoming feeling. An eagerness to be with the long-legged man striding through the dusk toward her. He held her tight. She felt herself relax against his warmth.

After a moment, she lifted her face. "What is that heavenly smell?"

"Pulled pork. I think I've finally got the dry rub right, and the mop. Your John's working on the beans. We're also having Mexican street corn. And deviled eggs. I called M.A., told her she owed you for that flare gun shot."

"Did you ask if she'd give you her recipe?"

He grinned. "She would not. She said, and I quote, she 'wasn't a bit scared by that gangster.' However, she said she'd give me a hint."

"Yeah?"

"She asked if I'd ever considered adding a pinch of dry mustard."

"So sly. That way she can keep claiming she doesn't give away a recipe."

He held open the door for Alice. Kinsear had combined his living room and kitchen, creating a vast stone-floored room with a fireplace at one end, flanked by leather wing chairs and a long leather sofa. Logs were burning, cedar and oak; firelight gleamed on the books lining the walls. Between the seating area and the kitchen stood a much-used mission oak dining table. "It can seat fourteen, with the inserts," Kinsear had told Alice. "A hundred years ago the cook fed all the hands and all the family."

The kitchen end held a six-burner stove, a commercial refrigerator, and a long kitchen island. Alice's son John stood at the stove, stirring a large pot. Jimmie was mashing avocados. "Guacamole?" Alice asked.

Jimmie nodded, with a smile, glancing at Kinsear. "He's a stern taskmaster."

Alice hugged John, busy at the stove with his beans. "It's your recipe, Mom. Start with bacon and onions, then add the beans—kidney, ranch-style, and regular, plus a little molasses, and hot sauce. Right?"

"Some chile powder, not much, usually ancho. Some people add dried cherries," Alice said. "But definitely not when serving Mexican street corn."

She eyed the cast iron skillet simmering on the stove, golden corn bubbling gently. Her mouth watered at the smell of chiles and cumin.

"You've brought this boy up right," Kinsear said. "John knows his way around a kitchen." He laid a plate of warmed tortillas and a bowl of salsa on the kitchen island, next to a platter of deviled eggs, carefully covered with plastic wrap.

"Ooh!" said Alice.

"Don't touch," warned Kinsear. "Not yet." Alice reluctantly tore her eyes away from the deviled eggs. In her experience, one was never enough.

Kinsear poured her a glass of pinot noir. "Have some pulled pork wine. The rest of us are drinking beer."

She glanced at John and Jimmie, wondering how dinner would go. Jimmie held out his bowl of guacamole. "What next?"

She heard Kinsear: "Okay, now add the juice from one lime, and a scant one-third teaspoon of cumin." Jimmie's hands, work-hardened, squeezed a stream of juice into the guacamole.

"Alice, Jimmie's gotten interested in barbecue," Kinsear said. "He wants to learn the fine art of the grill."

"You could teach him," Alice said. "I mean, your ribs..."

"No, he's serious. I was thinking about Conroy. You think Conroy might take him on? Teach him some basics?"

"Conroy's got his own food truck and traveling smoker now," Alice responded. The idea intrigued her. "In fact, he's providing official barbecue for the Beer Barn Holiday Bazaar."

Conroy Robinson, retired NFL pulling guard, still recovering from post-concussion syndrome, was right-hand man at Raptor Cellars, the winery run by retired NFL center Eddie LaFarge. Eddie not only made good wines with local grapes but had also taught Alice some useful defensive driving maneuvers.

"You think he'd take on a rank beginner?" asked Jimmie in his quiet Scots burr.

"I do," Kinsear said, his eyes meeting Alice's.

In that look Alice knew Kinsear had developed an alternative safe house for Jimmie, with Conroy as bodyguard, until Edwin Davies provided incontrovertible assurance that he not only would, but could, protect Jimmie. As she lit the candles on the kitchen island, she pictured Jimmie, spare and wiry (well, at least no longer skin and bones), scholar of the sea, working next to soft-spoken Conroy, a gentle but imposing giant, who'd devastated opposing defenders in the NFL...each an expert in his own field.

John held open the door to the patio. Kinsear, to applause, carried in the elegantly browned pork shoulder from the grill. John, Jimmie, and Alice gathered while he shredded the fragrant meat and set the dish next to the warm tortillas. He glanced at their waiting faces. "Let's go!"

Alice sat next to John, treasuring her son's closeness while trying to treat him like the grownup he apparently considered himself to be. A happy silence fell.

"Amazing," Jimmie finally managed. His plate was bare. "There's something about the combination, the tortilla, then the corn, then the pulled pork, then the avocado...plus that green sauce, and then a little sour cream..." His voice trailed off, and he began building another soft taco.

Later they refilled their glasses and adjourned to the fireplace end of the room. John helped Kinsear rebuild a satisfactory fire. Cedar and oak embers perfumed the air. Kinsear pointed Jimmie to the wing chair by the fire.

"Okay, buddy, you're on." Kinsear glanced at Alice. "Counsel, you may question the witness."

She was ready. "Jimmie, the Coastguard said you left on the offshore crew boat two days before Jordie's flight."

"Right."

"To catch your flight to Singapore?"

"Yes."

"So, first, give us the backstory, the history," Alice said.

"All right. Here goes." Jimmie took a deep breath. "Before I came out to the rig, I'd been geologist for a rare earths surface mine in Myanmar. Myanmar ships the ore over the mountains to China for processing. I hated that job. Probably asked too many questions, too. That's where I met Dickie Manners—he represented the company, was always prowling the site. Before I left Myanmar to meet Jordie, I'd signed on with GGI, geology consultants. My first assignment was the short project on the North Sea rig, where I got to see Jordie. NorthOil wanted me to evaluate the core samples they'd taken. But the big project was to map Pacific seabeds on their survey ship, *Following Sea.* After Myanmar, I was excited about that gig. For the next couple of years, I led GGI's mapping of the seabed, seamounts, volcanic vents, depths, and locations—and also tested samples of seabed sediments and sea water for metals and rare earths. We spent months in the South Pacific, off Australia, off Papua New Guinea, off the Cook Islands. Emma Linden came out during a couple of breaks, then I'd go back on the water."

His eyes got that faraway look. "The Pacific. It's mesmerizing. Occasionally terrifying, but so vast, so beautiful. Anyway, a couple of years ago, GGI moved the survey ship further north to Jakarta, and we did some more work around Indonesia. By then the market for rare earths was heating up big time. Interest in the seabed was huge. GGI was becoming known as the premier seabed sampler in the Pacific. And the reason was me. Not bragging, just being truthful.

"Anyway, after one long sampling tour, I finally got a break. When we docked at Jakarta, I checked into a hotel. No worries, we were heading next to Japan, I knew the drill, I knew the dock. But I had an odd feeling of being watched. The night we were due to reboard *Following Sea*, I was upstairs packing and spotted a guy watching the hotel. I took a picture of him. You know, the photo I sent Emma? I thought I recognized him."

Alice nodded. "Then what?"

His face reddened. "I still feel like an idiot." He took a breath, let it out. "Well, he worried me. So I ducked out the back door, sure I'd avoided him, and headed for the docks. And that's the last I remember. I woke up with a splitting headache and a big lump on the back of my skull, aboard a ship. Not the *Following Sea*."

"What ship?"

He gave a little snort. "The *Seabass*. Registered in Greece, chartered to some nameless company. Disguised as a fishing trawler, but it carried survey equipment and was run by some real bastards."

"Who?"

"In particular, Dickie Manners, the same guy I detested in Myanmar. His job? Keeping tabs on me, in my little bunk in my tiny stateroom—cell, really—on the Seabass. He locked me in at night, unlocked me in the morning, checked on me while I ran my tests and entered my data. He always made sure someone was watching my every move."

Alice shifted in her chair, horrified. Jimmie went on.

"I had a porthole. A cell with a view, you could say. I measured it daily. I thought if I could lose enough weight, lose enough muscle, I could squeeze out that porthole. If we ever returned to port, that is."

"Where were you?"

"We cruised broad swaths of the Pacific. North, northeast, and south of the Indonesian archipelago. Near the seamounts along the Mariana Trench. We weren't alone—other interests are prospecting out there. Some are legit, with a license to explore—not actually to mine—the seabed. Others? Not so legit."

"The people you worked for had no exploration license?"

Jimmie's eyes narrowed as he stared into the fire. "None. Did you ever read Robert Louis Stevenson? *Kidnapped*? That's how I felt. I'd been captured by pirates, pirates with deep-sea dredging equipment. They wanted me to locate and map areas that lay outside any country's exclusive economic zone, deep enough for the polymetallic nodules to form, but shallow enough for deep-water dredging. Around four thousand feet deep."

"You found some areas that qualified?" Alice asked.

He nodded.

"But dredging the seabed—that's potentially devastating for seabed organisms, right?"

"Yes. As I reminded them morning, noon, and night. They laughed. 'Just do your job.'"

"But weren't you out there for nearly two years?" Alice demanded. "Didn't the *Seabass* ever refuel? Take on supplies?"

"Oh, sure. We'd refuel in the Philippines. Indonesia. Sometimes a cruiser—military looking—would mysteriously appear to refuel us at sea. But like I say, they watched my every move. If I wasn't in the computer room below-decks, I was locked in my room with an armed guard outside." He pulled up his left pants leg, showing his calf. Alice saw a long white scar, jagged and irregular. "One night northeast of the Philippines I pried open the door. I'd smuggled a beer bottle into my room, under my shirt. I tried to brain the guard. He shot me."

"But how did you treat that—that wound?"

"Treatment? It was a surface wound. They handed me a roll of gauze and a tube of antibiotic. Shot me up with more antibiotic. No stitches." He paused. "I was terrified of gangrene."

Someone in the room blew out a breath.

"But you escaped. How?" Alice asked.

"I knew the *Seabass* was heading to Hong Kong." His eyes were fixed somewhere above their heads. "Being a prisoner—I could feel myself changing." The room was silent. "Growing up, I thought I had everything. A bicycle! A dog! Even when my parents died, I still had my big cousin Jordie, and I spent every vacation in Broadview with Gran, climbing Ben Cathair. A geologist's paradise.

"But being kidnapped—taken where I didn't choose to go, unable to leave, freedom gone, no phone, no passport, no driver's license, no money, no credit cards, no identity—that can change your soul. My captors promised they'd let me go—someday. But I worried they'd toss me overboard—that the kid who watched me all day was learning too much and I might become expendable. Plus I knew too much about Sone. They couldn't afford to let me go.

"I obsessed about escape, how I might survive on Asian streets, how I could reclaim my life. I realized I no longer felt any compunction about doing things I would never have done before. Like stealing..."

After a moment John said, "Tell about getting to Hong Kong. I gave Mom a short version."

Jimmie nodded. "I knew the bosses planned to meet in Hong Kong. We docked on the Kowloon side close to the container ships. I knew the crew would be drinking the night we docked. I'd been on a diet, remember? Could count my own ribs. Before we docked, I'd stolen some cooking oil and hidden it in my cell. But I needed something to trade. My guard was dozing. I stole a Game Boy some crew member had left in the computer room.

"I greased myself up, stashed the Game Boy and my, um, data records in a plastic bag, squeezed out the porthole and scampered away. I dodged and hid, moving from pier to pier along the shore. Finally slept under a tarp at a deserted dockyard."

"With no money?"

"Not a cent. I found one of the poor guys that haunt the harbor in small lighter boats, hoping for work. I traded him the Game Boy for enough cash for a ride to the Star Ferry dock in Kowloon—he wouldn't take me across the harbor to Hong Kong. John probably told you the rest—I managed to hide on a Star Ferry—first one out, at six in the morning, still dark.

"Then I met John. If I hadn't...I'd still be stuck in the monastery. At least, I hope I'd still be there, alive."

"John told us how you got to Hong Kong and the monastery," Alice said.

"Right. Jordie had sent me to the monastery on my first trip to Asia. I knew the old monk...though he was just a novice when we met. He remembered me, thank God. He let me work in the garden. My plan was to waltz down to the British Consulate and explain my plight, but the monk warned me. 'People are watching you.' I was getting desperate."

"And then you met John. Because of Gran's letter?"

He nodded.

Alice took a deep breath. "Okay, here's what I have to know. Who's after you? Who are the guys on the boat? The *Seabass*? What do you know that they don't want you to tell?"

Jimmie shot a glance at John. John nodded at him. "You've got to tell her. She won't quit till you do."

Jimmie looked at Alice and finally nodded. "There are two reasons they'd like to kill me—or anyone else who knows what I know. First, I've figured out who they are. You've got three crime groups. First is a retired general, Shwe Sone, from Myanmar. He got rich smuggling rare earths out of Myanmar. He knows markets, refiners, shippers. He wants in on the ocean mining but can't get a license because he's dirty money. He wants to harvest polymetallic nodules. Big profits right now, for the cobalt and copper. But he also wants to harvest some cobalt-rich ferro-manganese crusts that include rare earth elements. And harvesting either one? Illegal as hell.

"Second, Dmitri Novikov. He's Russian mafia, relocated to Miami. He got his start in shipping. He's well known in Asian ports; his group owns the *Seabass*. So he has transport. Third, Tino Vitale. He's Miami mafia. He's a financial guy, knows money laundering. He and Dmitri approached General Sone and cooked up this deal."

"How'd you learn their names?"

"Sitting in the office, entering my mapping and testing data twelve hours a day. I heard whispers. One day off Jakarta the big guys came out on a cruiser, toured the *Seabass*, inspected the dredges, made me show them the maps. I wasn't formally introduced, you understand. But I heard names, and they stuck."

Alice was thinking. No license to mine. No license even to explore and evaluate. Just a straight illegal mining and smuggling operation. "What's the downside if you report them to the International Seabed Authority?"

"I don't know. They did some dredging for several weeks southeast of Japan and harvested a bunch of polymetallic nodules. If legit rare earths developers negotiate for a license with a nation, like an island group in the Pacific, they've got to look clean. So my captors can't let anyone hear about their dredging profits. And given the price of rare earths these days, they've made a bundle. Also—"

"Yes?" Alice prompted.

"The second reason they'd kill me is—I copied my data."

"How'd you do that?" Kinsear asked.

"I had nothing," Jimmie said. "No iPad, no laptop, no phone. My job included not just analyzing the currents and the samples we took of seabed and minerals but also mapping everything and entering all the data on the ship's computer. Early on, I stole a notebook off the shelf, the waterproof kind engineers use." Like Jordie's, Alice thought.

"I started keeping a record of days, events, key data. I kept that hidden in my stateroom prison. Then one night, I was still trying to enter the day's numbers onto our spreadsheets. The guard fell asleep. I'd already spotted a loose thumb drive in a drawer. I downloaded all the mapping data—depths, latitude, longitude, sampling results. I hid the thumb drive in my underwear just as the guard woke up. Two days later, we docked at Jakarta. I'd found an ancient postcard in the crew lounge and bribed a guard to mail it to Emma. The night we docked in Hong Kong, like I said, I oiled myself up like a Chinese potsticker and squeezed out the porthole and down the hawser, with the notebook and thumb drive in a zip-lock bag in my briefs.

"At the monastery there's an ancient computer in the guest lounge. One night I crept out of my room and loaded all my data into that old computer."

"Then when we left," John broke in, "I downloaded all Jimmie's data from that computer onto my laptop. Just in case Jimmie got stopped at the airport. And there it is." John pointed to a laptop on the end table by the fireplace. "Plus, a thumb drive's in my bag."

"Holy cow," Alice breathed. Her stomach churned at the risk John had run. The laptop now looked immensely dangerous, ticking quietly on the end table, like a bomb. One that could blow her family to smithereens.

John finally rose. "Another beer, anyone?" Kinsear emerged from the kitchen, bringing wine and a plate of chocolate chip cookies.

"I made them, Mom," John said. "See the tops? I salted them, like you do."

A log broke in the fireplace, sending up a shower of sparks. Kinsear mended the fire, adding more cedar, then reclaimed his chair. Facing Alice, he said, "Counsel, let's list the causes of action."

Alice nodded. Suddenly she was back in the classroom, first year of law school. "For Jimmie as plaintiff? Damages and restitution. Damages for the kidnapping and enslavement. Restitution for his years of expert work. Plus theft of his passport, credit cards, wallet, and access to cash. But I wonder"—she frowned—"which court has jurisdiction of the causes of action? Or of the defendants?"

"Also, can Jimmie be sued for data theft?" asked John. "Or me? I mean, I've got the data he copied in my computer!"

"I think we characterize that data as *evidence*," Kinsear said. "Evidence of illegal mining, where there was illegal dredging and delivery of ores, without the required license to explore."

"Big whoop," Alice said. "Does that get smugglers a mere slap on the hand? A penalty? If there's evidence of smuggling, that would help—but smuggling where? Into which country? If it were the UK, or the US, I'd feel more optimistic."

Jimmie leaned forward. "But there is some evidence of smuggling. Where our sampling indicated the manganese nodules had REEs—rare earth elements—as well, the ship dredged them up. Those were taken to a newish smelter way south in Myanmar, on the coast below Mawlamyine. It's isolated but reachable by ship. We'd anchor offshore at night and unload the nodules we'd dredged onto a barge." He looked up, eyes bleak. "At least I heard the nodules rattling down the chute. But since I couldn't see them, could my testimony count?" His face brightened just slightly. "I've got the dates in my notebook, though."

"At that plant, what metals are produced?" Alice asked.

"I expect the plant can smelt nodules into cobalt, copper, and so on, or the ship wouldn't have delivered them. But my guess is that whoever wanted the nodules also knew how to produce REEs from the ores. That was what Sone wanted: for Myanmar to be able to produce the pricey metals and rare earth elements in country, instead of having to send their ores to China. I thought he'd been diverting some of the raw ores to that plant."

"Why are the rare earth elements so important? For magnets?"

"Just look at your phone, Mom," John put in. "You're holding rare earths in your hand. They're critical for cell phones, computer displays, and various magnets. They're in flat-screen TVs, lasers, missiles. Electric cars. Night-vision goggles. Like Jimmie said, most of Myanmar's rare earths ores go to China for processing, but a few years ago Myanmar threatened to quit sending ores to China. That caused a ruckus. I think Jimmie's right that Myanmar may want to do its own processing, get more profit."

"Let's follow the money," Kinsear said. "Jimmie?"

After a long silence, Jimmie said, "Right now people all over the planet are racing to figure out how to get raw materials for magnets. Seabed mining's only one possibility. Scientists are figuring out how to get rare earths from recycling electronics or processing waste from coal waste or aluminum mining. More ideas are coming. Demand's high right now, but if people figure out how to reclaim and re-use rare earths, the cost efficiency of seabed mining will decline."

"So piracy, smuggling, illegal mining—now's the time, right?"

"Right. Grab some quick, illegal profits before new technologies come online."

"Very greedy," Alice said. "And the current scarcity's a huge profit source, given the big push to electric vehicles."

"Think of the fortunes the mob made during Prohibition," Kinsear added.

"So it's yo-ho-ho time for seabed pirates," Jimmie said.

"How hard is it to police the high seas?" John wondered.

"The Pacific? Unimaginably vast," Jimmie answered. "Our ship was disguised as a fishing trawler. No one said boo to us. No coast guard approached. The International Seabed Authority lacks an armed navy. Smuggling was easy pickings."

Alice sat silent, remembering the printouts in the brown envelope and the potential for wads of illegal money from harvesting and smuggling seabed rare earths. "Money laundering." She thought of the Austin Financial Crimes Unit. "We can at least report this activity, can't we?"

Jimmie stirred. "My problem is, besides the people in this room, I don't really know anyone I can trust, or how far I can trust them. Here's a question you haven't asked me."

The room was quiet.

"You haven't asked why the British Consulate got John and me on a plane to Texas only hours after delivering my new passport."

Kinsear's eyes met Alice's. "Do they want to go after the bad guys? Do they want Jimmie available to testify about smuggling?"

Alice picked up the thread, eyes on Jimmie. "But don't they also want to protect you from your kidnappers? Because you—you didn't just upload the data on the thumb drive, did you?"

Jimmie looked steadily at her.

"You wiped the data off the *Seabass* computer," she finished.

Jimmie nodded. "You guessed it, Alice."

"And you did that so your kidnappers would have trouble trying to dredge the seabeds again," Kinsear suggested. "Because they wouldn't have the coordinates they needed."

Jimmie nodded. "Right. Nothing I'd produced, at least."

"And that's why Dickie Manners—or whatever his real name is—the fake Ian Blane—is still after you," Alice finished.

"So we need to decide the best places—safest places—to store the data," Jimmie said.

They looked at each other. "It's not just the data that needs protection," Kinsear concluded. "It's Jimmie's testimony about what happened."

*****

After John and Jimmie disappeared to their bedrooms, Kinsear looked at Alice and said, "Night walk." They put on jackets and walked into the chilly night.

Alice pointed up at the moon. "Cheshire cat." The silvery smile hid behind a cloud, then reappeared. They walked out the driveway toward the barn, holding hands.

"Is Conroy really going to teach Jimmie about barbecue?" Alice asked.

"He's definitely on," Kinsear said. "Says to bring Jimmie out to the winery tomorrow. Plus, what do you think about having Thanksgiving here? You and John, Jimmie, me, and the girls? Eddie and Conroy would definitely like to join us."

"Hallelujah!" Alice said. "How did Thanksgiving get here so fast? I've been stumped, figuring out what to do. Especially after Silla spotted the Ian Blane lookalike."

"But he won't know you're out here, and even if he did, I'd be here too." He stopped and turned her to face him. "Listen, Alice. We need to think about how to protect Jimmie's data, and Jimmie himself. He's right—who's trustworthy? You didn't seem sure even about the British Consulate guy. Anyway, let's all be here for Thanksgiving. I volunteer as your bodyguard."

"Tactful issuance of an invitation." She laughed.

"Conroy's bringing the turkey, plus some brisket. Eddie's bringing the wine."

"I'll bring—what? Garlic-lime mashed sweet potatoes with chipotle? And yeast rolls?"

"Just what I hoped. Plus cornbread stuffing, please? I'll get the boys to help make green beans and pumpkin pies."

Alice heaved a sigh of satisfaction. She'd assumed that since she needed to keep Jimmie under wraps, she'd buy a petite turkey and serve a low-key Thanksgiving dinner, just Jimmie, John, and herself. But that hadn't felt right. Thanksgiving was her favorite holiday, because of its inclusive "more the merrier" aspects. She always told guests to bring whatever gave them the warmest feeling. Even if this meant putting up with one cousin's fave—pumpkin mousse pie with pecans—someone else would bring traditional pumpkin pie with whipped cream. Some people liked dark meat, some wanted white, some opted for veggies instead. The world would not end if there were two kinds of stuffing (Alice believed in cornbread stuffing but had heard reliable reports that others couldn't celebrate without bread stuffing) and at least two kinds of gravy and at least three versions of cranberry relish. In fact, the world was a better place when people felt they could bring what they wanted, and what they needed, to a big communal dinner.

So a lonesome threesome and a petite turkey sounded sensible but felt depressing. Kinsear's offer got Thanksgiving right. Keeping Jimmie safe atop a hill overlooking Fredericksburg? Even better.

"Almost December," she said. "Can you believe the Beer Barn Holiday Bazaar starts this Saturday?"

"Holy cow. Maybe that's what Conroy meant when he said he needed Jimmie asap. Conroy's gonna put an apron on him. He'll be selling barbecue on Saturday."

Back inside, she and Kinsear sat by the fire until it was nothing but embers. Having agreed to spend the night at Kinsear's ranch, Alice felt a bit like Elizabeth in *Pride and Prejudice*, finally accepting Darcy. Kinsear had stayed under her roof many times. She'd never spent the night under his. She was a bit muddled as to why—something about it being too soon for his girls, her kids. Last night she'd refused. And she'd have to skedaddle early tomorrow. Meanwhile, here she was...

He was watching her face. He said, "I've had a great idea. Let's spend the night in the bunkhouse. It's above the stables. You've never seen it, have you? There's not a soul there. Come with me."

He took her hand and walked her back outside. Under the Cheshire cat moon, they crossed the driveway toward a two-story wooden building. Kinsear took her first into the stables, to check the horses. Then, outside, they climbed the exterior wooden staircase up one end of the building and around the corner to a landing. Alice could hear the horses below, quietly shifting in their stalls. A cool wind stirred the trees along the drive. Beyond, moonlight flooded the pastures.

At the landing, Kinsear held open the door to a short hallway. "The door on the left," he said. Alice walked into a small plain bedroom with one lamp glowing on bare wooden walls. Windows on three sides, a small desk, a battered old loveseat. The air smelled of hay, horses, and clean cotton sheets.

"Will it do?"

She leaned against him. "It's perfect."

Chapter Twenty-Eight

On My Watch

The Beer Barn sat between two one-way streets in downtown Coffee Creek: Hays Street and Travis Street. Early Wednesday morning on her way back to town, Alice detoured west down Travis, admiring the banner across the road announcing "Beer Barn Holiday Bazaar!" with dates and times.

She turned into the Beer Barn parking lot. Today the portable sign read, "Workers on the Giza pyramids got 10+ pints of beer a day! Workers unite—talk to HR!" She exited the parking lot onto Hays Street. Yep, another giant Beer Barn banner. She called Jorgé to congratulate him. "Looks great!"

"A new tradition—the Beer Barn Holiday Bazaar. You ready for this?" Jorgé asked.

"I think so. Silla's spreadsheet tracks insurance, vendor contracts, liability releases from participants, food truck licenses, as well as hiring officers to help with parking and security. How about you?"

"Portable toilets arrive Friday. The outdoor dance floor stage goes up Friday too. We'll block off one row of parking for the food trucks and extra trash and recycle bins. Inside the Beer Barn, we've set up the sellers' kiosks along the walls," Jorgé said. "Got vendors coming with hand-crafted items—pottery, wooden bowls, hand-blown glass, you name it. Even hand-crafted guitars. And Christmas ornaments out the wazoo. Okay, catch you later." He hung up.

Silla held out a note as Alice entered the office. "Call Files asap." Eyes wide, she asked, "You think he found a match for those prints?"

*****

"Files here."

"It's Alice."

"Thought I'd let you know that the prints on one of those glasses you dropped by..."

"Yes?"

"Match the prints on the victim's body. And on the laptop."

Alice shut her eyes at the image of Nanette being dragged under the shrubs by her slender ankles. Then her eyes popped open. "Whose prints matched?"

"First, tell me how you came by those fancy glasses."

"Um, it's a little awkward. You said the Simpson guys' office told you on Wednesday they were out of town."

"Yes."

"But my friend Miranda invited Silla and me to a shindig Madrone Bank was hosting yesterday for its wealth management clients and assorted hangers-on at that new French place on Highway 290."

"Yes?"

"We saw both Simpsons come in. I told Silla you'd been told they were out of town."

"And?"

"That made Silla mad." She described Silla's waitress act, including her departure via the kitchen with the Simpson brothers' champagne flutes.

"Wish I'd seen that," Files said.

"It was deeply satisfying," Alice said. She wasn't sure it was legal.

"Well, it was enough for me to send an officer out to each man's house early today. Assuming Silla correctly labeled the bags—can't imagine she didn't—Ron Simpson's prints match. But Ron Simpson's wife told my officer her husband left for the airport this morning and she's not sure where he was going."

"The day before Thanksgiving? Seriously?" Alice wondered if he'd really flown out—or was speeding toward Mexico.

"The officer asked which car he took. She had to look in the garage. 'Oh, he must have taken the Mercedes.' But the garage also held a white Land Rover SUV. Hers, she said."

"Can you test it? The grille?"

"We're doing that. And we'll be checking the tires to see if they match a couple of tire tracks Joske found out on Harrier Lane, near Limestone Lodge."

The carwash scene came back to her. "I keep thinking about the Land Rover I saw at the carwash the morning Nanette was found. Twice."

"The one that double-dipped? Circled back behind you to go through a second time?"

"Yes." But she hadn't gotten the temporary tag number, hadn't seen the driver. Could have been someone who simply wanted the car sinless and spotless, whiter than snow, for Sunday service that morning.

"We'll see."

"What about Pat Simpson? Did he disappear too?"

"Not so far. He's lawyered up and due to arrive here any minute. Okay, gotta go."

He hung up before Alice could ask more about Nanette's laptop. Even if Pat Simpson's prints weren't on it, couldn't he still have been present at the murder? A witting, or unwitting, accessory? Or would he throw brother Ron under the bus? Did Ron grab the laptop at the scene, or at the office? How did Nanette's laptop wind up on the IT guy's shelf?

She'd like to be a fly on the wall of the interview room. What would Pat Simpson tell Files? If he told him anything?

Silla stuck her head around the door. "Call Edwin Davies back."

She did.

"Mrs. Greer," Davies said, "I apologize for the delay. Some of the people I needed to include in the discussion of Mr. Greer's seabed studies have been unavailable. We'd like to send a car for him, if we could, this Monday morning. Will that work for you?"

"A car?" she said. Then she was struck by the oddity of what Davies had said. "Wait. Aren't you just interviewing him? You may certainly do that at my office." She wasn't keen on having the Davies entourage show up at her ranch. Nor did she plan to release Jimmie to the tender mercies of just anyone who wanted to participate "in the discussion of Mr. Greer's seabed studies."

"That works. Ten a.m., if all right with you?"

"Yes. But then what? Do you plan to leave him here after the interview, or help him get home to Scotland? Or elsewhere? Also, I need the names of anyone else who's coming." Before he could answer, she added, "Also, how will I know those attending are properly authorized? I think it's only fair to require you to send me, for delivery to Jimmie, a list of the names and positions of everyone who'll be here, along with a letter from the British government confirming proper authorization and Jimmie's safety. After what he's gone through, I don't want to lose him on my watch. Or yours."

After a moment he said, in that upper-class British accent, "I like your caution. I'll be one of the party. Thank you."

"And what about the letter I'm asking for? How do I know you'll keep Jimmie safe?" she blurted. Because she'd never felt sure of that. "If, indeed, he wants to leave?" She wasn't sure of that either.

A pause. "I'll bring a letter from the British ambassador. Will that do?"

Well, maybe. She'd ask Jimmie.

*****

"What the heck?" Silla snorted. She slapped some stapled papers on Alice's desk.

Alice stared at a letter from Louie Gumbert, attaching a motion for a temporary restraining order, set before Judge Sandoval on Friday at ten. The day after Thanksgiving, when the courthouse would normally be closed. Was Gumbert claiming this was an emergency?

Gumbert's motion asked the court to forbid the Beer Barn from using the words "Beer Barn Holiday Bazaar" in connection with the upcoming event. He asserted that the term "Holiday Bazaar" was already claimed on behalf of a planned festival by the Chamber of Commerce in conjunction with the City. He demanded that the Beer Barn banners be taken down forthwith.

"Oh lord. Send a copy to the Beer Barn."

"Yep."

"He lists the Chamber as plaintiff but claims it's 'in conjunction' with the City as well. Can you scan a copy of the complaint to John Dilley? I'll give him a call." She liked Dilley, a solo practice lawyer who'd served for years as counsel for the City.

"Alice! What can I do for you?" Dilley's slow deep voice.

"Silla just emailed you a copy of a TRO request Louie Gumbert filed. He's sued the Beer Barn, which I represent."

"Hang on, let me take a look."

Alice waited.

"Okay. I've read it. First I've seen of it."

"As you see, Louie's asking the court to prevent the Beer Barn from using the term 'Beer Barn Holiday Bazaar.' Our banners are already up."

"Yeah, I've seen them."

"He set a TRO hearing for Friday morning. He appears to claim that 'Holiday Bazaar' is part of this proposed joint festival. But he didn't name the City as plaintiff and didn't include you on the certificate of service."

"That's because as far as I know he's not authorized to do so. I've not heard a word from Louie Gumbert or anyone at the City about this."

"He's not representing the City, then?"

"If he is, nobody bothered to tell me."

"So far as you know, the City's not opposed to the Beer Barn using the term 'Beer Barn Holiday Bazaar'?"

"Not so far as I know."

She thought again. "And so far as you know, is there a 'Coffee Creek Holiday Bazaar' planned?"

"Again, not so far as I know. That doesn't mean the Council couldn't surprise me."

"Do you mind if I call the mayor and ask her?"

"That's fine, if you include me on the call."

"Deal. What time works for you and the mayor?"

"I'll set up a call and let you know."

She hung up and paced back and forth from her desk to the back yard window three times.

Too much. Worries about Jimmie's safety. Could she entrust Jimmie to Davies? And now Gumbert setting a hearing the day after Thanksgiving, the day before the opening of the Beer Barn Holiday Bazaar. Entirely wrecking a holiday weekend.

In an hour Dilley was back on the phone with Mayor Betty Wilson. "Alice," she rasped, "what the hell is Louie Gumbert up to? We have no agreement with the Chamber to put on a holiday festival."

"And you don't mind that the Beer Barn has organized the 'Beer Barn Holiday Bazaar'?"

"Heavens, no. You're paying our officers to provide security, correct? You're paying our trash service to pick up extra trash, right? You're bringing folks downtown where they'll spend money, and the City will get the sales tax. Right?"

"Yes, ma'am." What a relief. On impulse she said, "Um, Mayor, would you be willing to declare the festival open? Cut a ribbon? Or if you don't want to do that, judge the polka contest?"

"Yes to the ribbon. No to judging the polka contest. I never choose between potential voters."

Chapter Twenty-Nine

We're Lucky

On Thursday morning, building upper body strength, Alice hefted her biggest iron skillet and emptied its contents, buttery minced celery and onions, into her biggest bowl, full of crumbled cornbread, chopped fresh sage and parsley, and plenty of black pepper. She stirred in the chicken broth mixture and filled two baking pans. The scent of sage and pepper took her back to her grandmother's kitchen—the long white table, big enough for all the grandkids, the parakeet singing in its cage over the sink. With the stuffing taken care of, she floured her biggest cutting board and rolled out a ball of fragrant yeast dough. Just as her grandmother had taught her, she cut rounds with a biscuit cutter, then brushed on melted butter, and folded over each round into a little pillow, making two buttery dimples on each roll. What else? She'd already made mashed sweet potatoes, seasoned with boiled mashed garlic, chipotle powder, and lime juice, and cranberry sauce cooked with one of her home-smoked jalapeños—aka chipotle.

With these treasures loaded in the Discovery, she turned on Sun radio and hit the road. The Thanksgiving afternoon was blue, the air was a perfect sixty degrees, and Alice sang along with the radio almost all the way to Kinsear's.

On the way she called Ann, at her roommate's house for a New England Thanksgiving. "Miss you, Mom! Tell everyone hi!" Having her usual good time, Alice concluded.

At the top of Kinsear's hill, the driveway was busy. Jimmie was helping Conroy Robinson and Eddie LaFarge unload Eddie's big truck, with commentary from Kinsear's older daughter, Isabel.

"Hey, Alice!" Isabel called. "Come see this ginormous turkey Conroy's cooked!"

Conroy halted so she could admire the huge foil-swaddled bird he was carrying. "I believe it'll eat," he said in his slow deep voice.

"And if it doesn't, there's also brisket," Eddie added, lifting out another tray.

After hugs all around, Isabel and Eddie helped Alice carry in her offerings.

John and Kinsear's younger daughter, Carrie, were deep in conversation while setting Kinsear's long mission oak table. Alice eavesdropped. John was asking Carrie questions about classes, professors, her roommate. He'd always had that knack—drawing people out. She smiled to herself. Kinsear complained that Carrie could be notoriously uncommunicative. But not with John.

Alice felt Kinsear arrive at her side. They watched together as Isabel brought water glasses and candles to the table while Carrie and John chattered on.

"We're lucky," he said softly.

She nodded. "I thought Isabel's Sam would be here." Alice liked Isabel's boyfriend, Sam Brody. Just this past summer he and Isabel had helped rescue artwork stolen from Alice's client.

"Sam's coming over tomorrow," Kinsear said. "Probably will get here before breakfast."

"He and Isabel are still serious?"

"Oh, yeah. He'll get here before I can even get my robe on. Okay, let's gather our folks."

*****

The afternoon felt simultaneously relaxed and festive, like, Alice thought, the very best Thanksgivings. John, Carrie, and Isabel reveled in introducing Jimmie to new culinary traditions. "Sweet potatoes?" he asked, dubious. "Cranberry sauce with jalapeño? And must there always be turkey?"

Jimmie had never tasted pumpkin pie, or cranberry relish, much less with chipotle seasoning. But Alice noted he put away at least eight yeast rolls. He listened raptly to Conroy's discussion of the timing and temperature used for the day's brisket. Kinsear quizzed Conroy about the dry rub Conroy used and confided what he put on his own ribs. Conroy nodded approvingly.

In a quiet post-dinner moment, Alice was surprised when Jimmie slipped into a chair next to her. She smiled at him but waited for him to talk—if he wanted to.

"I don't know how I'll ever thank you," he said. "I feel—I feel in the midst of family. I never thought I could feel that way again. I've been an outsider for years. You've made me feel I belong."

She reached for his hand, squeezed it. “You are family.”

After a moment he asked quietly, “Tell me about Emma. You said she asked about me?”

“Jimmie. That woman flew from Antwerp to Edinburgh and drove to Broadview to ask about you.” She let a moment pass. “She teared up when she asked if you were there. She was so downcast that we couldn’t give her any news. Don’t you owe her at least a phone call?”

“She’s probably busy with her own life.” He glanced at her, his eyes uncertain.

“Hey. Don’t get a swelled head, but she mentioned that whoever she’d been dating wasn’t nearly so interesting as you.”

He gave a disbelieving half-laugh. But for the first time Alice saw him lift his head and stare into the future. “Wonder if she’d consider moving with me to Australia? Or New Zealand?”

“If you don’t ask, you’ll never know.”

The west windows glowed with sunset colors before Alice finally sighed and rose to leave. “That wretched Gumbert. I’ve got to get ready for a hearing,” she told Kinsear.

But first she took Jimmie aside to discuss the call from Davies.

Jimmie stood rigid, nothing moving but his eyes. “Can I trust him?”

Alice hoped he could trust a British Consulate official. “He’s promising a letter from the British ambassador.”

“I’ve been a burden on you much too long,” he burst out. “But will you be at this meeting on Monday?”

“Yes, and it will be in my office. If you feel the least anxiety, the least disquiet, we’ll just announce you’re staying here in Coffee Creek. As a barbecue apprentice,” she added.

“Thanks.”

She prayed Davies was an honorable man.

Chapter Thirty

Your Ox Isn't Gored

Silla was already in the office Friday morning when Alice arrived at seven. Jorgé arrived at eight in suit and tie, ready to prepare for the TRO hearing.

Mindful of the requirement to try to settle disputes, Alice decided Gumbert would be too sloppy with the rules to give her a call. So she called him. "Louie. Your claim is baseless. It'll be dismissed for lack of standing."

"Whaddaya mean, standing?"

"Well, your ox isn't gored. Rather, your client's ox isn't gored. Assuming you actually are representing the Chamber. In other words—" she stayed with her bovine metaphor—"your ox hasn't got a leg to stand on. So, how about dropping this claim before the court has to waste time on it?"

"Hell, no. I'm fully entitled to bring this suit. No way will I drop it. Unless you take those banners down and agree not to use 'Beer Barn Holiday Bazaar.'"

"You won't settle, then."

"Certainly not."

Well, that was clear enough.

She added a paragraph to her motion to dismiss, asserting plaintiff's counsel's refusal to settle. "Silla, let's file and serve this and deliver a copy to the judge."

"Yes, indeed. I've got my subpoenas ready. We want them to waive service and accept by email. Who are we serving?"

"Let's get the Chamber Secretary. This year, that's Miranda. I need a subpoena for the City Secretary, too. First let me run these affidavits by Miranda and John Dilley."

Alice got Miranda on the phone. "I'm sending you an affidavit, you lucky woman. As Chamber Secretary you affirm the Chamber, to your knowledge, has not authorized a joint Christmas holiday festival this year with the City?"

"Definitely has not."

"Read the affidavit. It's in your email. If you could sign and get this notarized, we'll come grab it. Like, now."

She emailed her very short affidavit to John Dilley and called him. "If this is okay, will you get the City Secretary to sign it and get it notarized? Saying the City has not authorized a joint Christmas holiday festival this year with the Chamber? And will you accept a subpoena for her for this hearing?"

"I will. I talked to Lizzie this morning and told her you'd probably need her for this hearing. And I, of course, am delighted to bill the City another hour or two."

"Okay. Silla will come by to get the original."

Silla, subpoenas in hand, left for Madrone Bank and the City offices. Alice and Jorgé walked through his testimony: how he'd come up with the name "Beer Barn Holiday Bazaar" and how the Beer Barn was using the name on contracts, ads, and correspondence. She asked him to describe the work the Beer Barn had put into the upcoming bazaar and the approximate costs of ads and contracts. She had him review the service mark application he'd signed.

At nine-thirty she sneaked into her office to check herself in the full-length mirror on the back of the office door. On Friday the judge would expect lawyers in boots, and she'd buffed her Goodson Kells. Her brown eyes stared back at her. Her hair needed taming; she gave her curls a fierce brushing, but some always snuck out of place. She'd dressed in her black suit and her scarlet silk shirt, a courtroom favorite ever since her best friend Red had informed her that red was the winning color. "Come on, Alice! Just look at the winning teams! You need more red in your closet!" Okay, Red.

Silla had served Gumbert, filed the subpoenas and affidavits with the court clerk, and delivered the judge's copies to his chambers. She brought Alice folders for each set of exhibits. Alice added her typed-up questions for Jorgé, plus the exhibits she planned to submit to show her client's commercial use of "Beer Barn Holiday Bazaar" on correspondence, contracts, ads, and bills, as well as the banners on Hays and Travis Streets. Miranda had emailed two years' worth of Chamber minutes.

Alice and Jorgé walked the two blocks to Courthouse Square, passed through security, then toiled up the limestone stairs, worn down for over a century by the feet of plaintiffs, defendants, witnesses, lawyers. The courthouse retained its familiar smell: paper, ink, adrenaline, anxiety.

In Judge Sandoval's third-floor courtroom, Alice claimed the defense table and told Judge Sandoval's bailiff she and her client were present. She heard the courtroom doors open behind her and turned to see her friend Miranda, tall, blonde, and cool as a cucumber in a pale gray suit with red heels higher than Alice dared wear. Miranda greeted Alice and Jorgé and sat down on the oak pew behind them. John Dilley arrived with City Secretary Lizzie Mikeska. Mikeska, forty-something, brown hair in a bun, wore her usual uniform—navy pantsuit, white blouse. Her reputation: accurate and detail oriented.

Dilley leaned over to talk to Alice. She liked Dilley—low-key, reliable, wry. "Did Louie Gumbert send you anything? Subpoenas? Affidavits?" he asked.

Alice shook her head no. "Not a single piece of paper. I'm interested to see what he says."

The big courtroom clock above the jury box, left of the judge's bench, said nine fifty-five. The bailiff poked his head around the door to the judge's chambers. "Mr. Gumbert here?"

Alice stood. "Not yet."

The court reporter took her seat below the judge's bench. Alice carried up two sets of her proposed exhibits, one for the reporter, one for the judge.

At five after ten the bailiff returned. "No sign?"

"No."

At ten-fifteen the doors to the courtroom opened. Gumbert bustled up the aisle and dropped his briefcase by the plaintiff's table. Alice rose and handed him a set of proposed exhibits. He turned, frowning, to stare at Miranda, John Dilley and Lizzie Mikeska.

At ten-sixteen the bailiff announced, "All rise," and Judge Bernie Sandoval, unsmiling, black robe billowing, emerged from his chambers, took the bench, and rapped his gavel.

"I have before me a request for a temporary restraining order and the Beer Barn's motion to dismiss that request, in part for lack of standing. Because standing is always required before this court will hear a case, I will first hear that portion of the motion to dismiss. Ms. Greer, you may proceed."

Alice walked to the lectern and adjusted the mike. "Your Honor, I called Mr. Gumbert this morning to discuss any possibility of settlement. He declined, and here we are.

"The named plaintiff is the Coffee Creek Chamber of Commerce, but the plaintiff alleges that the Chamber and the City of Coffee Creek jointly planned a holiday festival. You have before you the affidavit of Lizzie Mikeska, City Secretary for Coffee Creek. She affirms that she found no record that the City authorized any joint Christmas holiday festival with the Coffee Creek Chamber of Commerce. She further affirms she's found no record that the City authorized any holiday festival termed 'holiday bazaar.' At this time, I call Ms. Mikeska."

The court reporter swore in Lizzie Mikeska. She took the witness chair with the experienced air of a repeat witness.

Alice asked her first to detail her job as City Secretary. Then, "Does your job include keeping official minutes for the City Council?"

"It does."

"Are you familiar with all minutes of the City Council for the past, say, two years?"

"I am."

"Do any of those minutes reflect City Council authorization for City participation in a Christmas holiday festival to be undertaken jointly by the City and the Coffee Creek Chamber?"

"No."

"Are you aware of any authorization of such participation by the City that is not reflected in Council minutes?"

"No. I would have included such an authorization."

"Are you familiar with the tasks assigned to City committees?"

"I am."

"Is any City committee currently tasked by the City with considering participation in such a festival?"

"Not so far as I know."

"To your knowledge, has any City committee or body authorized such participation with the Chamber?"

"Not to my knowledge."

"Has the City, or any city official used the term 'Coffee Creek Holiday Bazaar' or 'holiday bazaar' for any proposed City event for this year?"

"Not to my knowledge."

Alice thought for a moment. "If any committee, or subcommittee, or individual Council member, acted to authorize such participation, would that be reflected in City records?"

"It would and should, if it were a valid authorization. But I know of no such records."

Alice decided to take a risk. "Ms. Mikeska, does the Beer Barn's use of the term 'Beer Barn Holiday Bazaar' cause any risk to the business reputation of the City of Coffee Creek?"

"Not that I can imagine."

Gumbert had risen to his feet on that question.

She quickly turned to Gumbert. "Your witness."

He lumbered forward. "Ms. Mikeska. Do you know everything the City does?"

Alice rose. "Objection. Vague and lacks required specificity."

"Sustained," said the judge.

Gumbert frowned. "Ms. Mikeska. Couldn't the City provide participation in a joint project with the Chamber without that winding up in your minutes?"

Mikeska frowned back at him, brow furrowed. "Do you mean, like provide garbage services or police services, in conjunction with a City project with the Chamber?"

"Um, yes."

Ooh, he shouldn't have let her rephrase for him, Alice thought.

"I would expect Council records to reflect a decision to provide such services." She added, "I don't recall seeing any such decision."

He knew he'd somehow missed a chance to muddy the waters. "What if the City just provides such services for free, for a worthy project?"

"Let me be sure I understand. You mean a project where the City is a participant?"

"Yes."

"Well, the City might agree to do so. But I'm not aware of any such agreement about a holiday project with the Chamber, which is my understanding of what you are asking."

"Objection," Gumbert growled.

"Denied."

Gumbert shifted from one large foot to the other. "Have you heard nothing about the City cooperating with the Chamber on a holiday festival?"

"Only when I read a copy of the papers you filed. Otherwise, no."

Ouch. Gumbert muttered, "Your witness," and sat down at his table.

"Nothing further," Alice said. She didn't want to ask Lizzie anything else; she had all she needed. Judge Sandoval did not look kindly on lawyers who retreaded paths already adequately trod. "I call Miranda Gray, manager of Madrone Bank."

Miranda looked the picture of poise as she reached the witness chair.

Alice walked her through her position at Madrone Bank, her membership in the Coffee Creek Chamber of Commerce, and her duties as current secretary of the Chamber. Miranda affirmed that the statements in her affidavit were true and correct.

"Ms. Gray, are you familiar with Louie Gumbert?"

"I am." Blank-faced.

"Did the Chamber ask you to serve with him on a committee to consider a holiday festival?"

"I was notified, after I was out of the room for part of our October meeting, that my name was proposed in that regard."

"Is Mr. Gumbert chair of that committee?"

"That is my understanding."

"Has your committee ever met?"

"Never, to my knowledge."

"Would it be correct to say this committee has never voted to recommend that the Chamber participate in a joint holiday project with the City this year?"

"Yes, to the best of my knowledge."

"Do your duties include taking minutes of Chamber board meetings?"

"Yes."

Alice had already given the court reporter two sets of Chamber minutes. She handed a set to Miranda. "Ms. Gray, can you identify these documents?"

Miranda leafed through them, once quickly, then more slowly.

"These are the minutes I've prepared for the Chamber board since becoming secretary."

"Your Honor, I move admission of the Chamber minutes."

The judge glanced at Gumbert, who was leafing through the minutes. No objection was forthcoming. "Admitted," said the judge.

"Ms. Gray, do your minutes reflect any Chamber board decision to participate in a joint holiday project with the City this year?"

"They do not."

"You say you missed part of the October meeting. Did you speak with others to be sure your minutes for that meeting were correct?"

"I did. I spoke with the president and vice-president and also sent copies of the draft minutes for their review." Miranda looked up at the judge. "They made no changes."

"To your knowledge, has the Chamber used the term 'holiday bazaar' for any joint holiday project with the City this year?"

"I have not heard that term used."

"Have you heard from any source that the Chamber authorized participation in a joint holiday project with the City this year?"

"No. Just to be sure, I called the president and the vice-president before this hearing to confirm there'd been no authorization."

"Did they confirm your understanding?"

"Yes. They said they didn't know what Louie was talking about."

"Objection! Hearsay," said Gumbert.

"Sustained, but only as to what the president and vice-president said." The judge leaned back in his chair.

Alice switched gears. "Ms. Gray, are you familiar with the print materials used by the Chamber? By print materials, I include correspondence, advertising, other business documents." She'd double-checked the initial proposal sent to Jorgé: no "holiday bazaar" verbiage.

"I am."

"Are you aware of the Chamber using the term 'holiday bazaar' on any print materials?"

"No. I've never seen those words on any Chamber documents."

"Ms. Gray, to your knowledge, did the Chamber authorize Mr. Gumbert to file this motion for a temporary restraining order?"

"Not to my knowledge."

Alice turned to Gumbert. "No further questions."

Gumbert trudged back to the lectern. "Ms. Gray. Are you telling this court you've heard nothing about Chamber participation in a holiday project with the City this year? Not a single word?"

"I'm telling the court that I've never heard that the Chamber authorized any participation in any such project. And I heard the comment from the president and vice-president that"—here she looked up at Judge Sandoval—"that the court struck." She paused, then added, "Otherwise, I've heard only one person mention the possibility of a Chamber holiday project with the City."

"Aha. And what was this mention?"

"The only person I've heard mention the possibility of a Chamber holiday project with the City is you."

"So you've heard me mention such a project."

"Yes. But even when you mentioned the possibility, you never said the Chamber had authorized such a project."

"Objection."

Alice stood. "What's the basis for the objection?"

Gumbert: "Uh, it's not what I asked."

"Overruled," said Judge Sandoval. "Any further questions, counsel?"

"No, but—" He halted, stumped.

"The witness is excused." Sandoval looked at Alice. "Any further witnesses?"

She'd thought about calling Gumbert himself, but he wasn't the plaintiff. "I call Jorgé Benavides."

Jorgé strode forward, was sworn in, and took the witness chair. Alice walked him through his roles and tenure at the Beer Barn. Then she asked, "Who came up with the name, 'Beer Barn Holiday Bazaar'?"

"I did."

"Has the Beer Barn been using that name?"

"Yes. On banners, on our invitations to vendors, on our advertising, on our contracts connected with our upcoming Holiday Bazaar."

Alice approached the court reporter, handing her two more packets of exhibits, marked 1 through 5, including photos of the banner, invitations to competing dance groups, advertisements, and band and vendor contracts.

Alice turned to Jorgé. "Can you identify for the court each type of the documents marked Exhibits 1 through 5, including the actual use made by the Beer Barn of these documents?"

Exhibit by exhibit, Jorgé explained when and how the Beer Barn had used each type.

She handed the court reporter copies of the Beer Barn's service mark application, marked Exhibit 6.

"Mr. Benavides, can you identify Exhibit 6?"

He explained that the Beer Barn had applied for a service mark for "Beer Barn Holiday Bazaar" in connection with the upcoming festival.

"You signed this application, did you not?"

"I did."

"Do you affirm that the statements in the application are true and correct?"

"I do."

"Your Honor, I move admission of Exhibits 1 through 6."

"Any objections?"

Gumbert stood. "These are irrelevant, Your Honor."

"How so?" asked the judge. "Aren't you trying to prevent the Beer Barn's use of the term 'Beer Barn Holiday Bazaar'?"

"Yes, I am, but..."

"Isn't the use in commerce of the term 'Beer Barn Holiday Bazaar' the focus of your motion? Aren't you asking this court to forbid its use?"

"Yes, but..."

"Objection overruled. Exhibits 1 through 6 are admitted."

"Your witness," Alice said.

Gumbert stood. "You claim this term, 'Beer Barn Holiday Bazaar,' was your own idea?"

"I do," said Jorgé.

"Well, how do I know you didn't steal that from the proposal I sent you for a project with the Chamber?"

Jorgé looked puzzled. "You sent a short proposal, but it doesn't use the words 'holiday bazaar' anywhere. I suggested 'Beer Barn Holiday Bazaar' when we came up with our Beer Barn festival."

"Weren't you aware that the Chamber was going to use the term 'holiday bazaar' for a joint project with the City?"

"No. I never heard that."

Gumbert furrowed his brow, picked up his papers, looked at them, looked at the judge. "No further questions."

"The witness is excused. Ms. Greer, any further witnesses?"

"Not at this time, Your Honor."

"Mr. Gumbert?"

Louie Gumbert paused, then shook his head. "No, Your Honor."

Alice asked, "May I proceed to my argument on our motion?"

"You may."

She claimed the lectern and squared her shoulders. "Your Honor, the Beer Barn, as Mr. Benavides testified, came up with the idea for a holiday festival it named the Beer Barn Holiday Bazaar for the last weekend in November and several weekends in December. The Beer Barn has invested its resources to bring this event to Coffee Creek. The Beer Barn contacted vendors to sell crafts inside the building and contracted with bands to provide music. The Beer Barn arranged for local food trucks and is providing an outdoor stage for a polka contest and other dance competitions. The Beer Barn arranged to pay for additional services from the City, including added trash pickup, security, and parking.

"The Beer Barn properly applied for a service mark for the name 'Beer Barn Holiday Bazaar,' which begins tomorrow, Your Honor. Tomorrow! The Beer Barn has already used 'Beer Barn Holiday Bazaar' on contracts, banners, ads, and other materials for the event, as shown by Exhibits 1 through 5. Based on its use, it filed a service mark application for 'Beer Barn Holiday Bazaar,' Exhibit 6. It's unconscionable for Mr. Gumbert to wait until today to demand that the Beer Barn stop using its service mark.

"As you heard today, neither the City nor the Chamber has authorized any joint project using the term 'holiday bazaar.'

"Mr. Gumbert is, to use a non-legal term, way ahead of his skis. He purports to sue on behalf of the Chamber, but testimony shows the Chamber didn't authorize him to file this action.

"In first-year contracts class at law school, we heard the term 'officious intermeddler' for someone 'off on a frolic of his own.'" She looked up at the judge. "Mr. Gumbert is indeed off on a frolic of his own.

"Which gets us to standing. Both the City and the Chamber have disavowed participation in this lawsuit. So who's the plaintiff? Because Mr. Gumbert fails to establish standing to sue, this action should be dismissed forthwith."

"Mr. Gumbert, it appears to the court that this case should be dismissed. Any response?" asked the judge.

"I came up with the name 'Coffee Creek Holiday Bazaar'!" Gumbert said.

Alice was still on her feet. "I believe evidence will show that he used that term only after he learned the Beer Barn was already planning and publicizing the Beer Barn Holiday Bazaar, Your Honor. Mr. Gumbert has offered no evidence whatsoever that any party but the Beer Barn, including Mr. Gumbert, has actually used 'Holiday Bazaar' in commerce."

"Mr. Gumbert?"

But Gumbert was silent, then blurted, "The whole thing was my idea!"

There was a pause. "Anything further, counsel?" The judge glanced up at the courtroom clock, waiting. Gumbert stood for a long, awkward moment. Finally, the judge rapped his gavel. "Case dismissed. Ms. Greer, please prepare a draft order for my review."

"All rise," called the bailiff. All rose. The judge disappeared into his chambers. Gumbert stood for a moment at the plaintiff's table, then threw his copies of exhibits into his briefcase and huffed down the aisle, red-faced. He ignored Alice and Jorgé. He didn't glance at Brad Dilley or Lizzie Mikeska. But he threw a bitter look at Miranda.

"Good grief," Alice said to Jorgé. "Of course, Gumbert could still challenge your service mark application, claim it's too descriptive, argue you should disclaim part of the mark. But he'd have to file that objection with the Texas Secretary of State, not Judge Sandoval."

"I wish we could get our fees and costs from that guy," Jorgé said. "But frankly, this was worth the price of admission." He grinned at Alice. "Kinda fun."

Alice snorted. "I'm glad you thought so." She disliked wasting her time or her client's money. She also hoped Gumbert wasn't cooking up another move.

Normally after a successful hearing or deposition she allowed herself at least a few moments to celebrate. But she couldn't, today. Nanette's parents were due at her office any minute.

*****

A dusty tan Ford Explorer with New Mexico plates sat in front of the office when Alice returned. Silla had installed the Ferrises in the conference room and brought them tea. When Alice entered, both stood. Mid-fifties, tall and wiry, slightly stooped, Tyler Ferris had a rancher's weathered face and penetrating blue eyes. Alice shook his hand—rough with outdoor work—and then the softer hand of Nanette's mother, Jean Ferris, a slender dark-haired woman with gray eyes. Like Nanette, she stood very straight, still but watchful.

Alice got them settled in their chairs, then told them how she'd met Nanette and Mischa at the UT Law Moot Court competition, how much she admired and respected Nanette, how they'd become close, what a loss this was—not just to the profession, but to Nanette's colleagues and friends.

What can you say to parents whose beloved daughter has been murdered? A gifted daughter on the brink of finding happiness in love as well as success in work? The faces of her own children flashed before her as she imagined what the Ferrises must feel.

Sober-faced, Alice began walking them through their duties as Nanette's executors. They nodded dutifully.

She could feel the weight of their grief in the air.

Then Tyler Ferris said abruptly, "We had a call from that Detective Files. He said one of Nanette's bosses—Ron Simpson—is a suspect. He hasn't been charged yet."

"I expect Detective Files told you that Ron Simpson's prints were found on Nanette's body? And her laptop?" Alice asked.

"Yes." His voice shook—rage, grief. "When is Nanette's murderer going to be charged?"

"I don't know," Alice said. "Maybe the Sheriff's Department still needs to confirm the—the murder weapon. Would you like me to call Detective Files to ask?" She wanted to know too. Ron's prints were on

Nanette's ankles. But who drove the murder car? She debated mentioning the email Nanette had stashed in the ink cartridge box but decided to wait until Files had actually filed charges.

Before they left, she mentioned Michael Greene, saying he seemed truly devoted to Nanette. Both leaned forward, faces intent.

Alice went on to say that Michael Greene had begun tutoring Benjy Patch, the child Nanette had tutored at Coffee Creek Elementary. "She'd already bought Christmas presents for Benjy. Michael made sure to get them wrapped and delivered them to Benjy just before the Thanksgiving break."

Jean Ferris closed her eyes for a moment and let out a slow breath. "Nanette told us how much she liked him. She'd never been serious about anyone before." She teared up, then managed, "Do you think we could meet him?"

Alice made sure they had Michael's phone number.

When the meeting ended, the Ferrises picked up the materials Silla had prepared for them—probate procedures, executor duties—and drove off to the Tea Garden House, where they were staying. Alice called M.A. "They're on their way. I know you'll take care of them."

"If I get my hands on the sorry bastard that ran over that poor young woman—"

Alice thought M.A. could deliver some rough justice.

She called George Files. No answer. She left a message: "Nanette Ferris's parents just left my office. What's going on with the case? Did you locate the car that hit her? What's Pat Simpson's status? Did you find Ron Simpson?"

Chapter Thirty-One

Louisville Slugger

Saturday morning brought sun, a mild breeze shaking the last golden leaves off the cedar elms, and the holiday feel of Thanksgiving weekend—students home from school, families reunited, Christmas just ahead. Perfect weather for the first annual Beer Barn Holiday Bazaar. Alice had donned her Goodson Kell boots, her best-fitting jeans, and the denim rodeo jacket, embroidered with yellow roses, that made Kinsear smile. She planned to check on Conroy, then work at the office awhile before meeting John and Kinsear at the Beer Barn.

She carried three apples out to the waiting burros, asking herself when they'd trained her to deliver morning as well as afternoon treats. Was she spoiling them? Or were they manipulating her? Yes. Oh, well.

Files hadn't yet returned her call. Otherwise, her list of morning worries was mercifully short. Daughter Ann: safely back at college from spending Thanksgiving with her roommate's family. Son John: returning to Coffee Creek with Kinsear for the opening of the Holiday Bazaar. Jimmie: safe with ex-NFL pros Conroy Robinson and Eddie LaFarge at Eddie's vineyard, Raptor Cellars, where Conroy kept his new food truck. Conroy had enlisted Jimmie as sous-chef for the barbecue he'd be selling tonight at the Beer Barn.

Alice worried about Jimmie's safety, given the danger suggested by the British Consulate's efforts to spirit him out of Hong Kong. The white rental car outside her office, with the driver taking pictures? She had no certainty that was the man calling himself Ian Blane. Nevertheless, she warned Eddie and Conroy.

"That guy hasn't met us yet, Alice," Conroy growled. "Don't worry."

She hoped he was right. She'd like to see that imposter trussed up like a turkey, delivered to—to whom? British authorities, for impersonating a Coastguard officer and, maybe, imprisoning a British citizen? Messy jurisdictional issues.

But what of Ron Simpson, whose prints were on Nanette's ankles, who'd dragged her under a hedge to die? Where was he? And where was Pat?

By the time Alice reached Coffee Creek, downtown was so crowded she called Kinsear. "Come park at my office! You and John and I can walk to the Beer Barn."

"Are you looking festive?" he asked.

"Definitely. You?"

"Boots are polished. Are we entering the polka contest?"

"No! Two-step, maybe. Polka, no. I run out of breath after thirty seconds. Besides, the competition's ferocious. Same for the Spanish folklórico contest, though I love their costumes. Especially the men's." She thought for a moment how charming Kinsear would look in the folklórico costume: black pants, white shirt, black hat.

"We'll meet you at what—three?—at your office," Kinsear said.

"Deal."

By the time she walked down Live Oak to the Beer Barn, Conroy's barbecue rig—a food truck with the enormous cast iron grill on the trailer behind—was ensconced in the Beer Barn parking lot, with its smoke coiling out across the venue. She walked up to the food truck window just after eleven. Inside she saw Jimmie, chef's toque askew, busy chopping something, and Conroy, large as a live oak, eyes scanning to make sure all was ready. Both wore blue chambray shirts, sleeves rolled up, and red bandanas. She inhaled the addictive aroma of barbecue.

"Conroy, you'll sell out. Smells incredible."

The big man settled his brown eyes on her, a smile on his lips. "Smells right to me. I'll put some aside for you tonight."

She and Conroy went back awhile. She'd met him when he recuperated at Eddie's vineyard from concussion injuries in the NFL. What a contrast, she thought, staring at the two men: Jimmie, worn and sunburned, thin and wary-eyed; and Conroy, an impeccable professional athlete, combining strength and what Kinsear announced was amazing speed for an offensive lineman: "Forty-yard dash in less than five seconds."

"How's your sous-chef?" she asked Conroy, shooting a smile at Jimmie.

"For a Brit, he's got a knack. Must be all his time in Asia. He says he didn't grow up with barbecue in Scotland but that it's starting to catch on there. Anyway, I'm glad of the help." He looked at his watch. "We open in ten minutes."

Indeed, an eager line was forming behind Alice.

"I'll see you two later."

She made her way to the Beer Barn entrance, joining a throng of people of all ages—grandparents with grandkids, couples pushing strollers, young people glancing speculatively at each other. Inside, the Beer Barn echoed with music and chatter. Down each side of the big hall stood booths where craftspeople were displaying their wares. Alice saw Christmas ornaments, hand-turned wood bowls, knitted and felt Christmas stockings, as well as all manner of blacksmith work, hand-blown glass, jewelry, hand-made paper, photographs, paintings, and angora and mohair shawls. She found a hand-woven embroidered scarf made in Guatemala for Ann, a leather vest for John, and then stopped at a booth displaying San Antonio creches with hand-painted pieces. Little lambs, shy shepherds, the Magi with camels, and the parents with their swaddled infant—but the donkeys got her. She watched as the saleswoman wrapped each precious piece. At a vintage Western wear booth she snapped up a 1940's cowgirl shirt for Silla, black satin with white fringe, still in mint condition. Just imagining Silla wearing it made her smile.

She'd already squirreled away Kinsear's gift. A package had arrived from Paris containing a hand-colored map dated 1660 of "Mexique et Nouvelle Louisiane." She particularly loved the depiction of Texas, with hand-drawn tiny figures that appeared to be bison (as drawn by someone who'd never seen one), and rivers with names like "La Dure" and "La Maligne." Yep, sounded appropriate. She couldn't wait for Kinsear to see it.

Arms full, she caught sight of Bill Benke next to the Beer Barons' office, leaning on the wall and watching the crowd. He grinned at her. "Hi, Alice. What do you think? Pretty okay, right?"

"Home run," she agreed. "I'll be back in a bit."

At her office she stashed her treasures, dutifully answered emails, and waited impatiently for three p.m., wishing she'd stayed in line for Conroy's first barbecue sandwich. Finally, she looked out the window to see Kinsear's Land Cruiser parking at her curb. He and John wore boots, jeans, and down vests. John looked unexpectedly cheerful. Hmm.

When they reached the Beer Barn, John disappeared. She and Kinsear toured the craft booths. Then the music called. They squeezed through the growing throng, up to the stage where a band from Kerrville was playing. To her surprise, nearby, gazing intently at each other, stood her son John and a pretty girl with auburn hair. John apparently felt his mother's eyes. He turned and walked over, holding the girl's hand. "Mom, Ben, meet Sara McKee. Sara, my mom and Ben Kinsear." After John admitted he'd known Sara in high school and Sara admitted she was at the LBJ School of Public Affairs, the parental grilling ceased, and the two young people vanished into the crowd.

Kinsear pulled Alice close. She closed her eyes, feeling his warmth, enjoying his pleasure in the music, rocking gently back and forth to the drums.

When the song ended, he said, "This beats worrying about who's trying to grab Jimmie. Is he okay, out there with Conroy?"

"He's in the food truck, hard at work."

As the afternoon wore on, Alice and Kinsear walked outside to the temporary dance stage erected by the Beer Barn. They watched the polka contest, then the folklórico contest—tapping heels, flashing skirts, insistent rhythms. At November's end, sunset came early, painting the western sky orange. The crowds thinned. Cars pulled away, heading east and west on Hays and Travis Streets. Near the entrance to the parking lot, Alice and Kinsear ran into M.A., all alone, her white hair gleaming under the city streetlight at the curb. She was about to leave.

"I'll be back," Kinsear said, "as soon as I walk M.A. to her car."

That was one of the things she loved—his kindness. "Meet you at Conroy's food truck," Alice said.

Now the sky was dark, save for a faint orange streak in the west. The Beer Barons, members of the Coffee Creek dark sky chapter, tolerated the city streetlight but insisted on lighting the parking lot with lamps that didn't throw glare and were shaded to throw light downward, dappling the parking area with circles of light and shade.

Inside Conroy's barbecue truck the lights were still on. Alice peered through the front window.

"Hey, Alice! We're totally sold out! But I saved you enough chopped beef for a couple of sandwiches. Here you go." Conroy handed her two warm plump sandwiches wrapped in waxed paper. Grateful, Alice carried the sandwiches across the parking lot to an empty picnic table that sat beneath the low-hanging branches of a large oak and climbed up to sit atop the table and wait for Kinsear.

The aroma was so compelling, so irresistible, she couldn't wait to taste the barbecue. Carefully she laid Kinsear's sandwich on the wood planks and picked up hers. Oh, that first bite. Smoke, dark spice, almost indescribable. She took another bite, watching the door open at the end of the food truck. She saw Jimmie backing down the steps, tugging a big black garbage bag. Then he turned, slung it over his shoulder, and started toward the dumpster at the inside front corner of the parking lot.

Alice watched Jimmie's progress, thinking of this seabed geologist, now studying barbecue, far from his native land. She glanced toward the adjacent street, wondering how long before Kinsear would return. M.A. adored him and would talk his ear off.

Sitting tucked under the branches, she heard footsteps to her rear. A man walked toward the dumpster, apparently oblivious to her presence. As he passed under one of the light standards, she saw he was fairly tall with short bleached hair beneath a ball cap. Watching him walk into the shade between the lights, she was suddenly in the hallway at the Aberdeen Mortuary, following Ian Blane. What was it about that walk—

For a moment she was frozen, unable to process the information. Then he moved into the light again. Something glinted in the man's hand. "Jimmie!" she yelled, scrambling off the table. "Jimmie!" She ran.

Standing at the dumpster, holding open the lid with one hand, garbage bag in the other, Jimmie turned. The man in the ball cap broke into a run, the streetlight shining on the object in his hand.

"Jimmie!" Alice screamed, running toward him. The dumpster lid clanged shut.

The man lunged at Jimmie. Jimmie swung the garbage bag at him. Alice heard breaking glass bottles. Jimmie swung the bag again, backhanded. It split. Garbage flew out, splattering the man. "Shit!" he hissed. He was taller than Jimmie, his arms longer. Arms extended, he leaped forward.

Jimmie dodged sideways, reached down and grabbed the neck of a broken bottle, the cut end glittering in the light. The man in the ball cap, his back to Alice, danced back and forth, right arm cocked. Now she saw in the streetlight what he gripped in his right hand: a glass syringe.

Footsteps thudded behind her. "Move!"

She skidded sideways.

Conroy Robinson raced past, a wooden baseball bat high in his right hand. The man in the ball cap took his eyes off Jimmie and spun around. Conroy swung the bat straight at his midsection.

"Unnhh!" The man flew backward onto the ground. Conroy stood over him, breathing hard. With one foot he carefully nudged the syringe out of the man's reach, then stepped firmly on his right hand. The man groaned.

Kinsear walked into the parking lot. "What the hell?"

The man's ball cap had fallen off. Jimmie, Alice, Conroy, and Kinsear stared down at the attacker's face. The streetlight turned his peroxided hair an odd yellow-green.

Here in Coffee Creek, he wasn't sporting the Coastguard uniform he'd worn at the mortuary.

"Ian Blane," Alice murmured.

"Dickie Manners," Jimmie answered.

"Don't anyone step on that syringe," said Kinsear.

Jimmie looked up at Conroy. "Thank you."

Conroy said, "No problem, man. Thank my Louisville Slugger."

*****

Alice called 911, asked for an ambulance, then called the Sheriff's Department. "George Files, please."

"He's not on duty at the moment."

"We need him at the Beer Barn. There was an attack in the parking lot. The attacker was caught, and I called an ambulance, but this may relate to Detective Files's investigation of the Ferris murder."

"I'll convey the message. Hold, please."

In a moment the deputy said, "He says he'll join the party."

Flashing lights, sirens. Two Coffee County Sheriff's Department cruisers rolled up, then an ambulance. Files unfolded his long legs from the first cruiser. "How I spend my weekends," he said.

Followed by a young, uniformed deputy, Files walked over to

Jimmie's attacker, flat on the ground. Jimmie, Alice, and Kinsear stood nearby, shivering in the chilly night breeze. Alice wished she'd brought something warmer than her embroidered rodeo jacket.

Conroy still had one foot resting on the man's right hand. He shifted his baseball bat to his left hand and pointed with his right at the syringe lying on the gravel parking lot.

"I hit him," Conroy said to Files. "I heard Alice screaming. I looked out of the truck and saw him going after Jimmie with that needle."

"Bag that," Files said to the young deputy hovering at his elbow. The deputy—nametag "Evans"— complied.

Two EMTs trotted up to the man on the ground, examined him, eased him onto a gurney, and knelt at his side. "Can't tell whether that's blood or barbecue sauce," one man observed. "Smells more like barbecue."

Files squatted by the gurney. "Name?"

The attacker squeezed his eyes shut but didn't answer.

Files looked up at Deputy Evans. "ID on him?"

After a careful search, Evans shook his head no, but held up a key. "Only this car key. No tag on it. Pockets empty."

"Okay, get him to emergency," Files told the EMTs. He beckoned the two deputies who'd arrived in the second cruiser. "Stick with this guy. If the ER wants to keep him overnight, I'll interview him there. Call me if they threaten to discharge him. If he's discharged, bring him straight to the jail."

As the ambulance pulled out, followed by the cruiser, Alice said, "He had a rental car. White sedan. I don't know what kind. He was taking pictures of my office the other day."

"Call in a search for an empty white rental. And get everybody's contact info," Files told Evans. He turned to the group. "Did anyone see the whole thing?"

"I did," Alice said.

"We'll go over this again, but first, who's the guy with the syringe?"

"He's the man I first saw in the Aberdeen Mortuary wearing a Scottish Coastguard uniform, calling himself Ian Blane. But the Coastguard says he's lying. Jimmie says he knew him in Asia as Dickie Manners."

Files frowned, shook his head. "Scotland? Asia?" He turned to Jimmie. "Can you identify your attacker?"

Jimmie was trembling in the chill breeze. "That's the man who kidnapped me in Jakarta. The man who held me captive on the *Seabass.*"

"Did he threaten you tonight with the syringe?" Files asked.

"Yes. I picked up a broken beer bottle." He shivered again. "Pretty big syringe. But Conroy got him before he could get me."

Files looked around at the waiting faces. "I'll need statements from everyone." He turned to Jimmie. "Do you plan to file charges?"

Jimmie glanced at Alice, who nodded. "Yes," Jimmie said.

By now the three Beer Barons had emerged from the Beer Barn and joined the onlookers. Jorgé spoke up. "Detective, it's getting cold. Can we offer you some warm office space inside? And hot coffee? Luis is opening up the kitchen again."

Files nodded, thanked the three men, and turned, indicating the witnesses should follow.

Alice whispered in Kinsear's ear. He reversed course, striding back to the picnic table under the oak. "Got it," he muttered when he caught up with her. "I do love a woman who understands the value of a barbecue sandwich." The waxed paper packet stuck out of his pocket.

Inside, Luis served hot coffee and cheese quesadillas. Files interviewed them one by one, with Evans taking notes—first Conroy, then Jimmie, then Kinsear, then Alice.

Alice described how she'd left the Beer Barn to check on Conroy and Jimmie, how Conroy had given her two barbecue sandwiches, how she'd sat on the picnic table under the live oak, waiting for Kinsear to come back.

"Why was Jimmie in the truck?"

"He wants to learn barbecue."

Files nodded. "Why not."

Alice went on. "Jimmie headed for the dumpster with the garbage bag. I saw a man appear from the back of the parking lot, walking toward Jimmie. Something about his walk—I recognized it. I yelled at Jimmie. The man sped up, running toward Jimmie. Jimmie swung the garbage bag at him. Then I saw he had a syringe."

"Why the hell was he chasing Jimmie with a syringe?" demanded Files.

"What's in the syringe?" Alice asked. "I assume he wanted either to kill him or dope him up. My guess is—the latter."

"But why? Why did you tell the duty officer this relates to the Ferris murder?"

Alice took a deep breath. "You've already got Anton Ivanov and Tim Lemmon aka Bennie Vitale in jail, right? They're small fry but should get you the big fish investors—from the Florida and Russian mafia. But Dickie Manners is your connection to the third leg of the stool—the guy who knew how to smuggle rare earths. Jimmie says that's General Shwe Sone, from Myanmar. Dickie Manners was working for Sone when Jimmie met him."

Files's brow furrowed. "You're saying this smuggling scenario relates to investors in the Simpson's big investment deal? The one Nanette Ferris was working on?"

Alice nodded, watching Files's face. "It could be that's where the dirty money comes from. The proposed laundry job? Maybe using smuggling money to buy Lacey's ranch."

"Good lord." Files shook his head. "Have I been teleported out of Coffee Creek into an international financial crime scene?"

"Feels like it."

Chapter Thirty-Two

With A Bang

On Monday, the Beer Barn Holiday Bazaar had been declared a success—by the mayor (who indeed cut the opening ribbon), by the Beer Barn (which survived two days of happy crowds and excellent ticket sales), and by the Sheriff's Department (only one potential fight between polka contestants, and the odd incident of the man with a syringe).

At quarter to ten, Silla had set out coffee and breakfast tacos. "They may be English, but I don't do tea," she said. "And what the heck are crumpets?"

"No need even to ask. Besides, they'll be dumbstruck, admiring your outfit. New boots?"

"Mm-hmm," Silla said, peering down at her vintage blue boots with white stars. They matched her denim culottes and white cowgirl shirt. She tossed her ponytail. "Bring'em on!"

Files called. "Ketamine," he said. "That's what was in the syringe."

"Isn't that like a date rape drug?"

"It makes you compliant. Looks like Dickie Manners wanted Jimmie up and walking but ready to tell him everything he knew."

Alice blinked at the memory of the man dancing back and forth, syringe raised... "Thank God for Conroy."

Jimmie arrived in Conroy's pickup. Conroy stood in the office entry, making everything around him look small. "I've got a little shopping to do. Call me if you need me. Especially if these English dudes get fancy. Got to take care of my man, here. My sous-chef."

Jimmie grinned. "I'm not ready to leave, Alice. Conroy's teaching me barbecued ribs next."

"I mean it. Call me if they lay a hand on this guy. Be back shortly." Conroy left.

Alice got Jimmie settled in the conference room. "So what have you decided? Are you sticking around awhile?"

"Maybe. I like the peace. I miss the ocean, but you know, the way the hills out here wave up and down, those limestone seabeds heaving up from the ground, it's kinda oceanic."

That made her laugh. "Not my business, but what about Emma? Did you get in touch?"

He nodded, face more serious. "I called her. She said—"

But Silla stuck her head in the door before Alice could hear more.

"They're here."

Three suits entered the room—one gray, one pinstriped navy, one plain navy. Davies (gray suit) introduced Horace Banks (bifocals, bald, navy pinstripe, from London) and a sturdy man named Andrew Douglas (plain navy) with ginger hair, bushy eyebrows, and a Scottish accent.

Davies handed Alice a sealed envelope. "As you requested."

She opened the envelope while Silla introduced the group to the idea of breakfast tacos and coffee. The three men appeared both curious and pleased as they carried plates and mugs back to the table. "Don't overdo the hot sauce," Silla warned.

Then Silla asked to see their credentials—asked all three, even Davies. Davies nodded at Banks and Douglas who—surprised and hesitant—finally produced their identification cards. Which Silla photographed.

Alice scanned the letter. Satisfied, she passed it to Jimmie, and nodded at Davies. At least she had the British ambassador's written commitment to protect Jimmie. "Before we get started," she said, "tell me how Dickie Manners knew Jimmie was in Coffee Creek, Texas?"

"Our best guess?" Davies began. "The trip to Hong Kong airport. Jimmie, you and John Greer traveled to the airport by the Hong Kong Mass Transit Railway, right? Took the MTR from Hong Kong Central?"

Jimmie nodded.

"And you or he checked a bag, correct?"

Alice remembered waiting for John's bag at the Austin airport.

Jimmie nodded.

"It's surprisingly easy to follow someone who's busy at a counter—like the counter at the MTR, where you can check your bag before you even board the train," Davies said, "and see the bag as it's placed on the conveyor with the destination tags attached. Plus, your enemies knew you and Jordie shared the same surname. Knowing the name 'Greer,' knowing the Austin destination, perhaps using Jordie's name to track down Alice—well, how many Alice Greers are there in the Austin area?"

Damn, thought Alice.

When all were settled, Davies began. "I'm here on behalf of Her Majesty's Government, via our Houston Consulate. Horace Banks is with the Border Force, concerned with maritime border control, and Andrew Douglas liaises with the Royal Navy, including seizures of smuggled goods. I'd like these men to hear Jimmie's story of his incarceration on the Seabass. Then, when we're all on the same page, we'd like to discuss what to do with this information. Our joint goals are these: protect Jimmie against repercussions from his kidnappers—or anyone else; prevent further illegal use of the collected data; and, if possible, prosecute the wrongdoers profiting from smuggling. These are big goals, perhaps not feasible. But do they suit, as a starting point?"

Alice glanced at Jimmie. His face was serious, his eyes moving back and forth among the three men. Finally, he nodded. "Yes."

Davies glanced around the room. "First, we'd like to hear your story, and, if agreeable, to prepare a sworn transcript."

Made sense, Alice thought. In case the witness somehow became... unavailable. "Before we begin," she said, "I need to tell you that General Shwe Sone's presumed smuggling accomplice, Dickie Manners, is now in the Coffee County jail. He tried to grab Jimmie again and drug him with a syringe full of ketamine."

"He's *here*? In jail?" Davies sounded stunned.

"Yes." She gave details. "Given the ketamine, he and his handlers apparently intended to make Jimmie give back the data. But let's start with Jimmie's story."

An hour later Jimmie had told the tale to Davies' tape recorder (as well as a tape recorder brought in by a mistrustful Silla—always alert to potential unauthorized edits). The details brought raised eyebrows and astounded faces. When Jimmie finished, there was silence. Then Douglas said, "Straight out of Robert Louis Stevenson! But far more dangerous."

Banks leaned forward. "The data on the thumb drive? You still have it?"

"Yes. We left Hong Kong with the data on John's—Alice's son's—laptop. He also had the thumb drive."

"So it's not here?"

Alice spoke up. "The original thumb drive's in my safe, with a couple of copies. The version on my son's laptop was removed to a hard drive and deleted from his laptop."

Davies asked, "What do you want to do with the data, Jimmie?"

"I've thought about it a great deal. If you prosecute the bad guys for smuggling, it'll be evidence, of course. If the data gets out into the world, other people will want to use it—for good, for evil. One idea is giving it to the International Seabed Authority, but I read their security is crap." The three men nodded.

"I want it used to increase our care of the sea," Jimmie said. "So I thought about giving the original to the National Oceanography Centre, in Southampton, to expand our knowledge of the seabed."

That got Andrew Douglas's attention. "What an amazing idea."

"But could they keep the data safe?" Banks demanded.

"Probably not," Douglas acknowledged. "It's likely to get out somehow, whether from the Seabed Authority, or any institution—even the Home Office. Hacking's an international industry."

Reluctantly, Davies and Banks nodded. "Still, if we can get jurisdiction over the smugglers, if we can prove illegal dredging," Banks said, "it might at least discourage some folks."

Jimmie spoke. "I'm willing for the authorities to have a copy to prosecute the smugglers."

Alice leaned forward, staring at Davies. "And I have your commitment to protect Jimmie before, during, and after any prosecution of these guys?"

"You do."

Alice thought, but didn't say, that fully protecting Jimmie's data was a pipe dream. He might not have successfully deleted it in the first place. His kidnappers might already have used some computer genius to retrieve every bit, every byte. But Jimmie's notion of a gift to an English research facility—she liked it.

Meanwhile, she wanted Jimmie protected. Nice that Davies had agreed. But who could best do it? As she gazed at the three suits—she had to admit they seemed bright, committed, competent—her vote still went to Conroy and Eddie.

Jimmie might stay here a little longer. But he wouldn't stay forever.

She heard Conroy's deep voice in the hall, and Silla's laugh. When she opened the conference room door, there stood Conroy, massive in his jeans, faded blue chambray shirt, and red bandana. She introduced him to the Brits. He shook their hands, looming over them.

"Conroy's teaching me the fine points of barbecue," Jimmie explained. "As well as Hill Country wine culture and animals unknown to the British Isles, like raccoons and porcupines and possums. And armadillos."

Alice laughed and explained Jimmie and Conroy were helping out at Raptor Cellars. Davies—who was tall—looked up at Conroy—even taller. "Thanks. We need Jimmie alive."

"No kidding." Conroy handed him a business card. "Call any time, night or day."

Davies thanked him and turned to Jimmie. "So, you plan to stay at Raptor Cellars for a bit?"

Jimmie glanced at Alice, then nodded at the British contingent. "Yes, I do. Meanwhile, thank you gentlemen for coming. I'll keep you posted on my whereabouts."

"We'll alert you to any new concerns," Davies responded. He and his companions shook hands with Jimmie and Alice, and again with Conroy. They left with one thumb drive, having signed Alice's receipt, which described it as evidence for use in punishing illegal dredging and prosecuting Jimmie's kidnappers.

Jimmie announced he was ready for her to send one thumb drive to the research center in Southampton.

"Let's call first and let them know what you're thinking."

"Right."

"And Jimmie? What about Gran?"

He grinned. "You're right. Now I can call her." He glanced up at Conroy. "My aunt. In Scotland."

"Your aunt?" Conroy handed him a cell phone. "Go right ahead."

He and Conroy left.

Alice intended to use the third thumb drive in Jimmie's civil damages lawsuit against the kidnappers—if he decided to go that route. The hard drive? Locked in her safety deposit box at Madrone Bank. Not foolproof, but...

*****

Alone, back at her desk, Alice stared down at her cellphone. No message from Files. No email from Files. What about the grille on the white Land Rover SUV?

She was about to dial him when her phone rang. Finally, Files.

"You know that brand new fancy Land Rover you saw that Sunday morning?" Files sounded smug—almost smiling.

"Yes?"

"Ron Simpson's wife's car. Even had those twin carwash receipts in the console. But the big thing is, the lab found material from Nanette Ferris on and behind the front grille—and along the wipers."

She didn't want him to describe the nature of the "material." "Was Ron driving? Wait, have you found him?"

"Yeah, hiding out in Houston. I'm expecting him to be delivered here in an hour. And yes, his prints and DNA are in the SUV, including the driver's side. I expect he'll claim he 'often drove her car.'"

"And she says?"

"We'll see. I'm sure they'll challenge our testing."

"I can imagine him saying it was an accident; he followed Nanette home to be sure she was safe after working so late; she ran out in front of his car; he didn't know what to do, thought she was dead..."

"You may be more creative than he or his lawyer will be, Alice. But thanks to you and Mischa, we know he had motive."

"What about Pat Simpson? I assume his prints weren't in the Land Rover?"

"No. But..."

"But what?" Then she guessed. "What about on the papers Anton wanted Lacey to sign at her ranch?"

"You got it. Pat Simpson's prints are on some of those pages, along with Brett Bradley's."

God, Brett must be terrified, Alice thought. She felt a moment—a nanosecond—of sympathy for the little twerp—in way over his head on the "rescission mission."

Again she wondered about the email Nanette had hidden in her ink cartridge box. What would Pat Simpson say about that?

"Okay, wanted you to know. By the way, Joske and his team are out at Simpson Strategic Assets, serving a warrant for the brothers' laptops, emails, and other stuff. Later." Files hung up.

*****

One last task before she could call it a day: finalize the draft inventory of Nanette's possessions to be filed by Nanette's parents, as executors.

She heard the front door open with a bang. Without warning, Pat Simpson barged into her office. Silla came racing from the kitchen, behind him.

Alice shot to her feet, looking at the face of the man who—she was sure—had wanted Nanette dead.

"You—you conniving bitch," he spat. "I'll see you disbarred! If you use one single piece of my work product—if I see one piece of paper you stole from our offices—you'll be sued for damages so big they'll make your head swim!" He took another step forward, his face growing redder and more furious each second.

"You're an accessory to murder," Alice said through clenched teeth. "You violated every tenet of the law that applies to you. You utterly failed to live up to your ethical requirements. You want to know who'll lose his bar license? And any other license you've got?" She stared at his apoplectic face. "Not to mention sending your boy Anton out to my client's ranch—with those so-called rescission documents you drafted? And a knife?"

"Those documents were perfectly legal! And I didn't know about any knife," he sputtered.

"Oh? Like you didn't know about Anton's Mafia connections?"

His eyes widened. "How did you—what are you talking about?"

"You knew your investors were dirty, so you ordered Nanette to skip any due diligence."

"There was no need! I already knew about these investors!"

"Yes—you knew they're Mafia—the Vitales and the Novikovs. When Nanette figured out what you already knew, she put her resignation letter on your desk. And then she was toast."

"What do you mean? She was incompetent—"

He hadn't denied the connections, Nanette's letter, or his instruction to skip due diligence.

"You told your brother Nanette had to go, didn't you?" She paused. "By the way, did your baby bro have a nice Thanksgiving? Out there on the run?"

"I'm telling you, if you think you're getting away with this—if you make trouble for me—if you testify—if you—I'll get you! I'll destroy you! I'll make sure you lose everything! I'll make your life so miserable you'll wish you were dead!"

"Like Nanette?"

She thought he'd explode. He shook with rage. Instead, he turned, shoving Silla out of the way.

Silla stuck out her booted foot, hooked his ankle, and tripped him.

Probably a long time since he's been on his knees, Alice thought.

As he scrambled to his feet in the entry hall, Silla said, "Oh, excuse me. Let me show you the door."

Which she slammed and locked. Then she stood with her back to the door. "Whoo-ee." But she held up her phone. "Got it on here, everything he said."

That Silla. What a woman.

"I think we each deserve a cold beer," Silla said, turning toward the kitchen.

Chapter Thirty-Three

I Don't Want To Wait

Nearly Christmas; late afternoon in late December. The weather was unusually warm. A late rose was still blooming by Alice's front porch.

She and Kinsear stood in the driveway with the burros, watching Alice's Discovery pull up as Big Boy brayed his traditional welcome.

John and Ann popped out of the front seat. Ann ran to Alice and hugged her. "Whee! Free at last! Only one more semester!" She was halfway done with senior year.

Kinsear opened the back of the Discovery. He and John began unloading baggage.

Jimmie held open the car's back door for a woman with straight blonde hair, who climbed out, her face jetlagged but curious. Jimmie's own face was a study: anxious, thrilled, and still disbelieving.

"Emma!" exclaimed Alice. "Wonderful that you're here!" Emma offered her the *bise*, the near-kiss on each cheek, left, right, left.

Alice introduced Kinsear. "Emma, you and Jimmie will be in the casita. The guest house." She pointed to the small cabin that sat near the house, above the creek. "After you get settled, come to the house and we'll celebrate!"

The champagne stood ready—already set out by Kinsear. Celebration was in the air.

Sam Brody's old brown and cream Bronco rolled down the driveway. He'd brought his girlfriend, Kinsear's daughter Isabel, and her sister, Carrie. Kinsear hugged his daughters and shook hands with Sam.

Ann took Isabel and Carrie to get carrots for the burros. Kinsear and John delivered bags to various rooms. Alice took a deep breath. Her kids were home. Emma was here. She went to the porch and turned on all the Christmas lights.

*****

Inside, her house was alive with music (at the moment, Lukas Nelson) and with such excited voices that Alice couldn't stop smiling. To the tune of "Come On Up to the House," Kinsear poured her a second glass of champagne. Jimmie took Emma out onto the deck and waved his hand at the landscape. "Seabed!" Alice heard him say. "But it's pretty old seabed. Cretaceous."

"You love having your kids back under your roof, don't you?" Kinsear was watching her face.

She thought about that. "Yes. Not because it's my roof but because we're together, and I cling to the belief that I can keep them safe. Because I know where they are." She laughed. "Most days, of course, I have no idea." She watched Ann's merry face, deep in conversation with Carrie and Isabel, and Sam Brody, talking to John, over by the bookcases.

Kinsear looked out the doors to the deck, watching Jimmie and Emma. His face grew serious.

"What are you thinking about?" Alice asked. "What Jimmie's going to do?"

"You mean, whether he'll accept that offer from Southampton or head for New Zealand? Maybe the latter, if the university there comes through with a teaching job for Emma."

After a moment he said, "No, what I was really thinking was, life's dangerous."

She nodded, thinking of Jordie, falling from the sky. Jimmie, kidnapped and held captive. Nanette, hit by a car and dragged away to die.

After a pause, he smiled and pulled her to him. "Yet we're so damn lucky to be here."

He and Alice got busy arranging a buffet dinner around the kitchen island. Tamales, Mexican street corn, pulled pork, deceptively incendiary green sauce, warm tortillas, guacamole, salsa. Chips, beer, wine, iced tea. People filled their plates and perched on sofas, on the deck, at various tables, and on the screened porch, lit by Christmas lights. A faint whiff of Fraser fir from the Christmas tree competed with the chiles from the buffet.

Alice listened to the voices, watched the faces: Jimmie's, softening more and more as he watched Emma. Sam Brody, eyes on the future as well as on Isabel. Ann, eyes laughing as she made some wisecrack to her brother. No telling what they were talking about.

She felt Kinsear take her hand.

He pulled her out the front door, out to the treehouse, draped in its own Christmas lights. She followed him up the ladder. They sat on the bench, looking out through the branches toward the lit-up house, the dark vale that held the creek, the stars bright above.

Alice thought, it's the turning of the year. The winter solstice. She thought again of Jordie, wrapped in the lovely shroud painted by Robbie. A ghost laid. We move from dark to light. As we always have, as we must.

From his pocket Kinsear tugged a small box, handed it to her.

She looked at his intent face. She opened the box. Did the sparkle come from stars, or Christmas lights, or something more? She saw a ruby, flanked by two sparkling diamonds, on a plain gold band.

"I wanted to get you a ring," he said. "I was afraid after all that's happened the last two months you might think it was too soon, but I don't want to wait any longer." He paused. "What are you doing, say, New Year's Day?"

She was tugging the ring from its box, putting it on her finger. It felt new, different, interesting.

She took his face in her hands. Kissed him.

"Mom! Where are you?" Ann called from the porch.

She kissed him again, again, again.

THE END

ABOUT THE AUTHOR

I live north of Dripping Springs, Texas, in the stunning Texas Hill Country, loosely supervised by three burros, with occasional visits from other inhabitants: gray-backed foxes, jackrabbits, deer, armadillos, skunks, raccoons, owls, hawks—and porcupines. This landscape won my heart years ago. I left Texas for Wellesley College, then entered graduate school at UT Austin and later the University of Michigan Law School where I grew intrigued by dirt and water law. Current preoccupations: Texas water issues; achieving a perfect barbecued brisket; boogie-woogie piano.

HEARING FROM YOU

If you enjoyed meeting Alice and her Coffee Creek companions in *Ghosted*, please consider rating it or putting up a short review. You can also stay in touch with Alice and her adventures at www.helencurriefoster.com, and sign up on the email list there for updates and news about upcoming books. You can find the entire series and follow me on Amazon. Upcoming events as well as pictures of the three burros and various aspects of the Hill Country appear on Facebook at https://www.facebook.com/helencurriefoster.

Check out my blogs at https://austinmysterywriters.com and https://inkstainedwretches.home.blog//
Happy reading!

THANKS AND MORE THANKS

To all who read *Ghosted* and put up with my questions—Virgil Yarbrough, Suzanne Wofford, Keith Graham, Grace and Bill Bradshaw, Sara Stinnett, Ann Barker, Megan Biesele, Diana Borden, Stephenie Yearwood, as well as fellow writers Kathy Waller, Kathy Gresham, Fran Paino, and D.L.S. Evatt, and always Larry, Sydney and Drew Foster—thanks for your invaluable help. This book couldn't have taken shape without you. Any errors are mine alone. Many thanks to Susan Wittig Albert for her kind comments. And thanks to my father, Stuart Dickson Currie, who gave us the run of his library, and usually had a mystery in his pocket.

Finally, to Judy Cohen for superb copy-editing, and to Bill Carson for cover, design layout, and sheer professional brio, thanks and more thanks.